"What's a girl li... doin' with some...

His blunt question stunned Jamie, and she stammered, "I don't understand."

His brown eyes were angry. "Sure you do. You're no fool. I'm not exactly handsome. Or rich. Or anything. Girls don't fall over me like they do Ben Dalton."

She tried to sidetrack him. "Oh, come on, Ren, you can't tell me you've never had a girlfriend before."

"No, I can't. I've had 'em. But that's not what I'm talkin' about. You're... you're beautiful. And there's something about you that says pretty plain you've had a lot of money. The men in this town are right on the edge of makin' fools of themselves over you."

He paused, then continued slowly. "You came after me. You know you did. Nobody would believe it. Hell, *I* don't even believe it." He yanked at the grass beside him impatiently. "I want to know why."

Dear Reader,

Welcome to the Silhouette **Special Edition** experience! With your search for consistently satisfying reading in mind, every month the authors and editors of Silhouette **Special Edition** aim to offer you a stimulating blend of deep emotions and high romance.

The name Silhouette **Special Edition** and the distinctive arch on the cover represent a commitment—a commitment to bring you six sensitive, substantial novels each month. In the pages of a Silhouette **Special Edition**, compelling true-to-life characters face riveting emotional issues—and come out winners. Both celebrated authors and newcomers to the series strive for depth and dimension, vividness and warmth, in writing these stories of living and loving in today's world.

The result, we hope, is romance you can believe in. Deeply emotional, richly romantic, infinitely rewarding—that's the Silhouette **Special Edition** experience. Come share it with us—six times a month!

From all the authors and editors of Silhouette **Special Edition**,

Best wishes,

Leslie Kazanjian,
Senior Editor

DANA WARREN SMITH

High Stakes

Silhouette Special Edition

Published by Silhouette Books New York

America's Publisher of Contemporary Romance

SILHOUETTE BOOKS
300 East 42nd St., New York, N.Y. 10017

ISBN: 0-373-09563-5

First Silhouette Books printing November 1989

Printed in the U.S.A.

DANA WARREN SMITH

is a seventh-generation Tennessean who married her high school sweetheart and now lives within hollering distance of all sorts of cousins, aunts, uncles and great-grandmas. "We believe in roots," she says. She grew up fascinated by regional authors and, at sixteen, became interested in writing. For the past two years she has been working on a criticism, based loosely on her master's thesis, of the Western as a genre. *High Stakes* is her first novel.

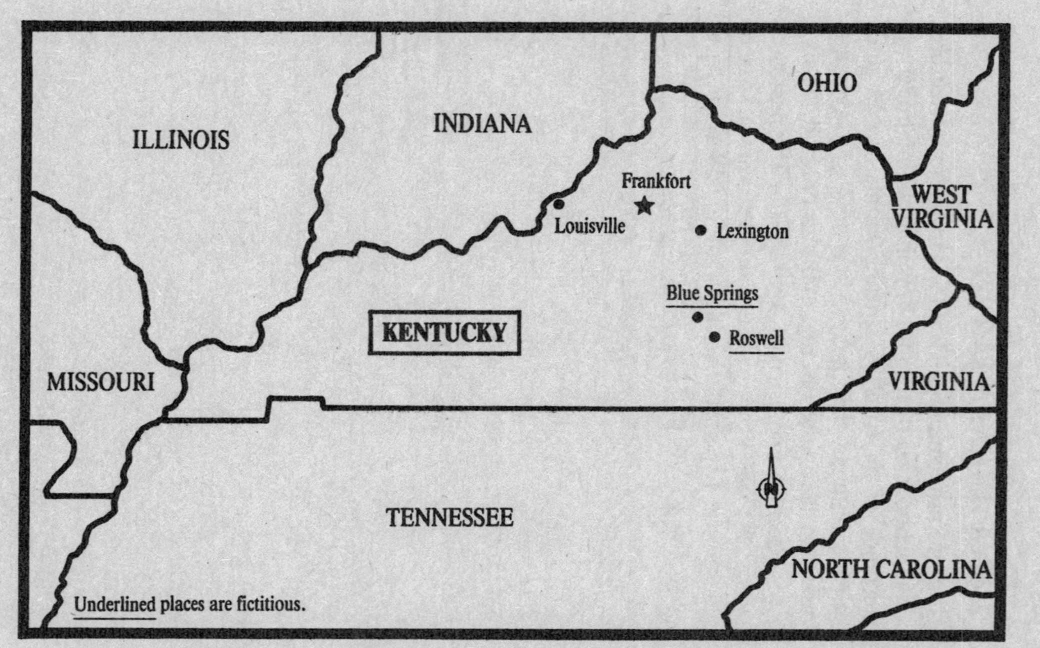
ILLINOIS
INDIANA
OHIO
Frankfort
Louisville
Lexington
WEST VIRGINIA
Blue Springs
KENTUCKY
Roswell
MISSOURI
VIRGINIA
TENNESSEE
NORTH CAROLINA
Underlined places are fictitious.

PART ONE: The Setup

Chapter One

He was ugly. Well, maybe not exactly ugly. His nose was crooked, his hair a sort of bushy brown mane that looked hard to control, his mouth lopsided when he smiled. But he wasn't scary-ugly. Sometimes he was even strangely attractive. That was because his brown eyes looked gentle and his conversation was slow and teasing—or it was when he made it. Jamie had been watching him, following him unobtrusively in her cousin's car for several days now, and he never seemed to talk much.

She observed him mostly at work. Sometimes he answered the store owner's query about a customer; once in a while he spoke to a farmer who'd come in, usually one who'd spoken to him first. But in general, he just went about his business, managing Enoch Johnson's farm supply store. He did everything at the little place, from writing up the orders to answering the telephone and loading the big, heavy grain sacks into the back of the pickup trucks when they pulled in. Old man Johnson was nearly eighty, and he entrusted his entire business to the tall, shy boy.

The boy was actually twenty-five and his name was Wrendon Garrett, Ren for short. Jamie knew at least that much about him. Oh, she knew a few more things. He was single and always had been; he lived alone in a tiny white house on a farm at the edge of rural Calhoun County; he had lived here in the county for all of his life. She had gathered a lot of her information about him from a stack of old annuals from Calhoun County High School. His square, angular face looking up at her from the pages of the yearbook for his senior year had reassured her, just as had the corny saying his classmates had chosen to print beside his likeness: "His words are few; his heart is true."

He had nothing. No family to speak of, no money, no looks. Just a lonely existence as a clerk in a feed store in Roswell, the county seat of an area that was one-horse even for this section of mideastern Kentucky. That job, and the little farm. He was absolutely perfect for Jamie's needs, and the thought made her shiver.

What made people like him go on living? she wondered. His life was flat, empty. Everything about him was austere and stark.

But Jamie didn't waste too much time or energy thinking seriously about Ren Garrett and his situation. He was going to be her means to an end, just a handy way to get something she wanted. In fact, she would have gone on living her life in complete and happy ignorance of his existence if she hadn't lost her temper with Beth Benton and if Todd hadn't been gone so long, for nearly six weeks.

And if Tory hadn't died.

But Jamie had, and Todd had, and Tory had, so here she was in trouble, and this awkward, shy, ugly Ren Garrett was her only ticket out of it. He just didn't know it yet, and if she handled him right, he never would. She would at least be more clever where Garrett was concerned than she'd been at the get-together that had catapulted her into this mess.

She remembered that occasion all too well. "Just some of the girls," her cousin Sharon had said when she'd urged Jamie to go with her. Over at Claire's parents' cabin down on the far side of the Danton River. The guests had turned out to include Beth. Jamie liked very little about the woman. Jamie's sister, Victoria, had despised her, but Tory was gone and Jamie was lonely, despairing and angry, so she'd gone to the cabin and stayed despite the presence of Beth Benton.

Tory had been dead for two long, empty months, the victim of a terrible car crash. Jamie's parents, Eli and Eve, were in Europe, where her mother had begged to go after the accident and where Daddy had reluctantly taken her. Leaving his farm, his business and his family had been hard. He had wanted Jamie to go, too, but Jamie had seen Europe more than once, and she wasn't in the mood for the Louvre or the Sistine Chapel. Tory would have loved it; Jamie wanted only the rich, green Kentucky grass under her feet. Eli had finally left, mumbling that at least she'd have his brothers' families close if she needed anything, and, of course, Roberta, the housekeeper who'd been a part of their lives for twenty-five years. Jamie had added quickly that she'd have Todd, too, so Eli wouldn't have to worry. Her father had frowned, but Eve had murmured something about Todd being "a wonderful young man."

The "wonderful young man" had been around all of four days after her parents' departure, then he'd voluntarily accepted a deal that required him to go to Alaska, of all places, to finalize contracts for some company. The house got bigger and emptier every day, even with Roberta's friendly presence. Jamie had needed someone to help her through the loneliness.

Then Todd had called, but he'd called at the wrong time and with the wrong message. What he'd said was that he'd be in Alaska at least another month. And when Jamie got angry, Todd had reminded her that he had his own problems. Jamie was furious, and by the time she'd told Todd in no uncertain terms what she thought of his "problems," his own temper was up. After he'd worked his way through several adjectives, words like *overemotional* and *excessive*, Jamie had slammed the receiver down so hard she hoped all Alaska heard it. But even in the midst of her hurt and anger, she was aware of a spark of satisfaction somewhere deep within. Todd had at least shown some honest, real emotion there at the end instead of his usual suavity. Her grief at Tory's death had unsettled him. She suspected that her emotionalism had helped to send him north to ice and snow. That was a good place for him, she thought angrily.

Nevertheless, she stood fuming after she hung up, trying to fight down the urge to strangle somebody. She and Todd were nearly engaged, she hadn't seen him since shortly after Tory's death, and her world was frighteningly unstable and lonely these days.

In that mood of hot temper, resentment and aching hurt, she had decided she would indeed go to Claire's. Sharon had been relieved and delighted until after they arrived. Her teetotaler cousin Jamie had calmly picked up and swallowed one drink, and then another, and had then begun working on a third.

Sharon had nervously tried to object, and her unobtrusive warnings had eventually been noticed by the others present. Most of them were already anxious about Jamie's morose behavior in the past few weeks. Finally Claire had tactfully suggested that her guests might like to go outside and see the lake by moonlight, in a clear attempt to give Sharon time to speak to her cousin. One by one they drifted out after Claire until it was just Sharon and Jamie and Beth, and Sharon had waited impatiently for Beth to do the same.

But Beth simply stood there, finally drawling, "What's the matter with our upright angel tonight, Jamie? You're the one who always protests when there's too much drinking, remember?"

Jamie eyed Elizabeth Benton with dislike. The woman was pretty, the daughter of a prominent family who'd fallen on hard times in the past few years. Rumor said they were all waiting for some rich relative they had somewhere here in the state to die and leave them a tidy inheritance. Beth was several years older than Jamie, closer to Tory and Todd's age, an established career woman whose small law practice was beginning to flourish. Todd was a lawyer, too, so maybe that was why Jamie just kept running into Beth these days, though Todd's firm was in a much larger city an hour's drive away, and Beth's practice was more rural, her work sprawling across most of neighboring Calhoun County. Looking at the woman now, Jamie felt the antagonism rise in her. She wished Beth would get lost.

Jamie could remember the glitter in her blue eyes. Funny how the three drinks she'd gulped down hadn't taken effect until too late.

"There's nothing wrong with me. I'm just joining the human race. That's all."

"Joining it? Or trying to get away from it?" Beth had set down her own glass and circled Jamie's chair like an alert shark. "Don't tell me you and your precious Todd have had an argument. Trouble in paradise and all that!"

Jamie stiffened. "Leave Todd out of this. He's got nothing to do with it."

Beth smiled. "You can't fool me, Jamie. I know you. You always get a certain look when you two quarrel, and you've had it a lot lately. But you don't usually get drunk. What's the matter? Todd found some Eskimo he likes better?"

Sharon tried to intervene. "Come on, Beth. Stop it. Jamie's just feeling bad tonight. She's got a right to. She's had a hard time since Tory di—"

Sharon swallowed her words too late. Jamie said dispassionately, "It's all right, Sharon."

Beth chose to ignore the warning. "Seems to me that those short chains you and Todd have had each other on for the past few months are about to break. He's been in Alaska for more than a month now, and I heard today he's planning on being there longer."

"News travels fast, doesn't it, Beth? If Todd's business there takes a few days more, it's fine by me."

Beth gave an incredulous laugh. "Really? This is a surprise. You're turning loose the man your daddy's redneck money bought for you?"

Sharon's gasped "Beth!" echoed the shout in Jamie's own mind. She had known Beth disliked her, but not to this venomous extent.

"Daddy's money didn't 'buy' anybody for me, Beth," she said slowly, trying to concentrate on the other woman's movements. She had not eaten much and was not used to liquor at all; now she was beginning to feel dizzy and a little sick.

"Do you really think that you—little Miss Virginity—could hold Todd if it weren't for all those oodles and oodles of dollars Eli Logan's going to leave someday, all to you now that Tory's dead?"

After the first stunned second while her mind registered incredulously what Beth had said, Jamie came out of her chair as fast as her clumsy legs could get her up, and she slapped the face in front of her, hard. Beth's head jerked sideways at the blow, and in shocked pain she put her hand to her reddening cheek.

Tears in the back of her throat made Jamie's words come out harsh and choked. She didn't care what she said.

"You leave Tory out of this, Beth Benton. You always hated my sister. And I know why. You were jealous. She was beautiful—and she took Adam Ralston from you. Everybody knew you wanted him, that you'd dated him off and on for years."

"Don't be ridiculous. I couldn't have cared less when they got engaged," Beth spat back angrily, her hand still on her face. "Or, for that matter, when they broke up."

"Don't lie to me. I know Tory was upset with you in the weeks before she died. She even wrote you a letter. I saw it on her table—saw the name on the envelope."

Beth glanced uneasily away from Jamie's passionate, accusing face. "Adam wasn't the first man Tory ever stole from another woman and then dumped. She probably wrote more than one letter, too."

"This time was different. Tory changed. The last month—she was quiet, too quiet. She pulled away from me. It had to be Adam. There wasn't anything else," Jamie said on a hard sob.

"So? Why tell me?"

"Because I asked her after I found the letter if she had had trouble with you. She tried to get away from answering, but I knew. You're the reason she and Adam broke up, aren't you?" Jamie's voice dropped and slowed until it accused. Beth moved uncomfortably away from the threat in it.

"What was in the letter she wrote you? And don't tell me you didn't get it."

"So I've got a letter Tory wrote," snapped Beth, and two guilty red dots stained her cheekbones. "That's not a crime and what's in it is none of your business."

"I want to know. I *will* know."

"Why? Will it help you hang on to Tory? Or be like her?" Beth flashed back. "She was alive, Jamie. And she was a sinner just like the rest of us sometimes. Not a sweet innocent like you. She had one weak spot, though. But it wasn't Adam. It was you."

"I don't know what you're talking about."

Sharon came out of her openmouthed stupor and tried once more to end the whole nightmare conversation. "And neither does Beth. Come on, Jamie, let's get out of here."

But Beth was back in control, and she didn't want to turn Jamie loose. "She wasted a lot of time protecting you. Just like Sharon is doing now. Just like Eli does. They've got to keep their sweet little beauty pure. Miss Sweet Sixteen of the country club. Homecoming Queen at college. You're their ticket to respectability. And *that's* why Eli's buying Todd Jackson for you. Maybe the day you marry him everybody will forget your daddy's sharecropper blood."

"I never had any trouble getting men before Todd, Beth."

Beth said crudely, "You've never had a man, Jamie, not in any sense of the word. You wouldn't know what to do with the real thing. In fact, I'd bet hard, cold cash you wouldn't even put out the effort to attract some ordinary guy that Tory and Eli hadn't worked over, let alone crawl in bed with him for the night."

"All right." Sharon intervened firmly. "This is enough. Get lost, Beth. You've made everybody miserable, so now you can go home." She put her arm around Jamie's shoulder, murmuring, "C'mon, honey, let's just get to the car, and I'll—"

But Jamie pulled away. She said to Beth, "I'm not concerned with your opinions. In fact, there's not one thing about you that interests me." Then a thought struck her and her face and voice altered drastically. She said slowly, "Except—the letter."

"What?" Beth frowned.

Jamie had thrown Beth off balance and she pressed her advantage. "I want that letter. So I'll take the wager you just made. I'll spend the night with some 'ordinary' man, one who doesn't know or even care who I am. But not for cash. For Tory's letter."

"No! No, Jamie—you're half-drunk. You don't know what you're saying!" Sharon cried in alarm.

Jamie motioned her cousin into silence, never taking her eyes off Beth's face. "Well, what's your answer? Are you afraid? It's a perfect bet for you. Even if I win, you'll get a lot of satisfaction out of it. I'll have given up all that innocence and virginity you claim I've got, all that you resent so much."

Beth gave an incredulous laugh. "So you're Tory's sister, after all. All the same go-to-hell arrogance, the same reckless streak. How long have you been hiding it, Jamie?"

"Not long. Just since I saw Tory and knew she was dead. Her life is wasted, and I want to know why."

Beth opened and closed her mouth in shock, then said, "You really mean it, don't you? And if you lose? What's in it for me?"

"I won't lose. But—name it. What do you want? I'm willing to listen."

The other woman said slowly, "I want a job, one at the law offices of Trevor and Harrison over in Tyler. They need a rising young female attorney, anyway."

"I can't guarantee you that," Jamie said, thinking fast. It made sense that Beth should want the position. It was home to the most prominent lawyers in the area, especially those with political ambitions. Todd had been elated to join the firm. Beth was notoriously aggressive, determined to get ahead.

"I have faith in you," Beth replied calmly. "Everybody knows Eli says 'jump' and Martin Trevor says, 'How high?' You can do it."

"All right," Jamie answered finally. "But I get to set the terms for the bet."

"Not the man," Beth objected quickly.

"Listen to yourselves," Sharon burst out. "This is wrong. It's not fair to you, Jamie, or to Todd. Think, for heaven's sake."

Beth drawled, "Yes, please, for one time think for yourself. Sharon, that means you stay out of it." Then she turned back to Jamie. "It's no good if I don't choose the man. Otherwise, how do I know it's not a trick? But I'll tell you what—I'll give you a fighting chance. I'll make up a list of several men, give you a week or so to decide on one, even make a new list if you have good reasons to dislike all of them."

A tingle of fear and disgust went through Jamie's stomach. She wished she'd never started this, but it was too late now. She couldn't back down in front of Beth. Tory wouldn't have. So she nodded. "All right. But he can't be tied to another woman in any way. He can't be somebody from here in Claiborne County."

Sharon interjected, "He has to be a normal, decent human being. Oh, Lord, what am I saying?"

"Well, that eliminates half the males in the state," Beth answered dryly. "But okay, I agree. I choose the man, you approve him. And you walk into his home one night and don't come out until the morning. Whatever you do while you're in there...well, I'll use my imagination."

"Jamie wouldn't do anything *that* bad," Sharon snapped.

Beth laughed. "I think you're right. I doubt if she's got the nerve. So how long will it take you? A week? A month?" She added suggestively, "Or only a day?"

"One month," Jamie said firmly. "And when I win, I get not only Tory's letter but also an explanation of anything in it I don't understand."

They had written it all down in stark black and white, an infamous contract that was now in Sharon's nervous possession. Beth had left for home confident and elated.

"You won't win. Miss Purity isn't about to crawl into bed with a one-night stand."

"Shut up, Beth," Jamie said distinctly through the roaring and throbbing in her head. Then Sharon drove her home while Jamie tried to think clearly and escape the feeling that she had just played Faust, right into Beth's devilish hands. Sharon worried and fussed during the whole of the trip.

"...and heaven only knows who she'll pick out. Jamie, how can you do this? And Todd—poor, poor Todd. I never liked him much, I'll admit, but nobody deserves this. You're ruined. Let me tear this paper up. I'll swear it never happened."

"Sharon, please hush. I don't have to go to bed with this—this unknown."

Sharon gave a derisive laugh. "Just what gives you that loony-tune idea? It's there in writing. It says plainly—"

"That Mr. Unknown will spend the night with me. So? Let him. I don't have to sleep with him just because he stays all night."

"Jamie, you are so dense sometimes. Just how do you propose to get a stranger to stay all night without you and bed?"

"That paper doesn't say a thing about sex. I know. I signed it. All I have to do is make Beth think I've got this man interested in me. Spend time with him. Then we stay one night together. Maybe I'll get sick and have to sleep on his couch or something."

"It won't work."

"Sharon." Jamie stared pointedly at her. "Do you want me to sleep with this stranger?"

"No, don't be silly. But she may plant somebody she knows."

"We have to approve him, remember."

"Or she might tell him who you really are, or after it's all over tell Todd or somebody else what you've done. And how do you know she'll really give this letter to you even if you win?"

"I don't. That's one good reason why I'm not sleeping with the guy. I never would have signed that paper if I thought I'd really have to go to bed with him."

"I don't like it, Jamie. She wants to bring you down. Why on this green earth did you do this?"

Jamie's face twisted painfully. "I don't know. Sometimes I want to stop thinking. Beth's right in one way: I'm sick to death of doing all the right things and the proper things. I've been good all these years, and what happens? I lose Tory. Her life is over, just like that. I want to understand why. And I want to live, before it's too late."

"Then do it with Todd," Sharon pleaded. "If you're really going to marry the stuffed shirt."

For once Jamie did not defend Todd against Sharon. "It's not sex I'm talking about when I say I want to live. I just want to—to be out of the cage for a while. To quit living up to my own reputation."

"Tory lived out of the cage, Jamie, and it never got her any real, lasting happiness," Sharon reminded her cousin slowly.

A dark shadow passed over Jamie's face. "I want the letter, Sharon. There was something wrong with Tory. She changed right before she died. She didn't talk to me anymore. She was edgy when we were together. When I questioned her, she got angry."

"So what? People do things like that."

Jamie said slowly, "The investigator asked us if Tory had been depressed, if she'd had any mood changes. Daddy and Mama hadn't seen any, but I..."

Sharon stared at Jamie, then she pulled the car over to the side of the road and killed the engine. In the sudden silence, she whispered incredulously, "You're not trying to say Tory committed suicide, are you?"

Wincing away from the word, Jamie put her face in her hands. She felt sick and wobbly from the three fast drinks, but she had to make her cousin understand. "She got killed because she went over a cliff into the biggest hollow in Claiborne County on a clear night on a road she knew like the back of her hand. The police said there was no sign she ever braked, and no evidence of any other cars. She was stone-cold sober."

"I don't believe it. Tory was too...too fond of herself and of living."

Jamie tried to speak dispassionately. "When she loved, she loved too much. Possessive and blind, and she expected a lot out of the one she loved. I know. She'd have given up everything for me, but she wanted me to be perfect in return."

"But you didn't do anything to cause her to get upset enough to kill herself!"

"I think Adam did. He and Beth. She knows something about Tory's death. Nobody seems to realize Tory was within a mile of Beth's house when she wrecked."

Sharon took Jamie's hands. "No, it's not even possible. Tory was a live wire. She always knew what she wanted and exactly how to get it, for herself and you, too. She loved you like you were her only child instead of her kid sister who was nine years younger. But none of that adds up to a suicidal person."

"And the letter?"

"To hell with the letter. It may—oh, Lord, here comes Cody Nichols." The sheriff's car slid in behind them, its lights blinding Jamie as they were reflected in the side mirror of Sharon's little roadster. "He'll have a heart attack if he thinks you've been drinking and have veered off the primrose path, Jamie. He'll be on the phone to Europe in a flat minute." She broke off to roll the window down. "Evening, Cody."

Cody was the local law officer, a skinny, wiry little man who looked lopsided from the weight of his gun. "Evenin', Sharon. Thought that was your car. Havin' trouble?" He bent down to peer through the darkness. "Miss Jamie! What y'all doin' out here?"

"Jamie was feeling sick to her stomach," Sharon said quickly. "We were on our way home from Claire's."

"You all right now?" Cody asked Jamie.

"Yes, I'm f-fine. I just want to go home."

He nodded approvingly. "It's too late for two nice girls to be out alone on the road. Eli would be worried if he knew. I'll follow you back to the house, Sharon, just to make sure y'all get there safe." He vanished from the window.

"He will, too," she said in exasperation. "Jamie, honey, maybe you do need to get out of the cage. Cody doesn't escort *me* around. Eli's got this whole little town hovering over you like they're some kind of guardian angels."

They pulled at last into the circular drive in front of the big white house that loomed under vast, spreading trees. In the dark night, in the honeysuckle silence broken only by the birds and the tree frogs, Jamie spoke.

"I want the letter. Tricking Beth into giving it to me won't cost me anything. So I'm going through with the bet."

Sharon called after her as she climbed out of the car. "Tory's dead, Jamie, and none of this will help her. You're getting into something that's trouble! Jamie!"

But Jamie had let herself into the quiet, empty house and shut the door on her cousin's imploring voice.

Chapter Two

So it was going to be this Garrett boy. Beth had promptly submitted a list of four names a few days after their little conversation. All of the men were from Roswell, thirty miles from Jamie's hometown and just over the county line. All of them were strangers to Jamie. One by one she and Sharon had eliminated three. She had to give Beth full marks—she had followed the rules and probably laughed every step of the way. One was a straitlaced, upright, stern young minister from one of the county's small rural churches. He was a little pudgy, but definitely decent. Another was a thirtyish widower with two children, anxious to find a wife and a housekeeper. The third one Sharon had urged Jamie to consider. He was new to the area, a clerk in the Roswell bank, rather handsome in a clean-cut sort of way. But something about his dark hair and brilliant blue eyes reminded Jamie uneasily of Todd, so she came at last to the fourth man.

She knew why Beth had chosen him. He was not only the farthest from her socially of all those on the list, but he also seemed well-nigh impossible to approach. He had no conversation; he was not attractive; he would not understand light talk, social graces or easy, meaningless flirtation. After Jamie had checked out his background, she knew exactly why he was on the list: a filler, a sort of last-minute joke. Beth was urging her toward the bank clerk, and that made Jamie uneasy. She turned to the fourth man as a sort of last resort.

She was even beginning to think this Ren Garrett might have real potential for her. So he was a little rough around the edges. Or maybe all the way through. He was quiet, unlikely to talk about any girlfriend; he was as far removed from her world as he could get in this county; he could be handled by a woman who knew the ropes. Good grief, he could be handled by *any* woman, as shy and backward as he was around them. Yes, indeed, Garrett was the solution to her problem. Jamie was nearly jubilant that it was going to be so simple.

Meeting him was easy enough. She realized quickly that coming on to this boy was not the right approach. He would not handle it well, would probably even run scared. But if she put him in the position of having to face her, of having to talk, he might come through.

So the following Friday afternoon, Jamie Logan drove out to her family's farm, parked her sleek blue convertible and took one of the farm trucks in its place. The one she chose was not as old as she would have liked, but it was covered with good old Kentucky dust, and it did not have Logan Farms emblazoned on its doors as some of them did. Sharon was left to drive the convertible back to the house, and Jamie pulled away with Sharon's dire predictions and last wails ringing in her ears: "Why didn't you take that boy at the bank? This guy worries me. He's nothing but trouble."

Jamie stopped the truck just off the highway a few yards down the long, dusty road that led to Ren Garrett's little house. From the truck she could dimly make out glimpses of the house through the trees that clustered around it. The pastures in front of it were green and open; a few cattle grazed in the left field, which gradually sloped away into a rich, deep, dark green hollow.

She took a screwdriver, raised the hood of the truck and deftly punched a hole in the water hose that ran to the radiator. She smeared one hand across the hose and then across her own face, making sure she looked smudged. Then she got back in the truck, turned on the engine and let it run until it got hot. Sharon and she had elicited all sorts of helpful information about this procedure from Sharon's unsuspecting teenage brother, Beau.

"Sorry, Dad," she muttered to her absent father as she shut off the engine. Next she left the truck, hood up, and started down the road to the Garrett house. She was good and sticky with perspiration when she got to the first tree; realism has its price, she thought philosophically, and sat down to wait.

Garrett should be headed home soon, she thought to herself. As soon as she heard him coming down this quiet stretch of highway, she was going to hop up and give every appearance of marching to his house for help. He *had* to offer help. And she'd made sure her problem would take time to solve.

The loud whine of flies hovering over the hot backs of the cattle in the nearby field was all she heard for a while. Then she glanced at her watch, impatient and nervous. He'd surely had time to get home by now. Suddenly she grimaced—the watch. She'd better take it off. Sweet young country girls in faded jeans and floppy T-shirts didn't wear watches that had diamonds glittering against the dull sheen of gold. She slid it carefully into her jeans pocket.

Her efforts to look as ordinary as possible had to be complete. She didn't resemble Jamie Logan, she was sure of that. Claiborne County had looked upon her with pride as one of its finest young beauties, though she lacked the exotic sultriness and reputation for fast living that had made men fall over Tory in droves. But from growing up in Tory's wake, Jamie had learned that being too pretty and too conscious of it made life miserable. To have friends she'd always just accepted her looks and ignored them.

Today she'd subdued them violently. The thick tangle of tawny hair, the perfect makeup, the expensive perfume and clothes were gone. The hair she'd battled into a thick plait that hung down her back. Sharon had made a face and said dryly, "Aren't you carrying this good old girl routine just a little too far? A braid?"

"This guy will never think a thing. Besides, I have to hide my hair somehow."

In the end she could diminish or alter every feature except the clean line of bone structure and the gray-green eyes. Still, she did not apply the makeup that accented her high cheekbones and made the slant of her eyes more noticeable. Sharon had finally admitted reluctantly, "You really do look different. Sixteen, maybe. Your face looks like it did when we were little girls. But you're still too pretty."

"Thanks—I think," said Jamie dubiously. "Maybe I'll frown a lot, or develop a nervous twitch."

So now here she sat, trying for all the world to act like a demure young farm girl who was desperately in need of a good strong masculine arm to help with the truck. And still Garrett did not come.

This was something she had never thought of. What if he did what a lot of men in the county did—went drinking every weekend? He sure didn't look the sort, but maybe she had been wrong about him.

She yawned and tried to relax, tried to get rid of that little niggling worry that said she should have gone with the banker. He was more her type. She could have given him a line and he would have come hotfoot after her. With this one, maybe she was running some kind of risk. Maybe... She yawned again. It was so comfortable here on the grass under the trees, and the heat of the day was giving way to cooler night air....

Somewhere in the distance she heard a low rumble. Thunder, maybe, she thought drowsily, or a car.

The rumble was close now, so close its vibrations tickled her ear. She put up her fingers to brush that ear, and suddenly something sharp and hard caught her hand. The rumble turned into a menacing growl.

Her eyes flew open and she came wide-awake, screaming as she looked up into the eyes of a—a wolf? A wolf! The next few seconds were a wild kaleidoscope of terror. In the dusk, the animal's eyes gleamed just inches from hers, his white, sharp teeth shone clearly in the twilight, and his vicious growl gave way to short, snapping barks as she jerked at the hand he'd caught in his jaws. He turned loose reluctantly.

She heard someone shouting commands at the beast somewhere behind her, but the blood pounding in her ears made the command unintelligible. She stumbled backward, away from the glittering eyes and dripping jaws, turning finally to run. Instead she banged hard into the body of the man who was hurrying toward her.

"You all right?" he asked anxiously, grasping her shoulders to steady her. He smelled of cattle and sweat. He felt hot and sticky.

Jamie's throat was so clogged with fear and her body was shaking so much she couldn't get out an answer. The wolf—the dog—whatever he was, gave another warning bark.

"Get quiet, King," the man snapped at him over her head. "Hey, you're not going to faint, are you? Steady, steady. You're okay. He won't bother you anymore."

Jamie leaned her forehead weakly against his shirtfront, dirt, sweat and all. She was not going to faint, but she had been scared to death.

"I thought—I thought he was a wolf. He was going to kill me." Her voice was a thin, high thread of sound.

"Not King," the man said reassuringly, patting her arm. "He's just a big German shepherd. He acts meaner than he is. I'll make him get in the back of the truck if it'll make you feel better."

Jamie drew a shuddering breath and pushed away from him. "I'd—I'd rather get in the truck myself, where he can't get me."

"Okay," said the man soothingly. They walked down the road to the truck, still running, the driver's door open where he'd left it. The man spoke.

"I left King in the barn today and went and got him on my way home. He was runnin' beside the truck when he started barkin'. Next thing I knew, I saw you gettin' up from under the tree and heard you screamin'. You sure gave me a scare."

He helped her up into the truck. It was dusty, and a Coke can and a pair of men's work gloves lay on the blue seat. The dim light from the truck's interior was enough for Jamie to inspect her injured hand.

She said, "We're even, then, because you and your dog frightened me to death. I must have gone to sleep. All I remember is brushing something from my face and then your dog tried to bite me. He had me by my hand." She shivered as she remembered those sharp white teeth so close to her.

"If he'd bit, you'd know it. He can tear the throat out of a—well, never mind. Here, let's see."

She twisted her hand in the light, then he took hold of it and did the same. There were teeth marks but no punctures.

"He just gave you a good shakin'. But I'm sorry. It's just that we weren't expectin' a girl. What were you doin' there, anyway?" he asked curiously.

Jamie was suddenly jolted back into an awareness of exactly where she was and why. She turned from her hand to peer into the face of her rescuer. He wore a cap, and its shadows and the heavy dusk around them hindered her view, but she could see enough of the face to realize that this was indeed the man she'd been waiting for. She stumbled into her story.

"My truck. It broke down, got hot. I think the water hose is messed up. Did you see it—out close to the highway?"

"Yeah. I stopped, looked around but couldn't find the driver. How hot did the engine get before you stopped? Did you try to drive it?"

So Jamie fed him the line she'd been planning to use. He listened, nodded, saw nothing wrong with her story until she told him she'd gone to his house for help and, finding no one at home, sat down to wait.

"Why didn't you just push open the screen and go on in?" he asked, climbing into the driver's seat.

"What?" Jamie answered blankly.

"The screen's not latched—the door's open. You should'a just gone on in and used the telephone. It's right there beside the door. Didn't you see it?"

"Uh—no. No, I guess not.... Aren't you afraid to leave your door open—afraid you'll get everything stolen?"

He shrugged. "Not much there to steal. Besides, I'm not that close to the road."

"Oh."

There was a moment of silence, and the man hesitated visibly before he finally spoke again. "It's pretty late. I might could fix up your truck enough so you could drive it a ways. How far are you goin'?"

Jamie was ready for this. She said smoothly, "Oh, only to Roswell. I've got an apartment there." And she did, too—one rented and paid for in cash.

"That's not far. Or you could use my phone and call somebody."

"Is there a service station open in town tonight?"

"Well, yeah, but generally on Friday nights there's only a kid there to pump gas."

"Oh, no," Jamie said in pretended dismay. "And I'm sort of new to town. I don't really know anybody to call...."

There was a pause, then he said hesitantly, "I could take you where you need to go, if you want."

"I'd hate to put you to so much trouble...." She let her voice trail off, a little wistfully.

"It won't be trouble."

"But you probably have a date or something planned, and I don't want to make you late."

He laughed a little. "You won't, 'cause I don't. But if you want me to drive you someplace, I'll have to go home first. I've got groceries in the back that have to be put up. It—it won't take but a minute."

"Well...I guess that's the best. Then I could call somebody tomorrow."

He sat quietly while she pretended to ponder. When Jamie finally said, "Okay. I'd appreciate a ride," he just nodded and started the ignition. She hastily shut the door of the truck.

The little frame house under the big oaks looked very small to Jamie, used to the grandeur and elegance of the Logan homes. There was a light on in the side kitchen, spilling yellow out over the dark yard. When Garrett got out of the truck, Jamie remembered belatedly to call, "Can I help you with anything?"

"No, that's okay," he answered, and he hoisted two sacks, one in each arm. Despite his answer, Jamie scrambled across the seat to slide out his door and run to open the kitchen screen. He muttered, "Thanks" and went in with his load of groceries while she climbed back in the truck. The big bulk of King sitting beside the tire scared her.

Through the screen she looked at the small kitchen. Its cabinets were freshly painted a creamy color, it was clean and a shiny new washer and dryer were just visible inside the door. But for all that, it was old. The linoleum was a worn blue, and no curtains hung at the kitchen windows.

Looking at the dirty, sweaty man wearing the cap pulled over his face and hastily shoving things in the refrigerator, and seeing the little kitchen, so plain and worn, made Jamie wonder for the first time if she could go through with this. She desperately wanted to know what was in that letter, but she did not want to try to flirt with this man.

At the moment the man in question came out the door and climbed into the truck. "Hope I didn't take too long," he said, then started the engine. "Now, where do you need to go?"

Jamie gave him the address of the apartment and they pulled out onto the highway in silence. Finally realizing that he simply was not going to speak, she gave a mental sigh and asked, "Are you just getting home from work? It's awfully late."

"Yeah, well, sort of. I work at Johnson's Farm Supply and today I had to stay later. Then I went to help a guy unload his cattle at the stock barn for the sale tomorrow."

"You must be tired."

"A little. Not too bad, but I have to be back at the barn at five in the morning to help with the sale."

Another pause.

"Can you tell me who I need to call tomorrow to fix my truck?" she finally asked.

"Guess Bob Daniels over at the Gulf station would be best. He keeps a mechanic on duty on Saturdays."

"I'm new in Roswell," she offered. "I don't know many people around here."

He shot her a curious glance in the darkness. "We don't get many new people in Calhoun County. Where you from?"

"Oh, Tennessee," Jamie said airily. "A friend got me a job here with the Farmers' Association office." And that was the absolute truth; she and Sharon had come up with it from one of Eli's files.

"You moved all the way from Tennessee for the job?"

"Yes, I start Monday."

"You must have wanted it pretty bad."

"Needed it is more like it," muttered Jamie. She knew absolutely nothing about what she was going to be doing, and the thought of typing all day behind some sterile desk did not appeal to her at all. But she'd have to look as normal as possible in order to catch this—this person sitting near her.

"You'll have to tell me how to get to your apartment," Garrett said after a few more minutes of silence. When they pulled up in front of the small brick complex, Jamie thought wryly that somehow this first encounter had lacked something. Still, she would see him again tomorrow when she went to get the truck. She'd make sure of that. She hoped he'd look better then.

"Well, thank you, Mr.—" She broke off in the nick of time. She wasn't supposed to know his name.

"Oh—Garrett, Ren Garrett," he said hurriedly. "And you're..."

"Ja-Jennie. Jennifer Lynn."

"Jennifer Lynn," he repeated.

"I really do appreciate this, Mr. Garrett. Maybe I'll see you again soon." She turned, opened the truck door and slid out into the darkness of the night.

"Yeah. Hey, do you want me to wait till you get in...or—"

"No, I'm fine. Thanks again." She slammed the door and stood waiting for him to leave. After a minute, he turned on the engine and pulled away.

Then Jamie went in, dialed Sharon's number, and when the answering machine came on, she left her cousin a short, concise message: "Well, I met him. And this is not going to be something to enjoy. The banker looks better every minute."

When Jamie awoke the next morning, it took her a few seconds to realize where she was. The little bedroom with its beige walls and its impersonal bareness was a far cry from her own luxurious rooms at home. But at least after she showered and dressed, Jamie felt better than she had last night. More confident. It would really be simple to talk Ren Garrett into her little scheme; look how easily things had gone yesterday. Only the scary incident with the dog had been awry.

Now for the day ahead. She had to get to a mechanic—maybe call one—get him to fix the truck and bring it to her.

She telephoned Daniels's station as Garrett had suggested, and yes, they could send a mechanic out to the truck if she'd go with him to find it and bring it back.

Jamie reflected as she checked her appearance—her country-girl jeans and shirt—that she was getting to meet a lot of different men these days. Very different. Then she went outside to wait for the mechanic.

There, sitting neatly at the curb, was her father's truck.

She gaped at it a minute. What in the world? But she already knew the answer: Ren Garrett. While she was still considering, a red and white truck proclaiming that Daniels Gulf was Open 24 Hours a Day pulled up, and a little bald man squinted at her in the morning sun.

"You the girl needin' a water hose fixed?" he demanded.

"Yes—no! I mean I think it's already been done."

His look became wary and told all too clearly his opinion of women around cars.

Jamie tried to explain what she thought had happened, that the man who'd helped her the night before had fixed it.

"Want me to check it out for you?" the mechanic finally interrupted to ask. "See if there's a new water hose?"

So he opened the hood, poked around a few minutes, then gave his verdict. "Looks fine an' dandy to me. And it's got a new hose, that's for sure."

"I don't see when he did it, though. Or why," Jamie protested to herself.

"Who was the guy?" asked the mechanic curiously, slamming the hood shut and wiping his hands on a rag.

"His name was Ren Garrett."

"Oh, Ren. You should'a said so. He'd know how to fix it, no doubt about it."

"Do you know him?"

"Sure. He grew up here. It's kinda hard not to know everybody when the town's only got eight hundred people. Well, I'll be gettin' on back to the station. No charge. I'll tell Ren next time I see him to quit takin' my business." But he grinned when he said it, and as he drove away, he flipped a friendly hand at the girl standing beside the truck.

She circled the truck warily. She was used to her father's concern, but she didn't know what to do with another man's. Not like this. He'd gotten up and fixed the truck. Given up his time. Todd would have had too many meetings and deadlines to have repaired her water hose. Not that he ever could have, anyway. Todd had trouble putting in gas himself. On that thought, Jamie climbed behind the wheel.

In this section of Kentucky, every little hole in the road had a stock barn; Calhoun County's was on the edge of town beside the fairgrounds. As usual, the smell nearly knocked Jamie down, but there was a sort of nostalgia in it and in the sights: the farm trucks, the hounds, the old overalled farmers and the younger blue-jeaned ones, the tomboy girls who came with their fathers and brothers and husbands. She had not been to the stock barn since she was nine, before Grandpa Logan had died. But it was in Eli's blood. Even when he'd made Sharon's daddy manager of the construction company and hired somebody else to handle his other concerns, he'd held onto the reins of the huge farm he'd amassed. He kept a foreman, but he refused point-blank to give up any other control; you held on to land, he vowed. It kept the family strong.

Eli was like his own father. Grandpa Logan had loved all of this. From his gnarled hands to his heavy boots, from his Washington, D.C. overalls to the old brown hat he'd worn on town errands, he'd been a farmer. Grandpa Logan had refused to set foot in Eli's fancy house, and Eli's in-laws had tried fervently to ignore his existence, but he used to come every Saturday morning to the back porch door and collect Jamie. Tory had rarely gone with them; she'd been far more interested in makeup and boys than in horses and mad romps in the fields. Jamie went to the sale with him, or to the horse show, or to the feed store. Sometimes she helped him with his planting.

Jamie smiled. There'd always been noise and laughter and children around Grandpa Logan. She had received no special attention from him because they had money and nobody else did; she'd tagged after him just like Sharon and all seven of her boy cousins. Funny how she hadn't felt this way—the memory of him so strong she ached—in ages. He'd died nearly thirteen years ago. Tory had been buried close to him.

With a hard jerk, Jamie shook off the rapidly mounting depression. She had to find Garrett.

She unobtrusively edged around behind the talking men, eyes searching. It didn't take long to locate him. He was helping another man unload cattle out of the back of a truck. She recognized him mostly because of the big dog trotting after his every step, and she stopped in dismay.

If anything he looked worse than last night. He still wore that dreadful cap and jeans, his gray T-shirt was stained and stuck to him in places where he was wet with sweat. He had on ugly, heavy brown gloves and was jerking violently, straining to pull a huge, reluctant animal out of the back of the truck. Jamie watched him and his friend struggle with their chore for a minute, and suddenly a great, weary revulsion washed over her.

She did not belong here, in this dusty, smelly barn with these country yokels and this farmer. She walked out, got in the truck and drove straight across the Calhoun County line into Claiborne County. She was going home.

She spent Saturday night alone, more depressed than she'd been since Tory's death. She felt completely isolated; the thought of Todd was not enough to help her during the long, hot night. Once she reached for the phone; she might get through to him in Alaska. But then she remembered their quarrel and backed away.

On Sunday morning, desperate to dispel the gloom from around her, she went to church for the first time in weeks. It helped a little.

The county's only stockbroker, Harry Sheffield, was also a very eligible bachelor; he'd made it plain years ago that he liked Jamie Logan, but when she turned him down, he'd let it go. He was with his elegant mother today, and Jamie was surprised to find that she was almost glad to see him. Harry picked up on her emotions quickly. When he asked her out to lunch, she went, and they spent an hour talking before he took her home.

Harry was clearly about to ask her out for a date as they stood on the front veranda of the Logan house, but he stopped when the front door was flung open. Sharon stood inside the foyer.

"Hi, Harry. I've been waiting for you forever, Jamie. I need to see you." Her expressive voice and face added silently, "Now."

"Sure. Well, thanks for lunch, Harry." Jamie smiled at him.

"I enjoyed it. Maybe we could do it again?"

His eyes were really nice, she thought idly, as she answered, "I'd like to, sometime."

When the door closed on him, Sharon said, "Don't tell me Todd has a rival."

"No, not really. I just felt a little lonesome and Harry was kind."

"Kind is not what Harry wants to be to you. He's been lurking around for years."

"You make him sound sinister," Jamie complained.

"I guess I'm worried. Oh, not about Harry. I got your message about the Garrett guy. You know you don't want to get mixed up with some creep you don't even know."

"He's not that bad, Sharon."

"Then why the panicky phone call?"

"I don't know. Maybe I got down because he's so...so different. So earthy, I guess that's the word. Guess I'm just into more sophisticated types." She tried to smile.

Sharon eyed her suspiciously. "Are you sure that's all? Some backwoodsman who throws a bunch of feed sacks around for a living is not my idea of an ideal date—or whatever you call what you've got planned. He sounds crude and loud and mean."

Jamie laughed for the first time in days. "I wish you could see him. He's so shy I can't get three words out of him. As for mean, the only things he's done so far are—let's see—he's saved me from a huge dog, driven me home and fixed my truck and left it parked right outside my door."

"Young Sir Galahad in the flesh," Sharon said dryly. "All this is one weekend?"

"All in twelve hours!"

"So you're determined to go on with it?"

Jamie thought a minute of how Garrett looked, then said slowly, "I can't believe it, but I guess I am. I want to know for sure if—if Tory meant to wreck. Why she died."

Sharon said impatiently, "Because. Isn't that good enough? Why did I fall off the roof when I was eight and not get a scratch? Just because."

"I want to know," Jamie said stubbornly.

Her cousin shoved her hand through her curly brown hair and sighed. "Okay. Have it your way. You always do."

Monday morning Jamie went to work at the Farmers' Association. Her job was better than she'd hoped. She was at one of three front desks, and she had to take payments, make appointments for farmers to see the officers and agents, type, file, run a computer and be a sort of general receptionist. Only one other woman worked in the front with her; the second was on maternity leave. Jamie didn't mind Mrs. Cheever. She was a dumpling of a woman, quick, efficient and warm. She called everybody "honey," from the oldest farmer to the boss himself.

Jamie didn't know what to expect from Mrs. Cheever. Jamie had, after all, gotten her job using distinctly underhanded methods. She and Sharon had lifted a letterhead from Eli's correspondence with one of his cronies, a state director of the association, and when Mrs. Cheever's boss had glanced at that unsigned but highly suggestive note from one of his superiors wondering if he could "find a place" for Jennifer Lynn for a while, he'd hastily done just that.

But the other woman either knew nothing of it or just accepted it philosophically as the norm, because she informed Jamie cheerfully that she was welcome to call her Cheever just as everybody else at the association did.

By the time Jamie got settled in and her head had stopped spinning, it was well past lunch.

"Nearly one, honey," called Mrs. Cheever. "You need to take your lunch hour soon or you won't get one. We go home at four."

"All right. I'm starving. Where do you go to eat?"

"I generally bring a sandwich and eat it in the conference room. But there's a little place down the road, and there's a Dairy Queen."

Normally Jamie would have shuddered at the sight of the brown little building that housed Mama Reba's Café, but today she was hungry. She wasn't used to getting up on a schedule and she'd been too late to eat. Her breakfast had been a Coke she'd had in the refrigerator and had drunk while she drove to work.

But she didn't have time to linger over lunch. She had plans, and when she rushed out of the café twenty minutes later, she turned the truck toward Johnson's Farm Supply.

"Drat!" she muttered to herself as she pulled into the parking area. There were several trucks; that meant several people inside.

The huge, drafty, barnlike interior of the structure was dim and cool, and it took her eyes a minute to find him.

He was at the counter, leaning across it to listen to the three other men who were talking. He was, she thought to herself in vast relief, clean and neat today. There was no cap hiding his face, and he looked quite—boyish—even pleasantly rough-cut.

There was no help for it; the lunch hour she'd been allotted was ticking away, and the men weren't about to move. Taking a deep breath, Jamie walked forward.

The talking died away. Three of the men eyed her with interest; Ren's face was blank, his voice pleasant. "Yes, ma'am?"

"Hello, Ren. I came to—to—say thank you for—" She broke off in embarrassment as he stared at her in surprise, a surprise repeated on the faces of the grouped men. Apparently girls just didn't walk in and address him, and apparently he didn't know her from Adam. This was definitely a new experience.

She tried again, flushing. "I'm the girl you—"

Comprehension broke over him. "You're the girl with the water hose!"

"Yes! Thank goodness you remembered."

"Yeah, I remember. You just look so—so different. I didn't really see too much of you that night—"

"Looks like that was your loss, Ren," said one of the men at the counter, a bold young one. He eyed the long lines of the girl before him.

Jamie knew his type immediately and ignored him. She spoke directly to Ren. "I—I wonder if I could talk to you a minute. Maybe just you and me."

His face registered shock and surprise.

"Whew, Ren!" hooted the bold one, and another, older one said teasingly, "Better watch it, son."

Ren just grinned at them but a flush spread up over his cheeks to match the one on Jamie's. He said,

"Okay," and edged out from the counter to follow her as she turned and walked away.

She stopped outside the store under the shade of the striped metal awning. He obligingly stopped beside her.

"Are they always so—"

He hastily said, "Oh, don't pay any attention to them. They're doin' it to get at me, not you, anyway."

"Oh. Well, I wanted first to tell you thanks for the repair job on the truck." She looked up at him, at the brown eyes, the crooked nose, the bushy mane of brown hair.

He smiled, shook his head. "No big deal."

"Yes, it was. You fixed it. I don't even know when you found the time or why."

He shrugged. "I just picked up a part from the station on my way back home. It didn't take very long. Then I drove it to your apartment on my way to the stock barn the next morning and a friend picked me up."

"But why? You don't know me. I could have had the mechanic do it the next day."

"You said you needed a job enough to move all the way here to get it." He gave another slow smile and a sort of half laugh. "That sounded pretty desperate to me. I just figured you needed all your money."

Jamie's mouth dropped, then she shut it. Money was not something she'd ever needed, and she hadn't remembered that to people who had to work for a small paycheck every week, the expense of a mechanic and an auto repair, no matter how minor, could be a real problem.

"Oh. Thank you. I do." She had to be more careful. "I'd like to do something for you in return."

He protested, "No, it's okay. I don't want—"

"I was hoping you'd let me take you out—" Whoops! "I mean," she amended, "let me fix you supper one night at my apartment. Maybe tomorrow night?"

He stared at her incredulously. "Do what?"

"Fix you—supper. You know," she said hurriedly. "Come over and eat with me. It's—sort of lonesome being new here and all."

"You want *me* to..." Suddenly a smile lit up his face. "Sure. I'd like it a lot. What time?"

She nearly heaved a sigh of relief. "How about six?"

"Okay. Six."

"I'll see you then." She walked away from him, and he stood unmoving, watching till she turned to wave. He threw up a hand in reply and reentered the store, where his curious friends still waited.

That'd give them something to talk about, she thought mischievously, especially if he told them about the upcoming date. They'd aggravate him to death the rest of the afternoon.

Chapter Three

Tuesday night found Jamie surprisingly nervous. The meal looked and tasted good. It should, she thought when she surveyed the set table in the tiny apartment kitchen. It had been nearly midnight when she'd finished the meal the night before and left it in the refrigerator, ready to be put in the oven and then served. Jamie did know how to cook. Her studies at the exclusive private college she'd attended had included an elaborate course concerning etiquette, household finances, gourmet cooking and entertaining on a grand scale. Those were the true keys to getting and holding a well-to-do husband, her teacher, Madame DeLeon, had insisted.

Jamie smothered a laugh as she waited for Ren. Madame would die if she knew that the only time Jamie had ever put her skills to the test was for a poor dirt farmer whom she hoped to seduce—or nearly seduce, anyway.

Jamie eyed herself critically in the mirror in the bathroom. It was hard to know how to dress and still hide her identity. She didn't want to come across as too provocative, either—she might scare him off. So she'd stuck to a pair of jeans. Well-fitting jeans, to be sure. And a wheat-colored cotton top that dipped ever so gently in front to reveal just a little of her lightly-tanned breasts. She'd brushed a hint of golden glitter across her exposed skin; if her hair had been arranged in its usual exotic disarray and if she'd worn her usual makeup, she'd have had her favorite golden-girl look, as Todd called it, instead of this sweet, innocent enticement.

Todd. Now there was one who was not going to be amused if he ever heard about this little escapade, thought Jamie. Then Ren knocked at her door.

As she ushered him in, she said in a friendly voice, "You look nice."

The flush that was already familiar to her rose along his cheekbones, under the clear tan of his face. "Thanks. So do you."

"I forgot to ask you what you like to eat. I hope I haven't made things you hate."

"I don't reckon there are any." He smiled. "It sure smells good. I cook for myself so much that I'm glad to eat somebody else's food for a change."

He hastily pulled her chair out for her. The meal was a success, but he was ill at ease and had little to say.

Finally Jamie asked him about his family. He was open, direct, blunt in his answers.

"My dad's dead. He died when I was in high school."

"And your mother?"

Something flickered in his face. "She's gone, too. She died when I was ten."

"Oh, I'm sorry."

"It's okay. It was a long time ago. Fifteen years."

"Who'd you live with after your dad died?"

"Live with?"

"You know, like a guardian."

He shrugged. "I never had one. An uncle of mine was ordered by the judge to look after me, but he had five kids of his own. So I just lived at home by myself, and he checked on me once in a while. At least, he did for a few months. When I didn't go to jail or starve to death, he quit worrying about me and left me alone."

Jamie stared at him, appalled as much at his simple, flat telling of the story as she was at the tale itself. "But that's hor—" Then she caught herself. "How did you survive?" she substituted instead.

"Worked for farmers hauling hay during the summers and for Enoch Johnson in the afternoons after school."

"Weren't you lonely?"

"Yeah. But I ran around with my two cousins sometimes. That helped." He tried to change the subject. "What about your family?"

This was tricky ground. "I've got a lot of cousins. Sometimes too many. Lots of boy cousins. They did—do—all the mean things they're supposed to. Once Shar—a girl cousin of mine and I were going to a party. Our first teenage party, with *real* boys and even chaperons. We spent hours getting ready, makeup and eyeshadow and hair spray galore. The minute we walked out the door, two of the boys hit us in the faces with the water from the garden hose. They soaked us. Shar—my cousin had mascara streaked to her chin, my eyeshadow had washed down on my cheeks. And our hair was ruined!"

He grinned. "They made you late?"

"Lord, no. We didn't even get to go. She was grounded and *I* went to the hospital."

He stopped eating. "You did? What for?"

Jamie began to laugh suddenly. She hadn't thought of the incident in years, but now it was as clear as if it were yesterday. "We forgot we were gorgeous, provocative young ladies and got into a terrible fight with them. They threw mud on us, but they were laughing so hard they couldn't run, and when Mama got there, I was after Joe with a hoe I found in the garage. I chased him right into a barbed-wire electric fence and we both got tangled up in it. I still have a scar from that fence, but it was worth it. I don't even remember the hurt too much. I didn't care. He was yelling so loud all I could feel was satisfaction."

He laughed with her, then said, "Sounds like the way my cousin treated us. She gave her brother a black eye when he told her boyfriend she'd put padding in her—" All of a sudden, he broke off and flushed hotly. Embarrassed, he tried to drop his hands from the gesture he'd made to show just where his cousin had thought she'd needed padding.

Jamie wanted to laugh, but she took pity on him. "Every girl in the world has done that, and every brother or boy cousin who ever found out has told. *I* know." She grimaced wryly.

"You don't look like you ever needed any help," he blurted out, then said quickly, "I'm sorry. I—" Then he accidentally dropped his fork. It made a clinking sound when it fell.

For a minute he just sat there. Then he took a deep breath and said quietly, "I'm not any good at this. I don't know what to do or say. It was a nice thing to do, to invite me. But I think I'd better leave."

He stood abruptly.

She stared at him in shock. No man had ever even expressed a desire to end a date with her early; this one was actually going home. Walking out on her.

But this one was shy. She didn't think he really wanted to leave.

"Ren."

He halted in his turning away.

"I'd rather you stayed. You can drop all the forks in the house if you want."

"I'd better go."

She stood, too. "Why? What will you do? I hope you'd rather spend an evening with me than with that dog of yours. I'm sure I'm as interesting as he is."

"You're fine," he said quietly. "But me—"

"Then why are you leaving? Unless you'd rather go. Would you?"

Her direct question brought his eyes up to hers. He shoved his hands in his hip pockets, then said haltingly, "No. I—I want to stay here."

She smiled at him. His plain answer pleased her, and her smile reflected the pleasure. "Good. I'll even let you help me with the dishes if you want, just to show how much trust I have in you."

Ren hesitated a second, then smiled. "I'm good at dishwashing," he said.

So she gave him a drying towel to help, and ran the dishwater. But just as she dumped the dishes in the sink the phone rang. It had to be Sharon; nobody else knew.

It was.

"I just called to see if you've made any progress with Sir Galahad. How's the job going?"

"Everything's fine, and the job is good."

Sharon caught the inflection and the restraint in her voice. "What is it?" she asked cautiously. "You can't talk?"

"I'd rather not, not right now."

Comprehension crept into Sharon's voice. "He's there, isn't he? At your apartment this instant! Are you all right? He didn't—he's not dangerous, is he?"

Jamie choked back a laugh. Ren had his back to her, but he was industriously washing dishes. Soapsuds rose around his arms, and the blue and white drying towel was hanging out of his hip pocket.

"No," she gurgled, "I wouldn't say that. Just—oh, ready and willing to help."

Sharon gasped. "My lord, you're not going to—not tonight! Beth has to see that he stays all night. Not this soon, Jamie."

"No. Sharon, for goodness sakes. Nothing like that. Look, call me back later."

"Swear I won't be interrupting anything," Sharon demanded.

"You won't. I'll wait for your call."

As Jamie hung up the phone, she watched Ren Garrett for a minute. He was whistling softly as he worked, and he hunched his right shoulder up to rub his cheek so that he wouldn't have to rub his soapy hand over it instead. Beneath the thin cotton of the blue plaid shirt he wore, Jamie saw the flexing and bunching of heavy muscles. Suddenly she realized that, though his jeans were worn and old, they fit him awfully well. She grinned to herself; she supposed there was more to a man than a pretty face. This one shocked her by looking good from this particular angle, anyway. He was not really slender despite his height. There was a heavy muscularity about his thighs and shoulders that probably came from handling those heavy feed sacks all day and livestock at night. Funny that she'd never noticed his attractive build before; ridiculously incongruous that she realized his strength, his masculinity, at this kitchen work. Work he did deftly, efficiently.

He glanced over his shoulder at her, and she started, afraid he'd catch her—well, assessing his attributes. He'd probably run for the border. Honestly, she was sure he had a sex drive. She just had to find it and operate on it a bit.

"That phone call was just in time, wasn't it?" she said as she started drying dishes. "Now if it had just been a little longer, you'd have had to do the dishes all alone."

"Couldn't you keep your friend talking?"

"I told her I'd rather she call back later. Even if it meant I had to do dishes."

When they finished, they went for a walk down the street. It was dusky and deserted. They talked mostly about work. She kept asking questions so he wouldn't lapse into another silence. At last they strolled back to her door.

"I really did have a good time. Thanks for the supper." He hesitated a minute, but Jamie had already made up her mind about this moment. She'd been cool and friendly all evening. Now it was time to add a little spice, hopefully to tantalize him into returning. He was a big boy—he'd take it.

"No, thank you for fixing the truck and for helping me get through a lonely evening. I appreciate it." She took a quick step into him; then, standing on tiptoes, she brushed a kiss on his warm brown cheek, oh so close to his mouth. "I hope I see you again soon."

He just stood there in silence and surprise as she shut the door. Jamie felt a stab of pure jubilation. She was pretty sure he'd liked it. There was definitely something here she could cultivate. She'd have that letter yet.

Wednesday passed uneventfully, and Thursday came as something of a shock. When Jamie got in to work, things were already in confusion. The manager of the association had been called unexpectedly to some hot meeting that afternoon with an auditor in Lexington. He had left Cheever to run his wildly disorganized office and meet with the agents.

In the middle of it all, while Jamie ran the front office alone, the door opened to admit a thin little lady dressed in violent purples. She hobbled on a cane, and her short hair was tinted nearly as purply-blue as her dress.

She let the door swing shut behind her and stared belligerently at Jamie, who at last ventured to say good-morning.

"Nothin' good about it, far as I can see. Where is everybody?" the little woman demanded.

"Nobody's available at the moment," Jamie said politely.

"Cheever. Where's she?"

Jamie glanced back over her shoulder. The door to the conference room was still firmly shut. "I'm afraid she's not available, either."

The old lady snorted. "Must'a got wind I was comin'. Well, they won't hide from me. I know they're here. Saw their cars in the parkin' spaces outside." To Jamie's surprise, she came determinedly around her.

"Wait, ma'am, you can't—"

The old lady raised her cane, not listening to Jamie at all, and whacked the conference door viciously several times. She was surprisingly strong and the noise was loud.

"Cheever!" she roared.

The door flew open, and the flustered Cheever demanded, "What in the world is going on out here? Sidney!" she exclaimed, her voice and face changing ludicrously.

"Yes, Sidney," the old woman snapped, pushing forward past her, poking her out of the way with her killer cane. "Thought you'd put me off with that twit of a girl out there, did you? I sent word to this office two days ago for you to send an agent out to see me!"

"Yes, but Sidney," Cheever began, "I can't send anybody now. The boss was supposed to go, but I guess he forgot. And he's on his way to Lexington. Let me get somebody out to your house tomorrow." The last was said in a cajoling voice.

"Now," Sidney demanded.

"No, not now," Cheever wheedled. "Whatever problem you've got, surely it'll wait."

The other woman said sharply, "You just march yourself out there with me and I'll show you what my problem is. Then you tell me what's goin' on."

"But—"

"Now." The old lady was implacable.

Cheever glanced around the room resignedly, then her gaze fell on Jamie, standing openmouthed behind Sidney. "Miss Lynn!" she said in sudden thankfulness. "Sidney, this is Jennifer Lynn. She's a—a—a new special assistant." Her voice sounded inspired.

Jamie could feel it coming. Cheever was going to stick her with this cane-happy old harpy. "No—no, really," she began to protest as Sidney turned to stare at her.

"She'll be happy to go out to your farm and help you," Cheever interrupted Jamie in relief. "Please, Jennifer." Her voice was pleading as she went back into the conference room and shut the door almost on Sidney's nose.

There was a moment of silence, then Sidney snorted. She started past Jamie, but something in her expression made Jamie realize that her feelings were hurt. That was no surprise, Jamie reflected. Nobody seemed to have time for her this morning.

"Wait," Jamie called as the little woman reached the door. "I really would like to help if I can. What's wrong, Miss—Mrs.—"

"Miss. Miss Sidney Hill," the lady said sharply.

"Miss Hill." Jamie smiled at her, but Sidney just glared back.

"Don't waste your efforts makin' friendly noises at me. If Cheever hasn't got the time to see me, I'm not gettin' fobbed off on any ignorant green girl like you."

The woman's derisive tone effectively cut off Jamie's feelings of compassion, and so she shrugged, retorting, "Miss Hill, green girls don't particularly like getting stuck with sour old persimmons like you, either."

There was a moment's silence while Sidney stared belligerently at Jamie. Then Jamie's good manners came back. "I'm sorry," she said reluctantly. "I shouldn't have said that."

"No," snapped Sidney. Then she turned back to the door. "Well, come on, let's go."

"Go where?" asked Jamie blankly.

"Out to the farm. You might as well. Nobody else is goin' to."

"Out to the—" Jamie cut off her dazed comment sharply. Apparently Sidney Hill had had a sudden change of heart. Grabbing up her bag and notebook, Jamie headed for the door in the wake of the unexpectedly rapid steps of Sidney and her cane.

So Jamie found herself crawling into an ancient Cadillac. What terrified her was the way Sidney's head barely reached over the dashboard, the way she pulled the long car out from the curb with never a glance for other vehicles.

"What did you want to see Cheever about?" asked Jamie politely, trying to take her mind off the weaving path of the car. Too late she realized her mistake when her question launched Sidney off into an explanation that took her eyes off the road. Jamie hoped she lived to see Roswell again.

"Lights. I saw lights out in my south pasture. I saw them once nearly two months ago, and I saw them again two nights ago."

"Lights?" murmured Jamie. Was this old lady for real?

"Don't use that tone with me, miss," snapped Sidney. "I've heard 'the old lady's crazy' just one too many times. From that fancy niece of mine, from that idiot boss of yours, even from Cheever a little."

"How far away were the lights?" interrupted Jamie, trying to be tactful.

"I told you. In the south pasture on the edge of Baker Hollow. It's a half mile or more from my house."

Sidney's south pasture was, in fact, a long way from everything. Jamie had a long, hot walk out to it, and halfway across its huge expanse, wet with perspiration, she stopped for breath and a good look around. There was nothing behind except fences and, a long, long way away, a mere speck in the distance, Sidney's house. In front of Jamie, another great green distance, there lay a heavily wooded deep hollow. She could see only the tops of the trees that grew up and down its steep sides.

"Lights," muttered Jamie to herself as she started back. "Probably a spaceship full of little green men who took one look at Sidney Hill and her purple hair and ran screaming back to Mars."

Then she saw it. A deep rut in a swampy, low section of the field where a fallen log lay. A track from a very big tire that had probably gotten hung up on the log hidden in the tall grass. And beside it the glitter of silver. Frowning, Jamie picked up the silver emblem; it said *orth*.

"Martian?" she asked the grasshopper who lit on her shoe, then she pocketed the metal piece. Back at Sidney's aging Victorian house, she gave it to the old lady.

"Means nothin' to me." Sidney shrugged. "I'll keep it. But you saw tracks, did you? When we get back to town, tell Cheever somebody's tryin' to rustle my cattle. That's exactly what's goin' on here."

Jamie shot one whimsical look at her and reluctantly climbed into the car. Staring out the window on the way back to Roswell, she suddenly realized where she was.

"Oh, there's Ren's house," she said in surprise, more to herself than anybody.

"Wrendon Garrett?" Sidney answered. "Know the boy, do you? He's my closest neighbor. Mows my yard for me. I can't abide that dratted dog of his. It chases my cats, or it did till the last time he brought it over. I caned it once and that was the end of that."

Jamie could believe it. When they pulled up in front of the office again, she climbed out, and Sidney followed her onto the little sidewalk.

"I appreciate your goin'," she said gruffly. "Don't you forget to tell them about those tracks you found. Surely they won't think *you're* senile."

So Jamie dutifully told Cheever what had happened, winding up with Sidney's claim that her cows were being rustled.

Cheever gave an exasperated groan and said, "I've heard that story before. I had it yelled at me once or twice by Sidney. But we sent an agent out and verified that all her cattle are accounted for. Not a one is missing."

Cheever had no more time to talk. She was doing the work of two people, so Jamie was left once more to run the outside office, and that was the end of the discussion about Sidney Hill.

Her night was, like the night before, lonesome in the tiny apartment. She thought about going home. And she again thought about calling Todd. Finally, she decided to drive over to see Sharon. It was a thirty-minute trip, and she was tired, but she wanted to do something.

The truck was hot, and she had barely gotten it out on the road before she decided against going. Instead, she circled the tiny town square. In the stillness, she could hear voices and laughter. Curious, she followed them. Driving down past the well-lit Dairy Queen Cheever had told her about, she saw a tiny park, and beyond that, a softball game going on.

It looked alive; the people were excited. Jamie stopped the truck, got out and strolled over. Her hands tucked in the pockets of her peach-colored shorts, she stood in the shadows watching the two men's teams playing. And in the middle of the screaming and yelling, she heard her own name being called. It took a minute for the "Jennifer! Jennifer Lynn!" to register.

It was Cheever, smiling and advancing toward her. "I thought that was you. Come watch the game. We can all use the rest after this day at work."

"I was just—driving by and saw all the people."

"I saw you walk up. My son's playing tonight, and I came to see him. I'm with my grandchildren. You're welcome to sit with us."

So Jamie let herself be led to the bleachers and introduced to the Cheever family. Cheever was especially proud of her three-year-old grandson, and pointed out Robert Cheever, Jr., who was playing first base.

It was a close game, and a lot of jumping and shouting went on. Jamie just sat and let the comforting feeling of being in a crowd sweep over her. The heat didn't seem to bother anybody much, and she amused herself by watching those around her.

It was the announcer who brought her attention back to the game. "Next up to bat is Ren Garrett, number 17." The name hit her unexpectedly, and she stood up to look for him.

He had the red baseball cap that the rest of the team wore, the same red jersey, and jeans. It *was* Ren; she recognized the tall figure, the long stride, the easy flex of muscle and limb as he stretched out to the bat. It was funny how she knew that build and walk. The recognition must have come from watching him work those three days before she decided to make him the object of the bet.

Somehow, it angered Jamie to think he was down here playing ball when she'd done her part to get his mind on her. What was he doing, having a good time and never even thinking of her—not even telling her he played ball?

Jamie laughed suddenly. This was ridiculous. She had only actually been around him three hours of his life, and she certainly didn't care what he did with his time as long as she got what she wanted. You're cracking up, Jamie, she told herself.

He had a strike and two balls against him when he finally made a low, hard hit out past second base. He only got to third, but two runners came in on his hit, so there was a lot of screaming and yelling. And Jamie suddenly discovered a new interest in the ball game now that she knew a player in it.

Ren was not on the team that Cheever's son was, and Jamie was apparently sitting on the wrong bleachers to be screaming for the red team, so she tried to be quiet whenever things got tense. But as the game wore down to its finish, and the score was 18 to 17, and the runner on second base was Ren, Jamie got as excited as everybody else. The batter hit the ball, and the runner on third came in to tie the score. Ren made a dash for third, slid in and lost his hat somewhere in the dust. The third baseman missed the ball an outfielder threw; it went over his head as he grabbed wildly.

Everybody was yelling and standing, and Jamie was on her feet screaming, "Run! Run! Get up and run!" Nobody heard her because they were shouting everything from "Get him out!" to "Throw it home!" Ren came in in a wild dash and a flurry of arms and legs and dust. Right behind him came in the third and last runner, and the game was over, Ren's team winning by two.

"That was a killer of a game," gasped Cheever, fanning herself with a handkerchief and wiping beads of perspiration from her face.

"It was exciting—and *hot*," Jamie said. "I think I'll get a Coke at the refreshment stand. It was nice to meet all of you," she added to the smiling girl and children who'd been with the older woman.

"See you tomorrow," Cheever called after her.

Jamie bought her Coke and sipped it, considering whether or not to approach Ren.

"Hey, doll," said the surprised voice of someone beside her. She jerked, and turned to face the young man who'd been in the store on Monday with Ren. "I remember you—you were in Enoch Johnson's place the other day."

"And I remember you," she answered dryly. He had on the same color jersey and cap Ren was wearing.

"Yeah?" His pleased smugness reminded her of Todd somehow, when some deal had gone right for him. "My name's Ben. Ben Dalton. Ren said yours was Jennifer. That you're new in town. You like ball games?"

"Doesn't everybody?"

"Sure. That's why I play. Look, I'm gonna get cleaned up and then go get something to eat." He pulled the cap off his curly hair and grinned down at her. "How about you go with me?"

Jamie eyed him sardonically. "One thing you've got a lot of is confidence. I'll say that for you."

He propped a hand on the wall of the refreshment stand beside her head and leaned into her to say suggestively, "I've got a lot of everything. Why don't you get to know me and find out?"

"No, thanks. You're not my type," she said uninterestedly.

A flash of irritation spread over his face, but he smoothed it away and leaned closer, right in her ear. "Listen, babe, I can be a lot more fun than Ren anytime. Hmm? How 'bout it?"

"No." She said it distinctly, and straightened to shove him away. But as she turned she saw over his shoulder Ren himself, standing just a few feet from them. He had stopped stock-still at sight of her and Ben. Some kind of emotion chased over his face, then he nodded to her and moved away.

Anger flared up in Jamie. Was he just going to leave her with Ben Dalton? He was about to learn a lesson about what you could do to Jamie Logan. Or Jennifer Lynn.

"Ren!" she called after him. He stopped and turned warily.

"You don't know what you're missing, baby," muttered Ben, catching at her arm.

She shook him off and said, "Oh, yes, I know exactly. Now let go!"

Ren stood waiting as she ran up to him. His cap was shoved back on his head and he was hot and dusty. His face was blank.

"I was driving by and heard the game. When I stopped, I saw you playing. It was exciting." She smiled at him.

"Yeah. But it's nearly too hot to play, what with all these lights on." He motioned toward the blazing boards of white lights on the field, where bugs buzzed and whirred heavenward. "Well, I gotta get home, I guess." The last was said awkwardly, and he lifted his cap to run his hand through his hair. It was wet where the edge of the cap had sat on it, and his raking fingers only made the thick, straight, short mane wilder. For all his size and face, he suddenly reminded her of a tired little boy. But he wasn't getting away that easily.

"Ben Dalton—is that his name?—just asked me to go get something to eat with him," she said boldly.

Her directness took him by surprise. He said, haltingly, "Oh." That was all.

She said softly. "I'd rather go with somebody else. If he'll ask me."

He jerked as if he'd been hit, stared at her in shock, then, after a minute, he smiled. It changed his face completely and revealed a dimple on the left side of his mouth.

Ren Garrett actually had a dimple, a very deep boyish version of one. It was the reason his smile gave him charm at odd moments, Jamie realized belatedly.

"I reckon—hope—you mean me."

Teasingly, Jamie mimicked, "Reckon I do."

"Would you like to get something to—"

"Yes, I would," she interrupted promptly.

He laughed. "I never met a girl like you before, Jennifer Lynn."

"Good. And I hope you never do. I want to be one of a kind where you're concerned, Ren Garrett." Somewhere in the back of her mind a small voice cautioned her to go slow. He was not used to this overdone flirting; he might not catch the spirit of the game. She didn't want to get too heavy.

They took his truck and did something Jamie had never done in her entire life: they ate under the bright lights of the Dairy Queen drive-in. A hamburger and fries tasted just as good in the front seat of his truck as they did served on china at home, Jamie concluded. And he was looser, more talkative. But he had to be, because people kept coming up to talk to him, mostly other ball players and their families who'd stopped to eat at the suddenly busy little drive-in.

"This must be the in place to be," she observed, after their third visitor at the truck window.

He laughed. "Only place, you mean. Nobody else stays open past seven. You're livin' wild in Roswell when you go out to eat after seven. Or you'd better have a good excuse for doin' it."

"If you don't want to set all the gossips' tongues to wagging, you mean?" Jamie grinned. "This sounds exactly like home. I'd better move."

"What's the name of your hometown in Tennessee?" he asked curiously, and Jamie rushed in to cut him off.

"I met a woman today who knows you," she announced, sucking her strawberry shake up through the straw. "Speaking of gossiping and things like that," she added teasingly.

"She must'a been out of people to talk about if *I* was it," he answered, but he looked at her with a question on his face.

"An old lady named Sidney Hill."

"Oh, Lord, not Sidney." He grimaced wryly. "I know what she said. I've been that 'dratted Garrett kid' ever since she was my Latin teacher in the eighth grade and I broke an ink pen all over a desk."

"Wrong," answered Jamie with a superior air that she spoiled by laughing.

"She didn't call me that?" he asked dubiously.

"No. She saved the compliment for your dog. She said she caned him, and I was in total sympathy with her."

It was Ren's turn to laugh, but before he could answer her, somebody slapped the back window of the truck roughly. The loud noise and the sudden jarring made Jamie jump, and she glanced around to see a man framed in the side opening grinning broadly at Ren.

"Hey, boy," he said affectionately. "You played a good game."

"Thanks," Ren answered. "I didn't know you were there tonight."

"Yep. We saw your truck and I stopped to ask you if you're goin' to the sale next week."

"Probably. I need to get rid of the extra horses before fall," Ren answered, then indicated Jamie, who sat in the shadows quietly. "This is Jennifer Lynn. She's new in town. This is my cousin, Dan Garrett."

Dan surprised Jamie by being older, much older than Ren. And he was handsome, with curly blond hair and sleepy blue eyes. The only way he resembled his younger cousin was in the slowness of his speech and the smile in his voice.

If Dan startled Jamie, he was equally startled by her. "Glad to meet you, ma'am," he said, surprised. He peered through the shadows at her inquisitively, through the thin, gold-framed glasses he wore, and his mouth dropped slightly as Jamie turned into the light and met his gaze head-on.

"Sorry, Ren," he said uncomfortably. "I didn't mean to butt in. I'll see you sometime this week about the sale, okay? G'night, ma'am," he added.

"Jennifer," she said. *Ma'am* made her feel like Whistler's mother.

"Jennifer," he repeated obediently, and melted away.

"What's wrong with him?" she asked in surprise. "He nearly ran."

Ren shrugged, a little uncomfortably. "I guess it's because he didn't know you. He's sort of, well, shy around strangers."

Like his cousin, she thought.

When they went back to get Jamie's truck where she'd parked it, Ren turned off his motor and in the silence of the darkened ballpark, Jamie could hear the crickets and the tree frogs singing.

"Must be late. I'll never get up on time tomorrow morning," she said in a hushed voice.

"Just think about it being Friday," he said lazily. "It makes a lot of difference."

"I had a good time," she said primly, reaching for the truck door. Surely if he wasn't dead from the neck down, he'd do something.

"Jennifer," he said quietly, and when she turned around, he reached out, took her hand and pulled her to him. Then, slowly, as though he was giving her time to consider and move away, he bent to her lips.

His mouth was warm and gentle, and aside from it and the hand he still held, they had no other contact. Maybe that was why all that Jamie was conscious of was the mouth pressed to hers. He pulled away an instant, then, with a low murmur of sound, kissed her again. Jamie had started to open her eyes, so he took her by surprise. She saw his intent face just a second before his lips claimed hers, and a sudden surprising sweetness swept over her heart. She felt warm inside, as warm as his mouth on hers. Her reaction was so unexpected she couldn't move until he let her go.

This time they parted slowly, lips clinging. They looked at each other in the thick darkness, and she said in a near whisper, "Good night, Ren."

He just watched her get out, then he said, "Hey, Jennifer. I'm glad you didn't go with Ben Dalton."

"Me, too," she replied, and smiled. She meant it, much to her own shock. She actually sort of liked this guy.

She felt that same liking for him from Cheever the next day. Jamie was surprised when he walked in the office at lunchtime, and he was embarrassed, because Mrs. Cheever hailed him loudly.

"Well, Ren, honey, we haven't seen you in ages," she said, standing up to help him. "How's that bull you bought doing?"

"Fine, Mrs. Cheever. I've had calves out of him all spring," Ren answered, but his eyes were searching for Jennifer. He found her behind her desk and she waved a little.

"What can we do for you?" Mrs. Cheever asked him briskly.

"Ah—" He motioned toward Jamie. "I—uh—I came to—to see her."

"Jennifer?" Surprise settled on Cheever's face when Jamie stood and said smilingly, "Hi, Ren. I see you survived our wild night at the Dairy Queen."

"I think I'll live. I just wanted to see if—if—" He flushed when Cheever leaned forward and listened avidly. "Have you had lunch, I meant to ask."

"No. If this is an invitation, I'd love to go," she answered promptly.

And as they ate together, he finally got to the point. "I work pretty late tonight. I don't get off till eight." He stopped: she said nothing. "What I wanted was for you—I mean, I was goin' to ask if you wanted to go to the movies. The late show."

"Sure. It sounds like fun."

When she went back to work, Cheever was waiting. "So you're seeing Ren Garrett, are you?"

"He asked me to the movies tonight."

"Well, Ren's a good boy, and a hard worker. He's had a rough time of it, what with his father dying. Nobody really wanted him. He was nearly sixteen when John Garrett died—too old to adopt."

"He told me a little about it," answered Jamie.

Cheever looked at Jamie, then said slowly, hesitantly, "This will sound awful, and maybe it's not any of my business, but—you're not just leading Ren on to have somebody to run around with till you meet somebody else, are you?"

A hot flush stained Jamie's cheeks and she stammered, "Of—of course not! I don't know why you'd ask such a thing."

Cheever frowned. "Sorry. But Ren's not the sort that just up and takes the eye of a pretty girl the first few times she sees him. And you're an awful pretty girl."

She paused, then continued, "He's quiet and a little shy. But you can't help caring about him if you get to know him. It's hard to describe the way he makes me feel; he makes me want to protect him. And I just don't want to see him hurt. He's too...too..." She searched for the right words.

"Sweet," Jamie said without thinking, and a secret smile tugged at her lips as she remembered the unexpected response she'd felt to his kiss.

"Innocent, too, maybe. Oh, I don't know that I mean about girls and sex. But there's a—a goodness in him. He's worth a dozen Ben Daltons." Cheever eyed Jamie, but added at last and with reluctance, "You'll probably do him good, no matter what."

That comment bothered Jamie so much that when she went back to the apartment, she took out a picture of Tory and stared at it hard. Was it right, what she was doing? Flirting had come so easily and been so meaningless to Tory, and, to a lesser degree, to Jamie herself. Surely Ren Garrett wouldn't be hurt by this. She didn't want his love; she wouldn't let him fall in love. She just wanted into his house to spend one night on some prearranged pretext, so Beth could see her enter and leave.

She was preoccupied most of the movie, and when Ren walked her to her door, he refused to come in. He had sensed something bothering her, and drawn the wrong conclusions, because he opened her door for her and turned to leave.

Jamie realized suddenly he was retreating back into the old shell, and that she had only herself to blame. She caught his arm and said laughingly, "Don't I at least get the same treatment I got last night?"

Startled, he finally said, "You mean, a—" His glance fell on her lips.

"Um, that's exactly what I mean," she said mischievously, bringing her lips closer to his.

He was quick to take her up on her offer, and in the shadows by the door his lips brushed hers once—twice—and then his arms went around her. She sighed against Ren's mouth, and let her own arms clasp around his neck. He was warm and good to the touch; his mouth was the same sweet brand it had been the night before. In fact, the enjoyment she felt from the contact was so great it only made her guilt stronger.

She pulled her mouth away and buried her face against his shirtfront. A hard sob caught in her throat, and panic-stricken with the realization she was about to cry, she stiffened.

"What's wrong, Jennie?" he asked quietly, above her head. "Is it me?"

She gave a hard shake of her head, swallowing tears.

"Are you sick?" he wanted to know. "Tell me. You've been different all night."

"Nothing's wrong," she whispered raggedly. "Just some old, sad memories, that's all."

"About a man?"

"No. About—about my sister."

"What's wrong with her? What's she done?"

"She—she left, that's what. Just up and left for good. And I don't know why it happened."

"Where'd she go?"

Jamie's laugh was harsh and cracked. "I don't know. All I know is that I'll never see her again." All of a sudden, she started to cry, all the ugly, tearing, wrenching tears she'd kept back in front of her parents and been denied by Todd. Her mother had gone to pieces during the ordeal, so Jamie had tried to hold back to help her bewildered father. Only Sharon had seen her cry at all, but even with her, Jamie had never really released her despair. Sharon panicked too easily. But here, before this quiet stranger who was solid and strong and capable of taking her grief and keeping it because it meant nothing to him, she fell apart.

He stood unmoving for a instant, then pulled both arms a little tighter around her. She felt his cheek on top of her head and the slow stroke of his hands down her back, and she let the misery swamp her.

They had been standing in her half-opened door. He somehow shut it with his shoulder, and they just stood there, locked together. He rocked her gently back and forth. At last when the hot tears and the agony began to recede, and all there was left were her gasping intakes of breath in the silence of the room, he edged his head back a little to look down at her half-hidden face.

"I'm sorry," she whispered in shamed embarrassment, wiping at her wet, burning cheeks. "I bet—you haven't ended many dates th-this way." She tried to smile.

"Your sister's dead, isn't she?" he asked quietly.

"Please, I'd rather not—"

"I know she is, because I've felt this way before. I've wanted to cry and yell and punch God."

Jamie half nodded and said, still sniffing, "Did it help?"

"Not much. But it gets easier with time. You don't hurt so much after a year or two."

It was what everybody had said to her; it was the same as the pious "Time heals, child" comment of her old Sunday school teacher. But from this still-faced, sad-eyed man she somehow knew it was a promise of truth.

"You may not believe this, but I feel better," she said, trying to smile, and she stepped backward. "*You* probably don't. I'm sorry I went to pieces like this, but—"

"It's okay," he said. "I mean it."

After he'd gone and Jamie lay in her bed alone, she thought he probably did mean it. It *was* okay with him. Todd hadn't wanted her to cry. He'd muttered something about being "no good at things like this," and had openly dreaded every second of the long ordeal of the week of Tory's death. And Jamie had found that she resented Todd's reaction.

She went to sleep with some of the bitterness washed out of her soul. Her only nagging worry was that somehow she'd revealed too much about herself and her inward state. She couldn't really figure out what had made her do that.

Chapter Four

Jamie saw Sharon when she returned home on Saturday and Sunday. They had lunch and went for a swim with friends. It was important that people see her around in case she ever needed to prove she knew nothing of Jennifer Lynn.

Beth was at the swimming party, but except for one exchange, she and Jamie ignored each other. Beth strolled up with a drink in hand as Sharon and Jamie emerged from the dressing room at the edge of the pool.

"How's the farm boy?" she asked, smiling brilliantly.

"Progressing nicely." Jamie's smile glittered as much as Beth's, but as the other girl strolled away, Sharon muttered, "Bitch!" under her breath.

Jamie told Sharon little or nothing about the past week. She said it was because nothing important had happened, but late on Sunday, driving back to Roswell, she faced the truth that that was not so. She hadn't wanted to remember how she, the cool, sophisticated debutante, had broken down and cried like an idiot in the arms of a man who should have been nothing more than a hired hand to her. She couldn't imagine revealing her inner self like that to Casey Evans, the foreman of the construction crew, who tipped his hat respectfully to Miss Logan on the rare occasion that he spoke to her at all, or to Jim Ed Bakewell, the guy who took care of the barns for Eli. They were both nice enough men but they were so distant, so far removed from her, that they did not even seem real. As a child, she had sometimes played with Jim Ed, whose mother had been Eve's cook, but as they grew up, they had drifted so far apart that they had nothing to say except a friendly greeting whenever they met.

Ren belonged in their world, didn't he? And she had blubbered all over him like a baby. So what, her cold, practical side said. She'd also kissed him and shamelessly chased him. Still, that was a game. It was not genuine, not like what she'd done Saturday night, when Jamie Logan—the real Jamie, not Jennifer—had revealed a personal excess of emotion, a piece of herself she'd shown no one else. All because she was starting to like the man she'd chosen as a pawn.

This bet, this game, had things all out of sync. She had only three more weeks to play it, and then, win or lose, she'd be through.

Until then, she'd better get on with it. She hated the sense of embarrassment that rode uneasily in her chest when she thought of facing Ren again, so she did exactly what Eli would have done: she went after it, determined to defeat it head-on.

She drove straight down the country road toward Roswell until she came to the turnoff that led to Ren's house. Looking down the gravel road, she could see little for the huge oaks and maples that shaded things from her view. She couldn't tell if he was home or not, and she wasn't anxious to meet King all by herself, but she turned down the road anyway.

His truck stood parked beside the house and there was no sign of King, much to her relief. The kitchen door was open and through the screen she could see that a fan was blowing. Somewhere back in the house she could hear a radio playing. She knocked; there was no response.

"Ren?"

She still got no answer and, puzzled, turned to leave. As she paused beside the truck, she glanced at the backyard of the house, fenced in from the wide fields behind it. It, too, was shady, the grass a deep green except for right around the bases of the big trees, where the shade made the grass patchy.

Suddenly, Jamie smiled, for under one of the trees was a chaise longue, folded out to its full length, and in it lay Ren, fast asleep. She stepped lightly toward him.

One leg hung off the side of the chair, as though he'd meant to get up and somehow had been trapped into sleep, and his foot in the grass was bare. He'd pulled on a light cotton shirt, but he had neither buttoned it nor tucked it into his jeans. One brown, broad hand was spread across his half-bare chest, and his face was turned slightly from her. The only movement came from the even, slow rise and fall of his chest as he breathed.

Jamie watched him sleeping, and as she did, that unexpected warm feeling of liking rose up in her again. She wanted to touch his face for a fleeting instant. She noted with a gentle amusement that he'd not only combed his thick hair into order but he'd also nicked his chin a little shaving.

Frowning, she realized that Ren had either just come in from someplace or was going out. If it was the last, she was going to be in the way. That thought, and the vague unease she was experiencing about her own emotions as she watched him, sent her backing away. She was almost at the truck when King came loping across the field and saw her.

He set up a loud, fierce barking at the figure edging stealthily away from his unsuspecting master and took out in a dead heat for her. Jamie remembered him too well; she cried, "Ren!" one time, then made a wild scramble for the hood of the truck. When King leaped up and his huge paws caught at the edge of the hood, Jamie went straight for the cab top. King, balked of his prey, gave several threatening snarls and leaps.

Then Ren was shouting, "King! Get down! Down!" His shirt flying out behind him, he ran to the truck. King's growls had subsided, and Ren jerked his collar. "Get out of here. Go on—get!" The dog reluctantly slunk off to one side, and Ren faced Jamie anxiously. "Jennie, you're all right?"

His worried brown eyes, his hands reaching up for her—they made her slide right down into his embrace. For a second, she stood thankfully with her face buried against the muscle and skin of his chest. Then she pushed away.

"I hate that dog. That's the second time he's tried to kill me." Her voice came out choked and broken.

"He's gonna have to quit barkin' at you and scarin' you to death. I'll lock him up in the barn." Ren looked her up and down. "He didn't bite you, did he?"

"Just because he didn't get a chance," she muttered. "He's dangerous."

"He's a guard dog. But I don't want him putting anybody in the hospital."

Jamie relaxed a little. "Just in awkward positions? I never climbed anything so fast in my life as I did that truck. I could have gone up Mount Everest."

He grinned at her and said, "I reckon I'd rather you came down, right here."

Jamie laughed. "It would have served you right if I'd bruised you up. Lying there asleep while your mad dog tried to chew on me. I'm going to try Sidney Hill's way with a cane one of these days."

"He must have thought you were gonna do something to me," Ren said apologetically. "He gets all worried and excited."

Jamie remembered then exactly how she'd wanted to reach for him, and her face flushed. She stepped quickly away from his hands and the warmth of his body. He glanced down and began buttoning his shirt.

"I—I was coming back from visiting—family and thought I'd stop," she offered. "But I saw you were asleep, so I was—"

"You were leavin'?"

"Oh, I don't know. You were sleeping so soundly. I thought you must be tired—"

Ren shrugged. "I was a little. I helped Old man Travers get his hay in yesterday. He broke his leg a couple of weeks ago and couldn't do it all by himself. It took me and two others till dark to get finished. Then when I got home, I had a cow down with a breech calf tryin' to be born. Dan came and we worked tryin' to save her till nearly daylight."

"Did she die?"

"No, and she's got a wobbly little calf for last night's work." Ren reached up one hand and rubbed the back of his neck.

"And you're exhausted," Jamie said in realization. "I'd better be heading on to Roswell. I just—"

"Don't go," he protested. "I slept some this morning, and I got dressed to go over to the cookout the ball team has every Sunday afternoon. I—" he hesitated a minute. "I don't usually go, but I called you to see if you'd like to. Anyway, when you weren't there, I sat down to wait and call again. Next thing I knew, King was barkin' and you—"

"I was climbing Mount Everest," she interrupted. It made her feel good to think he'd wanted to see her this afternoon; she might not need three more weeks.

He glanced at the setting sun. "Reckon we've missed the cookout. It was at four o'clock. I'm starvin'. Have you had supper?"

"No, and I'm starving, too. Want to drive into town and get something?"

He said slowly, "We could grill some steaks here, if you want to. Unless you'd rather go out to eat," he added uncertainly.

Without a pause Jamie said, "No, I'd love to eat here," and suddenly she smiled. If Todd or Harry or any other man she knew had asked her just to eat with them in their quiet, secluded bachelor accommodations in an intimate twosome, she'd have run screaming. She would have had to in order to protect herself. Now here she was blithely agreeing to Ren's suggestion. But then, he had King to protect *him*.

"What's the matter?" Ren asked, watching her face. "I bet you think I can't cook. But I can. Wait and see."

So he put charcoal in a grill in the backyard and took steaks out of the freezer. Inside his neat little kitchen she found pots to fix potatoes in and a bread pan to brown rolls on. His refrigerator held a pitcher of tea, and under a glass cover on the table was a pie topped by frothy meringue.

"Good grief!" she muttered to herself. "He's got me beat as a housekeeper and as a cook."

When Ren came back in to tell her the charcoal was nearly ready, she motioned to the pie and said teasingly, "When did you whip this up, Master Chef?"

He followed her glance and said, flushing, "You mean the chocolate pie? I didn't do that. Lucinda—Lucinda Travers brought that over this morning on account of the help with hay on their farm. I can't do that kind of stuff."

Jamie felt relieved. "That was nice of her. At least her husband is going to eat well while he gets over his broken leg."

He opened his mouth to speak and then carefully closed it. Jamie turned back to the potatoes.

"How long have you lived here, Ren?"

He looked up from the silverware he was collecting. "All my life. This farm was my daddy's, and my granddaddy's before that. I was born here." He motioned at the floor.

Jamie dropped the paring knife she'd been holding. "Here?" she asked incredulously. "As in right *here*?"

He grinned at her shock. "Well, not right on this spot in the kitchen. My mom made it to the bedroom."

"But why? Why not in the hospital?"

"There was a bad storm. The telephone lines were down and Daddy was out in the only truck tryin' to get some cows up. And I was early."

"Is that all?" Jamie asked dryly. "I'm surprised your mother survived. Did she deliver you herself?"

"No. Daddy got back in time to do that much." His smile faded. "She was strong in her own way."

There was a moment of silence. Then he turned away and so did she.

They ate on the picnic table in his backyard in the light of a lantern he lit and hung from a tree. The wet dew of the night cooled things down, and in the trees birds twittered sleepily. King kept his distance, staying just on the back edge of the dim yellow circle. Then they wandered around to the swing on the front porch and sat, creakily swaying and talking. He was a good listener. She told him about going out to Sidney Hill's farm, but he already knew most of the story. He told her belatedly, "She saw Dan and told him, then he told me."

"Do you know everything in this county? And everybody?" Jamie asked in disgust and a little bit of unease. "And how many of them are you related to?" It was common enough in this section of Kentucky for everybody to be somehow connected to everybody else. She herself had more connections than she could count back home in Blue Springs. Even Cody, the sheriff, was the brother of Aunt Somebody's second husband. But she and Sharon had been fairly sure Ren was a loner when they chose him. Where were all these relatives and friends and contacts coming from?

He smiled at her. "That's what happens when you live in a little town all your life. You wind up knowin' all the stories and most of the people. I'm not related to Sidney, if that's what you're askin'."

"Thank goodness," Jamie answered teasingly but in real relief on both counts. "I've never met such an old grouch. What's wrong with her?"

"She's not so bad." He shrugged. It was one of his characteristics, that shrug. Just a tiny lifting of his shoulders that hinted that he was a powerful man. "Lonely. Hurtin'. Her daddy had a lot of money and he wanted a son. Instead, he got three daughters. He was rough on 'em. Mean."

"She comes by it naturally, then," Jamie interjected, enlightened.

"No, I mean really rotten," Ren objected. "Her sisters left home, but Sidney stayed. She wanted to marry this man, I think his name was Roberts, but her daddy bought him off. Offered him a lot of money to leave town, right in front of the courthouse, and the man took it."

Jamie stared at Ren in disbelief. "You're joking," she breathed. "Nobody's got that kind of meanness in them."

"Judge Hill did. My daddy saw the whole thing," Ren answered quietly, and his face held a faraway regret. "So did a lot of other people. They expected

Sidney to leave town, too, like her sisters. But not her. Too much pride. She stuck it out."

"And her father?"

"I don't know. I remember the day he was buried. I was little. The whole town talked about how she never shed a tear." He pulled himself away from the story, and said apologetically, "I guess this is pretty borin'."

"No. It's not at all. I'm just sorry I didn't know before I told her she was a sour old persimmon," Jamie said regretfully.

Ren stared, then gave a shout of laughter.

"Well, she called me a green, ignorant girl," she protested defensively.

Still laughing, Ren replied, "Oh, Lord, I'd like to have seen Sidney's face."

Jamie grimaced. "No, you wouldn't."

"She's okay. Really. She just can't seem to trust anybody." He hesitated, fumbling for the words, then said slowly, "Sidney just can't see that somebody who really cares about somebody else won't deliberately make a fool out of them. Not a man—" and he gave the girl opposite him a slow smile "—or a woman."

There was a silence the space of two heartbeats. For one electrified moment, Jamie thought he was talking directly to her, but he turned away to watch a lightning bug that had lit on the edge of the swing and was glowing on the instant.

"I better go," she said abruptly, and stood up.

"Go!" His surprise brought him to his feet, too. "Not yet. Why, it's not even—" and he looked around at the intense blackness of the night as though he'd never seen it before. "Maybe it is," he said ruefully.

"I'll help you clean up," Jamie said, and picked up the glasses they'd brought around. Her nervousness made them rattle, but she carried them to the kitchen, and he followed.

"Leave 'em," he said, and Jamie obediently, desperately turned away. He watched her a minute, then said, "I said somethin' wrong, but I don't know what it was."

"No, you didn't," she protested. "I just remembered how—how much work I have tomorrow and how late it is."

"It is late," he agreed, then yawned. "Let me take you home."

"I've got my own truck here."

"Yeah, but it's still fifteen minutes to town on a curving road. I can bring your truck into town in the morning."

"And then you won't have a way home," she objected.

Stubbornly, he said, "Dan can bring me home from town. Or—you can." He smiled.

"And have this discussion all over again?" Jamie retorted. "I'll be fine. See you, Ren," and she started out the door.

"Uh-uh," he said, coming after her. "I'll follow you home, then."

Jamie wheeled around, exasperated, and bumped right into him. He caught her, then said teasingly, "Just get in my truck and let me drive you home. If you don't, I'm liable to get King to chase you back up on top and take you home that way."

Looking up at him, his face shadowed and smoothed in the gloom, she finally laughed. "And to think I thought you were shy! Just as bossy as any of them with a girl, aren't you?''

He sobered. "No. I don't mean to be. It's just that I'm different with you somehow. I wouldn't want you hurt."

His words struck her hard. Mutely she climbed in the truck. All she could hear was his voice saying, "Somebody who really cares about somebody else won't deliberately make a fool out of them."

When they got to Roswell, he glanced over at her and broke the long silence. "You goin' to speak to me again someday?"

His voice chased her moodiness away. He hadn't really done anything to upset her, anyway. Jamie felt the smile starting at the corners of her mouth, but she kept her eyes on the road and shook her head. They stopped at one of Roswell's two stop signs and he asked, "Then how are you goin' to say, 'Thanks, Ren, for drivin' me home'?"

She thought about that for a minute. Slowly she turned and looked at him, and her eyes twinkled. The smile that spread across her face was mischievous, tantalizing, suggestive. He did not move, just stared at her; comprehension dawned and he caught the promise in her face. A thin line of red spread over his cheekbones.

Then some man in a pickup behind them with his head stuck out the window yelled, laughing, "C'mon, Ren, I gotta get home sometime tonight," and Ren hastily looked back at the road and shifted gears. When they stopped at the apartment, he turned off the motor abruptly and they sat in silence. He fumbled with the keys, then she slid across the seat to him without a word.

Catching his hand with the keys in it, she pushed him back against the door. Then she did something that satisfied her immensely, something she'd wanted to do all afternoon. She slid her hands up around his strong brown neck and pushed her fingers into that thick, rebellious brown hair of his. Clutching it with both hands, she pulled his lips to hers. She ran her tongue along his lips and they parted instantly. And that was all she remembered, because the sweetness he'd set off lightly in her before exploded with this kiss. Her chest ached pleasurably, and she held him tighter. His hand was warm at the back of her head, his body pressed so closely to hers in the narrow space behind the steering wheel that she could feel the heavy thud of his heart.

When Jamie forced herself away from his lips and wedged a little distance from him, he opened his eyes and looked at her. "My God," he whispered dazedly.

Jamie felt her own heart racing, and her voice was uneven as she touched his lips lightly with one finger and said, "Thank you, Ren, for driving me home."

She pulled away completely and flew out of the truck and to her door. He sat and watched in silence till she entered, then he drove away. Jamie stood in the sterile little apartment watching him go, with an equal mixture of satisfied pleasure and surprised dismay with herself. She shouldn't have done that. Away from him, she couldn't imagine the things she did when he was at hand. Some devil was driving her, and she was afraid it was going to end in problems for everybody.

Chapter Five

Wake a sleeping tiger. That was the expression that kept running through Jamie's head all the next week. She'd meant to do it when she made the bet with Beth. That had been the deal. Get an "ordinary man" to want her. But somehow it hadn't seemed so dangerous, so *wrong*, then. It had just been a quick game of tease and retreat, one without consequences. A mild dalliance. The only trick would have been played on Beth.

But in Ren's eyes sometimes, there was a flash of something that made Jamie wince and worry. He had looked at her with an intensity, a near-knowledge, on Monday when she'd gone by the farm store at lunch to stammer out some absurd excuse about working late on the files. She'd been scared, that was all there was to it. Too scared to be alone with him if she drove him home.

He'd just smiled, said it was okay, that he'd ride home with his cousin. She didn't see him at all on Tuesday, but at lunch on Wednesday, he was waiting for her when she came outside the office. Her heart jumped wildly when he straightened off the wall where he'd been leaning.

"I thought you had to eat sometime today." He smiled at her.

She rushed into a babbled speech. "I'm starving. It's been a wild morning around here. Sidney came in again. Nobody ever went out to see her, and she's upset, to put it mildly."

"I know," Ren replied, as usual. "She came by the store on her way home and gave me a piece of her mind just in passin'."

"I don't understand this," Jamie frowned. "Even if there had been trucks or lights or whatever in her pasture, why? No cattle are missing. And where would they be going? There's sure no way down into that hollow for a vehicle; it just drops off into nothing. Who owns that hole, anyway?"

Ren started to walk toward his truck, and she slowly followed. Once in it, he answered her question. "It belongs to Jason Barnes. He's got a good farm on the other side of it, but the hollow's nearly two miles across. I've already asked him if he's noticed anything."

"And?"

"Nope. Not a thing. But you can't tell about Jason. If he's in the mood to talk, he will."

"And if he's not?"

"He'd knock you down as soon as look at you," Ren answered matter-of-factly.

"Well, great," muttered Jamie. "He and Sidney ought to make very compatible neighbors."

Ren grinned at her. "They do. She's one person old Jason never fools with."

"Smart man," answered Jamie dryly.

He laughed, and somehow, the initial meeting was over and the tension was gone. Lunch was pleasant—fun. But when they got back to the office, Ren said quickly as she started to get out of the truck, "Jennie, the team's playin' tonight. I'd like it if you'd come to the game."

Something like relief ran through Jamie's veins. Here was a nice safe way to be around him. "All right," she answered and he went away smiling.

The ball game was mean. It was apparently a grudge match between Ren's team and the one from Shining Rock, the ones dressed in blinding yellow jerseys. Most of them looked like close relatives of André the Giant in size. Jamie had to remind herself that this was softball, not football.

Ren's team lost ignominiously. The only one on it who managed to cover himself with glory was Ben Dalton, who got three players out before one of the enemy "accidentally" blacked his eye for him. There was a lot of yelling and scuffling; then both he and his attacker were thrown out of the game, and Ben finished up the night very satisfactorily, sitting like a self-righteous martyr among his sympathetic fans.

Jamie shocked herself by jumping up and screaming, "Knock him down! Hit him, Ren!" when one of the opponents chased Ren up against the fence and ground the ball against his chest to get him out. But

Ren just pushed him away with one hard shove and loped in calmly.

"What a bunch of rednecks," muttered Jamie to herself as she surveyed the yellow team. "Or maybe they're overgrown delinquents."

She agreed to go out to eat with two or three other couples when the game was over. She wasn't ready yet for more kissing in that truck. As they ate, she listened to their talk of jobs and farms and children. Ren was his usual quiet self, but Jamie found herself enjoying the lively talk and friendliness around her. In the middle of the uproarious laughter, she caught sight of herself in a window. The happy girl in the T-shirt and shorts with her tennis shoes and white socks and her hair in a long golden braid looked as if she belonged here. She resembled a wide-eyed teenager out too late.

But this was not her. If she'd been with Tory or Todd, she'd have been out at the country club in a designer gown. She'd have been having lobster or filet mignon or a delicate pastry. Those were the things that made girls like her happy, the things that everybody wanted, not hamburgers and fries.

And yet there, she'd have been as sterilely bored as always. Cool and elegant, waiting for something to happen to her. How many times had she waited? She'd thought when she graduated from high school, "This is it. Life. Now I start to live."

College had been interesting. But again, she'd been waiting. Preparing herself, keeping herself, for something. She'd sat through twenty-two years thinking, "My life is going to begin. Tomorrow. Someday." Desperation had set in.

Then Todd came along, and he was handsome and successful. Her mother had approved, and Jamie had thought, "Marriage will be the beginning. It will end the waiting. I'll be satisfied. Finally." But now, at this moment, she realized in sick despair that she wasn't sure of that. Tory, now—she had known how to light up the sky. So sure of herself and of what she wanted. She hadn't understood when her little sister had haltingly told her she wasn't happy, when Jamie had finally objected to bland men and glittering women and sanitary, neat little lives. Jamie had hated those statistics couples: Mr. and Mrs. John Doe the Third. Two point four children, two-story colonial home, one Cadillac, one Mercedes, two college degrees, one maid (uniformed), one collie (registered), and one goal—financial success. Jamie wanted to be alive.

Tory had laughed and said all she needed was a man. And, she'd added flippantly, it was just as easy to find one rich and handsome. Well, Todd Jackson met one of Tory's requirements: he was definitely attractive.

Jamie's gaze shifted to look at the reflection of the man beside her. He was bent over a little, listening to the girl on the end tell him about her brother, whom he apparently knew. No, he was not really handsome. But he exuded strength, from the slope of his neck down into the muscles of his shoulders. Wonder what Tory would think of *you*, she thought, and smiled to herself.

At that moment he straightened and his glance met hers in the window. Slowly, he smiled back at her. In another minute she felt his hand sliding down her arm, fumbling for and finding her fingers. Joined under the table like this, Jennie could feel the hard, callused palm, the big, square hand, the firm grasp. It reminded her of her Grandpa Logan's hand, and of Eli's. But her smile faded a little when the memory of another man's grasp slid into her mind: Todd had a slim, elegant hand, long fingered and artistic. And soft.

When they got back to her apartment, Ren unexpectedly climbed out of the truck and opened her door. Before she could slide out, he'd blocked her way.

"Jennie," he said, and he leaned toward her.

A warning, a sense of danger, clanged to life. She started to say, "Ren, I don't want—" but he spoke instead.

"You're thinkin' about your sister."

She gasped. "How did you know that?"

He touched her face tenderly. "I can see it here." Slowly, gently, as though he was afraid of her reaction, he leaned inward and brushed her lips with his. Then he let her go, and five minutes later, she was in bed and Ren was on his way home.

Somehow she wound up seeing Ren every night for the rest of the week. Thursday night she found herself loading two horses in a trailer with him. They drove them over to a small town on the other side of the county in preparation for a sale the next night, and on that Friday afternoon, he picked her up and they went to watch them being sold. While they were there, they met Ren's cousin Dan and his wife, Sylvia, and their children.

After the sale in the yellow-lit, big barn of a building, after the low laughter and hazy smoke and auctioneer's staccato voice, Ren and Jamie drove back to her apartment. It was late when they got there, and the bright neon glare of the streetlight on the corner swarmed with summer bugs as it poured a harsh purple light over Jamie's little porch.

She did not linger, but got out hurriedly. At her door, Ren said, "Jennie."

She glanced up at him warily. There was a note of entreaty in his voice. He stared down at her, one hand propped on the wall of the apartment.

"I got a lot of work at the farm tomorrow. I can't put it off or get away till pretty late."

This was so far from what Jennie had been expecting that she didn't know what to say. "That's okay, Ren, I understand. I was going home to see my... my folks, anyway, if that's what—"

He interrupted her. "What I was wonderin' was, would you—would you like to spend the day with me? Just around the farm, sort of."

"You mean, stay with you while you work?" she asked uncertainly.

"Yeah. I'd really like the company. Your company. I—" He looked away. "I like bein' with you."

His sincerity warmed her, but she did not like the idea of spending the whole day alone with him.

"I don't know, Ren. Maybe I'd better just go home like I'd planned."

"There's a horseback ride and a cookout tomorrow night at Dan's," Ren added quickly. "We could take some things and camp out with everybody."

He sounded extremely hopeful, and disappointed at her refusal.

"I—" she wavered. "No—no, Ren. I need to visit my family."

He nodded his head in reluctant acceptance and turned to walk back to the truck. He looked big and lonely and dejected striding away, and on the spur of the moment, Jamie suddenly relented.

"Ren."

He stopped and faced her.

"Okay. I'll wait about going home. I'll spend tomorrow with you."

She could see the slow smile start to spread even in the shadowy night.

Jamie Logan had one of the best times of her life on that June Saturday. Ren came to get her at the crack of dawn. He had to push the doorbell repeatedly before she answered it and then he waited patiently in her living room until she got dressed. She thanked her lucky stars that she did not need makeup in her role as Jennifer. She replaited her braid, washed her face and grabbed on her shorts and shirt.

She ate her breakfast in the truck, a biscuit and sausage he'd brought her, and by six o'clock they were at the farm.

She watched him milk the cow and deftly gather eggs before she decided she would help. He did the heaviest, most tiresome chores early in the morning while it was cooler. At the moment that translated into hoeing his small vegetable garden. They set out on the task, both industriously hoeing. But Jamie stopped every few minutes from lack of exercise and experience.

Once she stood looking around, suddenly soaking in the lush beauty around her. How many nights had she partied away, falling into bed in the wee hours and sleeping till noon? How much of the morning she had missed! The sky was blue and gold, the trees heavily green. The rich, cool, deep shadows under them sometimes hid honeysuckle and wild roses. Jamie could smell their piercing sweetness on the cool morning out of memory, something from a lost childhood.

The man hoeing the garden with her worked steadily, rhythmically, the muscles in his arms and shoulders like those of an athlete's in training. Once he interrupted his movement to look at her and ask, "Tired?"

She shook her head and said honestly, "I'm watching you." Funny how things changed. His shirt was already patchy with sweat across the back, and his brown face was wet. She had seen him like this two or three weeks ago and he'd seemed primitive, dirty. Today, though, the hard physical work, the sweat, seemed clean and purifying. He worked with an endless energy, his movements sparse and certain. She'd seen Grandpa and even Eli do much the same things in chores, but there was pleasure in watching Ren.

She got scratched up helping him get the huge rolls of hay stored in the barn, and surprised him by knowing how to drive the tractor.

"My grandpa used to let me drive his," she explained blithely, then let the clutch out too fast. It jerked violently and died, and Jamie added hastily, "But I was only nine years old."

They walked through part of a cornfield, and Ren shook his head over it.

"Looks like corn to me," said Jamie.

"It's corn all right, but it needs more rain. It's been a dry summer."

At lunchtime Jamie left him working in the barn. She found ham and sliced it for sandwiches, then she made a salad and cut up ripe, red tomatoes. The bag of lemons in the refrigerator made a delicious lemonade. She felt a little like a child playing house again. When she called him in to eat, she gazed at the table with pride. It looked good.

Ren thought so, too. He came through the kitchen door on his way to wash up and said in amazement, "You did *this*?"

"What did you want me to fix?" she asked, a little indignantly.

"This is fine. I'm just not used to it. Last Saturday I think I ate a box of sardines and crackers," he said, grinning at the face she made. "I'll like your lunch a lot better."

That afternoon he showed her a new barn that he'd just built, one not visible from the house, and beside it in a sturdily fenced-in area, his new bull. She backed away from the short, wicked horns of the animal.

"Why keep such a vicious-looking bull?" she asked, and Ren laughed.

"'Cause the cows like him. Farmers from all around here bring cows to breed to him."

"He doesn't look like a playboy."

"That's just because you're not a cow," he said mischievously.

After he'd plowed through a field with the tractor, they waded barefoot in the creek that ran along a big bottom on the farm. The water was from an icy spring, and Jamie cooled off enough in the wading that later when she sat down in the shady grass beside the creek, she fell asleep almost immediately.

She awoke in just a little while; the sun above her head had barely changed positions. Even here on the edge of the creek under the shade it was hot; the buzz of insects made it sound even warmer. She didn't know what woke her up, but there was a tingling feeling to her skin, as if—. She sat up quickly, and looking around, caught Ren's stare upon her. He was sitting just a few feet away with the still King by his side.

His gaze was dark, disturbing. She brushed off her cotton top and laughed nervously. "Have I been asleep long? You should have waked me up."

He shook his head, and lazily propped up one knee. He was tearing a piece of grass to bits. "I like watchin' you sleep."

That did not reassure Jamie. There was something odd, a feeling of restraint about him. She started to push to her feet, but with a quick spring, he caught her wrist and held her down at eye level with him.

"Ren, what are you doing?" she gasped. For one minute there was something—well, she would have said dangerous if it had been anybody except Ren.

"I was just thinkin'," he said slowly, his gaze traveling over her face. She relaxed back down onto the ground beside him, her wrist still held firmly by his hard hand. "You're the prettiest girl I've ever been around. I never saw such a mouth—" His other hand reached up, wavered, then his thumb brushed her lips lightly. "Your eyes are as green as grass. And your hair. I never saw it down, but it makes me want to touch it."

If another man—Todd, maybe—had said as much, Jamie would have been annoyed and embarrassed by his fulsome compliments. But Ren was clearly not trying to flatter. He said it matter-of-factly, with a trace of wary puzzlement in his voice and face. So Jamie made no response, just waited. He touched her face again, then pulled away and turned toward the creek.

"I've been sittin' here lookin', seein' all that prettiness. What I'm tryin' to say is, Jennie, what's a girl that looks like you and acts like you doin' with somebody like me?"

His blunt question stunned her, and she stammered, "I don't understand."

His brown eyes were angry when he looked back at her. "Sure you do. You're no fool. I'm not exactly handsome. Or rich. Or anything. Girls don't fall over me like they do Ben Dalton."

She tried to sidetrack him. "Oh, come on, Ren, you can't tell me you've never had a girlfriend before."

"No, I can't. I've had 'em. Had one when you came to town. But that's not what I'm talkin' about. You're...you're beautiful. And there's something about you that says pretty plain you've had a lot. The men in this town are right on the edge of makin' fools of themselves over you. Ben wants to punch me ever' time he sees us together, and I had to threaten one of those Sloan boys on the other team Wednesday night to shut him up about—about—" He flushed deeply, but his glance up her long legs let her know pretty clearly what the Sloan boy had found to comment on.

Jamie felt shock reeling her nearly sideways. Ren—quiet, good ol' Ren—had threatened somebody? And what was this about a girl?

"What girl? What d'you mean, you had a girl even when I came to town?" she demanded, shoving his loosened hand off her wrist and jumping erect to stare angrily at him. How had she and Sharon missed that piece of information?

He just sat looking up at her, brown and big and still. And he came stubbornly back to the point. "Dan says that something's wrong."

So that was the reason for this interrogation, Jamie thought in relief. "You listen to a man who's met me once or twice and believe him?"

He shook his head. "No. But—well, Jennie, you came after me. You know you did. Nobody would believe it. Hell, I don't even believe it." He yanked at the grass beside him impatiently. "I want to know why."

She watched his brown hand. It was a square, capable one, with strong, long fingers and calloused palms. Up his arms to the throat, where a pulse beat furiously at the base. His skin, that which was visible above the faded blue T-shirt that said Bluegrass Country, was damp and smooth. His jaw was strong and too pronounced, but his mouth was generous and well shaped. The nose—well, it was plainly crooked on one side, just as his forehead was too broad. But that hair was definitely a strong point. Wild and thick, it bushed up in the careless cut he wore. It begged a woman to touch it, smooth it. Just now, it hung down over his forehead and clung damply to his temples.

When she looked at his eyes, he was watching her assess him, and the flash of anger was there again. He had the brownest eyes she'd ever seen. Looking at him, her heart suddenly quickened its beat.

"Well?" he said impatiently.

"I don't know what to say," Jamie said slowly. "How can I tell you why I chose you—liked you. I only—" Some wild, uncontrollable, hot current of excitement licked up in her stomach. What difference did it make if she did what she wanted? He'd never tell. Like somebody in slow motion, she moved inch by inch until she was on her knees before him. He watched her warily, and she leaned up, into his chest. He drew back an inch, and she followed. Her lips hovered for just a minute near his, then she kissed him. When she leaned all her weight on him and relaxed against him, he said something, made some satisfied "um-mm" sound against her lips, and slid backward in the grass.

Lying atop him like this, her long, bare legs caught between his blue-jeaned ones, Jamie felt his whole hard body under her, under her hands. She ran her hands up his sides, up to his neck, and gasped for air against his lips.

He turned, shifted, carried her with him, until she was the one lying on the ground, partially held in one of his arms. And somewhere along the way, she lost control of the situation. He was no longer still and restrained, but was kissing the side of her face, her chin, her eyes with passionate lips. She felt his tongue tracing her ear and his hand was sliding down across her breast. She drew in a deep, shaky breath as he caressed her through the shirt.

His lips burned a path down her throat, between her breasts, and his hand, warm and hard, slid up under her loose cotton top to span her entire waist. Then he was bending, twisting away even as she caught at him to pull him back to her lips. His mouth was on the smooth skin of her stomach, and she whimpered as her muscles clenched in surprised pleasure at his touch.

He kissed her rib cage, her sides, and then his fingers found the thin line of the scar that lay just under one breast, the scar left from her teenage adventure with her cousin Joe and the electric fence. He traced it with his fingertips gently, then he lowered his mouth to it, and she wanted to cry and shiver.

Instead she reached for him fiercely, pulled his head up and tried to find his lips. He turned back to her willingly, and this time it was his mouth urging hers to open. They lay there kissing, again and again. There was an urgency in his touch that she responded to, clutching his shoulders and his hair. His kisses were deep and hot, and still she could not get close enough. His hand was like a brand on her skin.

Then King's face and cold nose was between them, and he was whining and dragging at his absorbed master.

"Go 'way," mumbled Ren, trying to shove the dog away, but King persistently returned. When Ren let go of Jamie and half sat up to push King down again, Jamie opened her eyes, stared up at the wide open sky and the trees all around her and felt like a bucket of cold water had been thrown in her face. What was she doing lying out here for God and the whole world to see, making love to this—this farmer?

She sat up rapidly, yanking the rumpled cotton shirt down firmly. Just as Ren reached for her, she knocked his hand away and rushed to her feet. He stood, too, and she took a hasty three steps away from the warmth of his body.

"Jennie, I—"

"Is this the reason you wanted me to spend the day with you?" she panted, her temper flaring. She was mad at herself, but Ren was handier.

"No! I swear it's not," he protested. "I just wanted you to tell me why, and you—" he broke off, but Jamie finished it for him.

"But I got carried away in my answer," she snapped. "Sorry. I'll try to control myself in the future."

He pulled her around to face him. "Not for me, you don't have to. I liked it." The teasing note in his voice faded. "I just wanted to be sure that I—that we're all right together."

She looked at him at last. His eyes were pleading, anxious. Her ridiculous anger melted away, and she smiled up at him a little.

"I'm sorry. Really, I'm not mad at you, just a little embarrassed that I...keep doing things when I'm around you. I don't know what's wrong." Her puzzlement was honest. "I just don't...haven't acted like this before to—other men." That was true enough: she usually left Todd swearing, and she winced away from some of his angry comments on her puritanical nature.

That blinding flash of awareness and excitement that had been in Ren's face the other night leaped up again, and he said thickly, "Good."

He tried to pull her up against him again, but Jamie resisted, suddenly remembering. "You never did explain that remark about having another girl, Ren Garrett."

He laughed and shrugged, but he was embarrassed. "I shouldn't have said that. She used to call me some, and I took her out two or three times. It wasn't anything."

Jamie watched him closely. "Men don't always tell the truth," she told him tartly.

"Do women?" he returned, but then he added, "We never—I never kissed her like—like we do, Jennie, I swear." His voice was earnest, his face sober. She believed him.

The horseback ride late that evening was fun. Jamie rode one of Ren's horses. He had patiently adjusted the stirrups for her as she sat in the saddle, and she had watched his bent head. The blood that had been flowing richly in her since the wild kissing spree this afternoon surged up in a new hot tide of emotion, and she reached down and smoothed his brown mane. Ren looked up, startled; he read her thoughts in her face, and his own features changed and darkened. He reached one long arm up, and cupping the back of her head in his hand, he pulled her face down to his lips, lifted to kiss her.

That was how Dan and his wife, Sylvia, found them when they walked around the corner of the barn, Jamie straining to touch Ren's lips. Embarrassed, the two broke apart, but Dan seemed to relax more after that. He was friendlier to Jamie than he'd been before. Evidently he'd seen something in that interrupted kiss that reassured him.

They cooked over an open grill, everyone for himself, and Ren showed Jamie how to handle her food while she fixed it. There were five couples, including Ren and Jamie and Dan and Sylvia. Three couples had kids in tow. They sat talking and laughing around a tiny fire under the stars blazing in the midnight-black Kentucky sky. Jamie was as comfortable as she'd ever been, sitting wrapped in Ren's arm. The coolness of the night air and the breeze that blew almost continuously made his warmth beside her pleasant. Neither of them said anything much, but he kept glancing down at her, at her lips. One of the young mothers left to put a baby to bed in a tent she and her husband had erected.

Jamie was tired, too. She'd gotten up early and worked hard most of the day. The voices around her came and went and, curled against Ren, she finally put her head on his shoulder. In a few minutes, she dimly heard Dan's voice say jokingly, "Looks like we've got another little baby asleep."

Ren must have carried her to her sleeping pallet placed not far from his, because all she remembered was the sensation of falling when he put her down. That and when he bent over her, kissed her cheek and whispered, "G'night, sweet baby."

Chapter Six

Jamie felt good beginning work on the following Monday. She'd gotten home from the camp-out late Sunday afternoon. A day on horseback was not something she had ever done, though she had ridden most of her life. She fell in the bed before six o'clock, and when she woke up at six the next morning, she moved cautiously. But little hurt. Just a twinge or two in an arm she'd scraped on a tree coming up out of the hollow.

Something inside her felt good, too. There was a low excitement mixed with a satisfied feeling. Maybe those two things combined to make her quick-witted that morning, because when she caught sight of the folder Cheever was working on, the name struck her memory sharply.

"Jason Barnes?" she asked Cheever. "What does he want?"

"Nothing," answered the other woman, glancing up. "He came in Friday while you were out to lunch and paid off a loan he had with us."

"A big loan?"

"You could say that," Cheever answered dryly, and held up the figures for Jamie to goggle at.

"Where'd he get all that money?" she gasped. "I thought he was a farmer."

"He is. But he also used to own a car dealership. And he's in the auto body parts business. He's got this huge store. It's over in Duval, where the dealership was."

"The car business is this prosperous?"

"I doubt it. I think all this money came from insurance. They had a big robbery and a fire at the car lot over there a month or two ago. It was weird. One night somebody got into one of his tractor trailers, parked at his lot that had all of these new cars straight from Houston on it, and just drove away, but before they left they set fire to his sales office. The fire department got there too late to salvage anything, and the truck and its load were never found. The insurance paid him off to the tune of a quarter of a million dollars."

"What?"

"Two hundred and fifty thousand." Cheever shook her head. "He just closed up the car lot. He said he was sick of it. And it's just as well. He did most of his business at the auto parts store, anyway."

"But tractor trailers full of cars don't just vanish," Jamie protested.

"That old Kenworth of his did. Those insurance men searched everywhere. It might as well have dropped off the edge of the world."

Jamie stared at Cheever a minute. "Kenworth?" she asked slowly.

"You know, Kenworth. It's a type of big truck."

Jamie just looked at Cheever, then she said slowly, "A man could make a lot of money from stripping down cars and selling their parts at an auto parts store. All he'd have to worry about would be getting rid of the identifiable parts, if there are any, and maybe the tractor trailer that he'd hauled them on and reported stolen."

Cheever dropped her pencil and broke the heavy silence. "You think..."

"I think the sheriff had better go to Sidney's south pasture and look off the edge of the world into Baker Hollow. There's no telling what he'll see down there," Jamie answered flatly.

Somehow the news spread all over town that the sheriff was on his way to Baker Hollow; then rumors flew as to why. By midafternoon, it had gotten out that a receptionist at the Farmers' Association office had tipped off the law as to Jason Barnes and a scam he'd worked. And by time to go home, Barnes himself had shown up at the office with his lawyer.

He was a big, barrely man with gray hair and lots of teeth. Jamie got a chance to notice them firsthand because he came in yelling and swearing, threatening retribution. He backed poor Cheever up against the wall trying to find out exactly who this "damned Lynn girl" was, and when Jamie said with all the courage she could muster, "I'm Jennifer Lynn," he turned on her. Jamie had the fleeting thought that she'd rather face Ren's dog again.

"I'd like to know who in hell you think you are, girlie," he roared. "Accusin' me of things I've never heard of, ruinin' my good name, tryin' to send me to jail. Do you know what happens to interferin' little busybodies like you?"

The lawyer tried to interrupt. "Look, Mr. Barnes, this is not the way to handle this."

"Shut up!" Then he turned back to Jamie, who was beginning to feel anger mix in with her fright. She was Eli Logan's daughter. Who did he think he was?

"Don't you dare speak to me like that," she flashed back, standing up from the desk. A door opened somewhere behind her—somebody had come in. "Being a crook and a car thief evidently doesn't require any manners, does it?"

"Why, you little—" he gasped out, turning purple. He raised one huge, meaty hand as if to slap her.

She flinched and Cheever screamed; then Ren, his voice angry and loud, said, "You touch her and I'll break your arm, Barnes."

Jamie collapsed inside, shivering in relief. Ren was here. She turned blindly toward his voice. He was right behind her, pulling her against him, into his embrace. She wanted to hide against him forever.

Barnes said nothing for a minute, then Ren spoke again. His voice was quiet, but it was deadly. "If you want to live to go to prison, you'd better stay away from Jennie."

The shaking girl heard Barnes suck in his breath, then move away. The door opened again, but this time it was Sidney and her cane and the sheriff and a warrant.

"You're under arrest, Jason," the sheriff told him. "You fooled me and the insurance people, all right. We all searched your farm with a fine-tooth comb, but we never thought about the back of Baker Hollow, because the only way in is through Sidney's pasture. If she hadn't reported the lights—"

"Damned old witch," muttered Jason darkly in Sidney's direction.

"Here, none of that," the sheriff said sharply. "There's enough in that hollow to convict a saint. Still, if you hadn't got greedy and tried to dump again a few nights ago—"

"I didn't!" blustered Jason. "I just went to see what was going on over there. Old lady Hill's had this girl, and farm agents, and Garrett here all out in that pasture lately. I just wanted to make sure—"

"To make sure you'd covered your tracks," snapped Sidney. "Varmint."

On his way out the door with the sheriff, Barnes said sullenly to Ren, nodding at Jamie in his arms, "So she's yours, is she, Garrett? You'd do better to keep her home in your bed. That's the only way to handle an interferin' woman like her. As for you, boy, you better stay out of my reach."

"I will just as long as you leave Jennie alone," Ren retorted, as Jamie straightened indignantly away at Barnes's remark.

Later, when Jamie got ready to leave, Sidney poked her with her cane as she went past. "I'm grateful, girl," she said brusquely. "Nobody else seemed to believe."

Then the old woman turned to Ren. "You haven't been out to see me in a good while. You come out to the house this Thursday night and we'll have supper. Bring your girl here with you." She glared at Ren a minute. "I've got a word or two to say to you, anyway, about that last bunch of feed you sent out for my cows."

It was very late when Ren got Jamie to her door, but he stood for a minute just inside looking at her intently. "Are you okay?"

"That Jason. Will he hurt you if he gets the chance?" she said, shivering at the thought.

Ren shrugged. "Forget Jason Barnes. The worst he can do is talk. Tell everybody that you're not his favorite person in the world."

"I'll survive," Jamie said dryly.

Ren smiled down at her. "Sure you will. I was proud of you tonight. You were really goin' to stand up to the old crook, weren't you? I thought, this girl is something special. And she's—she's *my* girl." He said it daringly, waiting for her reaction.

Jamie registered his words, but she was still too nervy and upset herself. "I was terrified for both of us. I thought you might get killed. Jason Barnes seems so brutal."

"I'll be okay," Ren said, then he added teasingly, "You know what, though? Jason's not so bad. He had one good idea." And he leaned down to kiss the astonished woman good-night.

Had shy, quiet Ren Garrett just made an—an improper advance?

Chapter Seven

At work the next day, Jamie was given the task of meeting as the association's representative with a week-long community board. She suspected it was an attempt to make sure she didn't "help" in any more explosive situations like the one with Barnes. But Jamie liked the people on the board and enjoyed working with them. She spent most of the rest of the week at the meetings, and went out every night for a little while with Ren. She also liked seeing him, telling him about her day and hearing about his. His biggest problem was lack of rain. His corn and hay needed it immediately. On Thursday it looked as if his worries were over: the day dawned heavily gray and gloomy, and Jamie could smell the rain in the air. By lunch it was pouring. Rain danced off the windowsills and ran down the road. Jamie got soaked fumbling with the key to her apartment door, and when she got in, the phone was ringing. It was Sharon, frantic and angry.

"Where on this green earth have you been, Jamie Lynn Logan?" she demanded. "I searched your house for you Saturday, and Roberta said she hadn't seen you in days. Then I tried calling you—you haven't been at this apartment one night this week." She said it accusingly, questioningly.

"I've been here every night, but not until late," corrected Jamie. She did not want a discussion about Ren, so she said instead, "You wouldn't believe what they've got me doing at work, Sharon. I'm meeting with this board here in town every day, and it goes on for hours. Monday night I was at the office until after ten o'clock."

"You've been working?" Sharon's voice was a mixture of shock and disbelief.

"What did you think?" asked Jamie, then added, grinning, "That I'd been partying and carousing? Living the wild life here in Calhoun County?"

"You've actually had to work in that dull, boring little office? Doing dull, boring things?"

Jamie's lips twitched. She remembered the shouting match two of the board members had had this afternoon and the exasperated way the mayor had threatened to "bash heads together" if things didn't get more civilized. There had been nothing dull, not today.

"Never mind all that, though." Sharon rushed on. "I'm calling because I found out something this weekend, Jamie. It bothers me. I think you should get out of this deal and forget this Ren thing."

Just for a second Jamie's mind was blank. "This Ren thing." Then all of that horrible bet rushed back into her memory, and the shock of realizing she'd forgotten it totally for a while took her breath away. She stared at the wall dazedly; only Sharon's impatient voice calling her broke through.

"...makes them cousins. First cousins. Did you hear me?"

"What? What did you say?"

"I knew you weren't listening. Jamie, this is important. I said, Todd is a first cousin to the man at the bank. The handsome one on the list that Beth wanted you to choose."

"He's Todd's cousin? But why would she do that?" exclaimed Jamie. "Maybe she didn't know."

"Jamie," Sharon said dryly, "get real here. Of course she knew it. And it makes me nervous. She wanted Todd to find out—wanted him to know you'd...slept with his cousin."

"So, what am I supposed to do?"

"Get out of Roswell, now. She's up to something. I just haven't figured out what yet."

"But I'm so close," objected Jamie. "I don't want to quit now."

"Tory is gone; and besides, she wouldn't like this one bit better than I do."

"No. I want to stay."

There was a pause, then a long sigh. "All right. Go ahead. Spend the night with this Garrett guy. But hurry up. Do it now. For heaven's sake, pretend to fall asleep on the couch and refuse to wake up. Or have amnesia and forget how to drive home. Just do it. Call me tomorrow—tell me when. I'll do the rest, at least as far as Beth is concerned."

Jamie said stubbornly, "I'll call. But—"

"Do it, Jamie. Please. I'm going to pull out all my hair and get wrinkles from worrying over you if you don't. See you Saturday."

Jamie dressed for the supper at Miss Hill's that night and barely knew what she wore. Her mind kept turning Sharon's words over and over. Outside, as dusk fell, a thunder and lightning storm burst upon the sky; the cracks and rumbles were deafening.

Ren was late. She glanced at her watch. It was raining too hard to drive in this with any speed. By the time he was an hour late and she'd been to look out the door several times at the curtain of pouring rain, she'd decided to call Sidney and try to apologize. Sidney was understanding enough as Jamie explained about Ren's lateness. All she said was, "Men are such problems. We'll just set it for some other time, girl."

Jamie dialed Ren's number repeatedly over the next two hours. No answer. Finally, an operator told her that telephone service in that end of the county had been knocked out by the rain, and that they were having trouble repairing it because of the terrific lightning and the blinding storm.

At eleven o'clock that night, Jamie called the sheriff's office. There the only deputy on duty informed her that the bridge between town and Ren's farm was standing in several feet of water. Still, he good-naturedly agreed to go look for Ren.

At midnight, he called her back; he couldn't cross the bridge, but there'd been no sign of Ren's truck stranded anywhere. He advised her cheerfully to stop worrying and to go to bed; Ren had probably already done that. That practical, realistic side of Jamie admitted to the sense of the deputy's words. Some other side of her remembered a mother stranded by a storm and a baby born unexpectedly while the rain poured down. She didn't sleep well, but she told herself it was the fault of the bolts of lightning and the cracking thunder.

By Friday morning, there was only a dull, overcast sky, wet, soggy earth and a thin drizzle of rain. Ren did not come in to work, but Enoch Johnson didn't seem upset. He said indulgently to her, "Bridge is still flooded and still no phones. He's all right. He'll be in this afternoon."

By lunchtime phone service had been restored. Ren again did not answer. Jamie listened to the ringing at the other end of the phone line, and then she made a decision. She had no time for lunch today. She got in the truck and pulled out onto the road in the misty rain. Something was wrong. She knew it.

The water on the bridge must have gone down a great deal. It was only six or seven inches high. She put the truck through it and drove on.

Her heart leaped when she saw Ren's vehicle parked in its customary place, and his door stood open and inviting on the other side of the screen. Jamie was beginning to feel foolish, but she got out and knocked.

"Ren?" she called, and just as on her other visit, there was no answer. But this time she pulled the screen open and hesitantly walked in. He was not in the kitchen or the living room.

"Where are you?" she called, standing outside his bedroom door. Cautiously she pushed it open. He was not here, either. The room had the neat look the rest of the house usually did—Ren was an unexpectedly neat man when he was at home. The bed was made, the quilt pulled up and tucked under the pillows.

There, lying on top of the made-up bed, were nearly new jeans and a button-front shirt. Ren wore T-shirts at home and to work. This must be what he was going to wear last night to Sidney's.

It took a minute for that fact to hit home inside Jamie's head. She stared at the clothes, knowing something was wrong but unable to put her finger on it. Then realization came: Ren had not slept in his bed last night.

Jamie tried to piece it together:

The truck was here.

The clothes were here.

The bed had not been used.

And she came up with a terrifying thought: something had happened to Ren.

The blood flowed back into her legs, and she ran out of the house, shouting, "Ren! Answer me! Where are you?"

He was not in the backyard, or the barn, or the tractor shed. She frantically searched each, the long wet grass clinging to her ankles and the rain that was coming down again in a light shower soaking her hair. Ren was nowhere to be found.

Finally she pulled herself to a panting halt and stood gathering her breath. All around, the fields stretched green under the misty gray skies, broken only by fences and rows of corn and, behind her, by the emerald belt of timber that the farm faded into before it fell into the hollow. Smoky fog was rising now from that deep ravine, swallowing up those trees and obscuring her vision. But the only thing over that way was the field with the new barn—and the bull.

Jamie disliked bulls even more than she did vicious dogs, but it was the last place left before she searched the creek. Oh, God, don't let him be drowned there, she thought and shivered violently. That thought made the long distance to the new barn seem like a reprieve. Ren had driven up to it the other day, but he had a four-wheel drive.

She shouted for him again several times as she hurried to the barn. At last, unexpectedly, she heard an answering sound. She stopped so fast her pounding heart felt as if it slammed into her rib cage, and she listened.

To her fright, it was King barking frantically. Now what was she supposed to do? He hadn't bothered her lately, but without Ren's protection she didn't know how he might behave. Then she caught sight of him through the swirling rainy fog; he was racing across the field of high grass toward her.

He was going to kill her this time. Leap for her head and grab her throat.

Jamie knew that, and stood frozen in terror. There was nowhere to run, no place to hide. She had to stand and watch him race toward her.

Just as he got within leaping distance and she could see his teeth clearly, her throat unlocked and she screamed, "Ren! Ren!"

But the dog came on, gave a mighty pounce and grabbed the bottom of her raincoat. Jamie tried wildly to kick him away, but he hung on. He jerked at her coat until it tore, and Jamie, straining away from the sharp white teeth, fell back in the grass.

There, as she lay braced for his attack, she heard his whine. Cautiously sidling upright, she saw King, head down, watching her. He whined and ran away a distance from her, came back and did the same thing again. His bark was urgent. And Jamie understood this time.

"It's Ren, isn't it? You know where he is."

She got to her feet and the dog, satisfied, took off again. She raced after him. He was heading straight for the barn.

Struggling for breath and holding her side with the stitch in it, Jamie made it to the barn. There was an eerie silence. She tried to take in the scene. The new barn was partially burned on one side; the fence was down beside it; the bull was gone.

She sucked in her breath sharply. Close to the burned end of the little barn lay a huddled shape. King was nosing at it, whining loudly. Jamie was terrified. She didn't want to see. She was afraid she had found Ren and he was dead. The still, cold face of her sister as she had lain in the hospital morgue flashed up before Jamie and her stomach lurched.

Then King barked at her sharply, reprimanding her for her cowardice, and she took stumbling steps toward the fallen man through the rain and her tears.

It was indeed Ren. He lay sideways, unconscious and drenched with rain, and his once white T-shirt was torn and stained red with blood on one side.

"God, not Ren. Please don't let him be dead," she whispered, dropping to her knees. She felt for the pulse in his limp arm while King watched. Nothing.

"No—no" she said in despair. She pulled him over off his side and he sprawled heavily like a limp rag doll. Jamie swallowed back her cry. Ren had a gaping, jagged red tear high in his left shoulder. His brown hair clung wetly to his head, his face was white and wan, as still as death. She reached out trembling fingers and laid them tenderly beneath the mutilated shoulder, against his chilled, wet skin. There was no heartbeat. She gasped harshly.

He can't be dead! Don't die!

Frantically she bent over him, her ear against his chest. For an eternity she listened. Maybe it was only her hope, but she seemed to feel a weak, erratic beat at moments. At last, lifting her head, she solemnly told King, "He's alive. He's *got* to be alive. What will we do—what?" She was shivering violently as she tried to think.

There was only one answer. He had to have help. She couldn't even lift him. Hurriedly she yanked off her slicker and laid it over his torso; she cupped it over and above his face to shield him from the rain. It seemed ridiculous considering how thoroughly wet he already was, but it made her feel better. Then she took off her soft cotton sweater and folded it up into a pillow that she slid under his head.

"I'll be back," she told King. "Just wait. Stay. Good dog." His tail thumped once, and he lay down beside Ren, just touching him.

In her silk camisole top and swirling cotton skirt she made a faster run across the fences and the fields to Ren's house than she'd ever made in a gym suit on a track. She slipped once on the wet grass and went sprawling. It didn't even hurt; she ignored the skinned palm of her hand.

At the house she dialled 911. This county had no hospital, just a tiny clinic, but surely they had something for a 911 call. They did. Through chattering teeth, Jamie gave her information. The clinic would send a doctor. The sheriff's office would be contacted, too, by the clinic.

Jamie broke down only once, just as they were hanging up. "Please, please, hurry—he—he's dying. Hurry!"

She grabbed up the shirt on Ren's bed and pulled it on. Next she pulled the quilt off his bed. Carrying it in a bulk under one arm, she started out, intending to run. Then she remembered his truck. The keys were in the cupboard so she grabbed them. The truck plowed down the muddy road under her wild guidance. She took the shortest distance to her destination, running through the half-opened gate and splintering it in two. Fences be damned.

He lay exactly as she had left him. Refusing to admit to her fears, she pulled the slicker off and wrapped the quilt around him as much as possible. Then she put the slicker over it.

She ripped off the bottom part of his shirt she was wearing to make a compress, and gently, she put it over the wound and pressed hard. If it was still bleeding, this had to help, but she knew dismally that she couldn't really tell too much about the wound. It was clotted around the edge; it seemed to have stopped bleeding.

She sat with her hands pressed over it, blood staining her palm, touching the coldness of the shoulders she'd often admired for their strength. The heavy muscles outlined under the torn, clammy shirt across the slope of the shoulder and running down into the powerful arm made her want to cry. His hand lay, open-palmed and helpless, on the ground before her.

She traced the cold outline of his face as he lay turned from her, watched his long chest for some rise of his lungs and shivered at the thought of how wet the rest of the clothes he had on under the quilt were.

"King! Look—I think he's breathing!" she tried to say, half laughing, but now her teeth were chattering so hard from near hysteria that the words came out all scrambled up. She had to touch his hand. Reaching out, she slid her fingers into his big palm, pushed through his unmoving ones.

I'm sorry, she wanted to tell him. I knew something was wrong. I should have come. Instead you've lain here all night, hurting and bleeding and maybe dying. Ren, forgive me. Breathe. Just move a little, and breathe, damn it.

So you can ease your conscience, part of her accused. You won't have to think of how you've lied and cheated and deceived him. So you can smooth things over.

You were stubborn and willful and angry when you made that ghastly bet, but worst of all, you were selfish. Completely selfish. And you're just as bad now. Wake up, Ren, so Jamie won't have to feel guilty, so Jamie won't have to hurt and be remorseful. The voice was a snake that coiled and hissed and struck at her again and again.

"Don't die," she whispered agonizedly again, looking at his face. "I swear I'll straighten things out if you'll be all right. What have I done? Ren, please forgive me. I didn't mean—"

But the confession she was pouring out to the man and the watchful dog was disturbed by the sound of an approaching vehicle. In the gray mist that was already beginning to fade into early evening, she saw it coming, following the rutted lane Ren had made with his tractor and truck to the barn. It was the ambulance, determinedly chugging its way across a well-nigh impassable field to stop close to the trio on the ground.

The doctor nodded to her and she tried to tell him what she knew, but she was having trouble speaking. He glanced at her sharply as he knelt on the opposite side of Ren and put his stethoscope against his chest.

Jamie watched and finally faltered, "Can you h-hear anything?"

The doctor slid the stethoscope down with a click and said absently, "He's alive. Heartbeat faint—irregular—but he's alive, at least for the moment."

A gush of warm blood—it felt like life—mushroomed out over Jamie's body. She laughed once, then twice.

"G-good. Good."

The doctor looked at her again, then turned back to the man on the ground. By the time the sheriff and a deputy got there, he was through. He told the sheriff briefly, "Best I can tell he's been roughed up by that ugly bull of his. And he may have a concussion. But the worst part of all is that he's been bleeding off and on all night. The girl says he's been out here for eighteen or nineteen hours."

"He's still alive?" asked the deputy, astonished.

"Barely. The bull didn't really do a lot of serious damage, but the exposure and the blood loss and shock will kill him almost immediately if we don't get busy. Get the stretcher."

So they carefully slid Ren's long body onto a stretcher and put him in the back of Roswell's only ambulance as Jamie watched, motionless. King whined and leaped at the doors as they lifted Ren away, and Jamie grabbed his collar to hold him back. But she felt an unexpected kinship with the German shepherd. These men had taken Ren from them, cut them off. Now who would make sure he didn't die?

The doctor climbed in the back after Ren, then he turned to the deputy. "Charlie, take that dog back to the house. And you, girl—what's your name? Lynn?"

"Jamie—I mean, Jennie. Jennifer Lynn."

"Jennie, get in."

"With—with Ren?"

"Yes. You're half in shock yourself. Face white, soaked to the skin, teeth chattering. That's reaction. So get in and sit down."

Jamie hesitated, then patted King's head, whispering, "Sorry. But I need to go. I'll be back, I promise." Then she scrambled up in the ambulance beside the still figure on the stretcher.

Chapter Eight

By two o'clock the next morning, the color had come back to Ren's skin, his breathing was regular and he was moving a little in his sleep. Jamie, who sat in the only chair in the tiny room, looked at him lying on the narrow bed between the IV bottle and the little table where the lamp sat giving out a very dim light, and she thought he looked wonderful.

Everything in this room was a contrast between white and brown: Ren's brown hair against the white pillows, his brown arms and shoulders against the sheets. The tear in his shoulder had been deeper than the doctor had at first thought, but high and rather clean. It had been stitched and covered with a smooth, white dressing.

Jamie didn't know when Ren would wake up, but she wanted to be there. Somehow being there would make up for all the other things she'd perpetrated. So she sat huddled in a hospital blanket, watching him, and the doctor let her.

She had nodded off, her forehead leaning against the side of the big chair, when the urgent sound of voices outside the room woke her. She glanced sleepily at her watch. It was 4:45 a.m. The commotion outside, the nurse's arguing voice, grew louder.

Then the door to the room flew open, and a flushed, distraught girl rushed in.

"Lucinda, it's five o'clock in the morning," the nurse protested.

"I don't care," she said flatly. She glanced defiantly at Jamie, then went straight to the bed. She sucked in her breath as she stood looking down at the still man. "Oh, Ren."

She touched his face gently while Jamie watched in shocked amazement. Who was this girl? She had short curly black hair and liquid dark eyes; her age had to be somewhere between eighteen and twenty-two or three. There was a clean preciseness about her that made her appear pretty, though her lips were too wide and her face too narrow for genuine beauty. Her huge eyes were her best feature, and when she faced Jamie from the side of the bed, they were gleaming with tears.

The nurse, standing in the door, said uneasily. "This is Jennie Lynn, who found Ren out at the farm."

"I know who she is," snapped the other girl. Jamie sat upright slowly, sensing trouble.

"I'm Lucinda Travers." She flung back her head as though that would mean something to Jamie. The name did sound familiar, but half-asleep and wary, she couldn't place it.

"I used to go out with Ren a lot, at least until three weeks ago when you came to town. He hasn't had the time to call me since."

Jamie didn't know what to say. She slowly pushed aside the blanket and tried to stand, but one foot was asleep. She half leaned on the chair for a minute, and when she straightened, Ren's shirt fell almost to her knees. It was torn and muddy; there were traces of his blood on it.

Lucinda began to cry silently. Then she scrubbed at the tears and said, "If—if Ren doesn't love me, I can't do anything about it, I don't reckon. But I love *him*. I always have. And before you, he at least liked me well enough." She drew in a shaky, sobbing breath.

"I-I'm sorry...."

"Don't be sorry for me!" she flared. "Be sorry for yourself. 'Cause if you don't love him, if you're not good to him, I think I'll kill you. I don't want to be hurt like you've hurt me unless... unless Ren really does love you, unless you really l-love him." She broke down completely, then she bent over and kissed the sleeping man's scratched face.

Jamie ought to have disliked the angry girl, but she felt like crying for her instead. Lucinda was hurting because she loved Ren.

Another heavy wave of remorse slapped at her. Jamie honestly had not known that Ren had a girl. Now, for the sake of a whim, she'd ruined that for him, too.

Lucinda looked down at him silently for a minute, then she spoke to the nurse. "I just had to see him. Daddy got a call this morning from Dan. He and Ren have been feeding and milking the cows while Daddy's leg heals."

The chocolate pie! This was the chocolate pie girl! And she knew Dan. Jamie knew now why he'd been so startled at her identity that night in Ren's truck. He'd thought she was Lucinda, and Jamie felt a sting of anger even at this moment.

"And he called to say he'd come by early so he could spend the morning with...with Ren. I had to see him."

"It's all right, honey," soothed the nurse, and she put her arm around Lucinda's shoulders as they left the room together.

Jamie had no time to think. Dan came in shortly afterward, shook her hand and thanked her earnestly for finding his cousin. She protested, feeling exactly what she was: an empty fraud.

It was while Dan was there that Ren aroused a little. He moved restlessly, the IV line jumped. He muttered something, and both Dan and Jamie jumped to the bedside.

"Hey," said Dan. "Ren."

The head turned on the pillow toward Dan's voice, and Ren opened his eyes dazedly. He looked silently, intently at Dan's face; his eyes were blank, uncomprehending.

Dan tried to tease, saying nervously, "What are you doing in bed when all the rest of us are up working?"

Ren's mouth moved. Jamie could barely hear his whispered words. "Where am I?"

Dan answered slowly and distinctly, "You got a lick on your head, and that bull of yours mauled you around. You're at the clinic, but Doc says you'll be fine."

"Clinic!" Ren tried to lift his hand, but he dropped it back weakly. For an instant he stared emptily at the

IV, his eyes wide and bright. That disjointed, soulless look made Jamie shiver. "I feel—tired . . . tired," he whispered.

"You were bleeding. You lost a lot of blood. Jennie found you and called the doctor." Dan motioned to the girl on the other side of the bed, who was nervously clutching the sheets. Ren turned his head, looked at her. There was not even a flicker of recognition in his face. "Jennie?" he said questioningly. Then he, like Lucinda, glanced at the shirt she wore.

He tried to grasp it. "My—my shirt." He frowned, wincing, "Got to wear that shirt s-somewhere."

Jamie spoke much as Dan had. "That's right. We had a date to eat supper with Sidney last night until you decided to jilt me for a bullfight."

He didn't even seem to register her words, just the teasing gentleness of her tone. He watched her mouth steadily, then he said, slow and intent, his words clear as bells in the thick silence, *"I love you."*

There was a long stillness in the room. Dan did not move. Those three syllables fell like ice shards into Jamie's brain, then she said chokingly. "Oh, Ren. Ren. I'm sorry for—" She hid her face on the pillow beside his, so close her hot tears burned his cheek as well as hers, and she caressed his face with her hand.

Her emotion, her tears, seemed to crack the wall Ren was behind. His hand—the one with the IV hooked into it—came up slowly to touch her hair.

"Jennie?" he said huskily, then he looked at his cousin. "What's wrong with her? Dan?"

At the knowledge in Ren's eyes, Dan smiled in relief. "Reckon you've scared her half to death."

Dan took Jamie home later that morning after the doctor checked Ren. She took a long, hot shower and climbed wearily into bed. Her mind went round and round in accusing circles until she fell asleep from sheer exhaustion.

The insistent, nagging ring of the phone woke her. Her head throbbing from a headache that made her feel sick, she finally fumbled for the receiver.

"Jamie! Jamie, this is Sharon!"

Jamie winced away from her cousin's clear, quick voice.

"I called because I had to tell you—Todd is home."

Todd is home. Words as simple and as shattering as Ren's. "I love you." "Todd is home." Two little phrases that ended everything.

"Jamie? Did you hear me?"

The girl sitting on the bed rubbed a hand over her beating, tom-tomming temple.

"I heard."

"He's been here twice already, looking for you. He said something about a fight you'd had—that he'd tried to call to patch it up—that you were mad and wouldn't call him. Then he wanted to know where in hell you've been, where you are now."

"What did you tell him?"

"A bunch of bull. That you'd gone to Lexington with me last week when I spent three days up there. That I thought you were visiting a friend in Nashville this weekend, but I conveniently forgot just who."

"Sharon." There was a note of despair in her voice. "Sharon, what am I going to do? This has all gone wrong."

Sharon sucked in her breath. "Then cut the losses and come home. End it now."

"I can't. I can't. Ren got hurt."

"Hurt? How?"

Jamie tried to keep the emotion out of her voice as she described what had happened.

"He's weak and a little disoriented still, but Dr. Chambers says he's going to be fine."

"He got gored and he's fine?"

"He wasn't really gored, just mauled around. They think lightning struck the barn and Ren went to put out the blaze. He must have forgotten about the bull, and it charged him."

"He lost his barn, too? This guy has all the luck!" Sharon exclaimed, but there was a trace of sympathy in her voice.

"No, not completely. It was only partially hit, just under the edge of the tin roof. Ren must have put out the fire, but he doesn't remember anything about it."

"All that is terrible, Jamie, but I don't see what it has to do with Todd and your coming home."

"I can't leave with him in the hospital."

"He's just a guy you've had a few dates with. Sure you can."

Jamie tried to speak, to explain her relationship with Ren, but somehow it was too much, too difficult. Instead, she said stubbornly, "I found him. I went to the hospital with him. He's expecting me back. I can't just leave this minute."

There was a long moment of silence on the other end, then Sharon said, "And Todd?"

"Put him off. I'm still in Nashville."

Sharon said nothing, then Jamie sighed. "I'll be home in a day or two for good. I promise."

Ren had a steady stream of visitors that night—Dan and Sylvia, Cheever, Ben and most of the ball team, Enoch Johnson, even Sidney Hill—until the doctor called a halt around eight. There was only one other patient in the clinic, a little boy recovering from an appendectomy, so when Ren said, "Can Jennie stay longer, Doc?" Chambers shrugged and said dryly, "Whatever's good for the patient."

They didn't say much. Ren was still too weak and worn out from his loss of blood. He pulled Jamie's hand up to his heart, said drowsily, "Thanks for comin' to look for me. Doc says you're the reason I'm still alive." She couldn't force out an answer. In a few minutes, he fell asleep, and at midnight, Jamie went back to the apartment.

The next morning he wanted to go home. He was adamant about it. He hated hospitals, he said. After listening to his arguments, Chambers finally gave in.

"All right. We've checked and x-rayed everything. I don't think you'll have anything except aches and pains. The stitches are okay if you don't break them. And I don't think you will. You're gonna be weak as a kitten for a day or two, then you'll feel draggy and tired for several weeks, but you'll be able to work. There's just one condition to your going home."

"What?"

Chambers jerked his head toward Jamie, who'd stood silently in the background.

"She goes with you. Or somebody does. And they stay with you constantly the next forty-eight hours to watch you and take care of you. You're too weak to fix meals, and you need to eat."

Ren turned his head to look at Jamie, but he didn't say a word. His eyes were questioning, a little pleading.

"I'll stay, Doctor," she said hesitantly, and Ren relaxed.

"Good—good." The doctor pulled his stethoscope off his neck and turned away.

Being alone with Ren had never been difficult before, yet when Dan got him in his bed at home and left, Jamie became nervous. Some fatal balance had been tilted, and she could not right it. But he slept most of the first night, victim of an ugly-looking needle the doctor had pushed into his arm just before he left the clinic.

While he was sleeping heavily, she called her boss at home to let him know that she wouldn't be in to work for the next few days.

She stood outside on Ren's porch before going to bed, and King, who'd forgiven her all her past sins, stayed beside her. The sky was a deep velvet-blue and the stars winked and twinkled down at her through the branches of the big oak and hickory trees in the yard. There was still a feeling of wetness in the air, and the grass was damp with dew. Somewhere in the still of the night she heard a lonesome whippoorwill call, and out on the distant highway a car passed.

The beauty of this night made her want to cry. It was all over but the crying anyway. Jamie had only felt this bad once before, the night they had led her to a white, cold room and pulled the sheet back from a face that was Tory's.

"I'm sorry," she whispered at the sky. "Tory's death, that's something I still don't understand. But I was wrong to do this. I should have let her go." As if she had a choice, she thought sadly. That arrogant, stubborn streak in her that demanded that God himself give her an explanation for the loss of her sister, that streak was going to destroy her someday.

The dog at her side whined, then stiffened. He gave a sudden bark and took off chasing a rabbit that ran across the yard. Jamie, startled out of her reverie, shivered and went back inside.

Ren slept peacefully against the pillow, one arm flung out from the covers. She looked down at him, seeing the red scratches standing out on the tanned skin of his cheek and neck, the dark bruising across his shoulders and chest. Gently she traced one long scratch across his temple. He slept on unconsciously. She got bolder and kissed the bruise just beside the white bandage on his shoulder.

Then she straightened, turned out the light and went to bed on the couch.

Ren was a good patient except that he tried to do too much. Early Monday morning as Jamie stood on the porch again, enjoying the cool morning sun and the mist that it had failed to burn out of the hollow to her far left, he actually pulled himself up to come outside and join her.

"Ren! What are you doing up?"

He opened the screen door slowly, wincing. "Dyin' I reckon. I feel like I've been used for a punchin' bag."

"Dr. Chambers said today would be the day you felt the worst. The soreness will start to leave tomorrow." She watched the play of muscles across the long, tight, sleek brown stomach as he reached up and felt gingerly around the edges of the bandage high on his shoulder. He had somehow pulled on a pair of worn, soft jeans, but he had not snapped the waistband, and he had on a loose shirt that was not buttoned. Then he touched his forehead, which had a vicious discoloration to match those on his side and back.

"I'm afraid to look in the mirror," he said ruefully.

"You look fine," Jamie said shortly. He did, she realized. He was alive, he was in one piece and he was Ren.

She fixed his meals; she laughed with him, talked to him, watched television with him. She listened while he and Dan talked about their work when Dan dropped by later that day. She came running when Ren tried to get up off the bed and got tangled up in the quilt she'd spread over him when she found him asleep like an exhausted child. That was when he slid onto the floor, knocking over a lamp and the clock with him. He groaned heavily.

"Why didn't you call me?" she protested, trying to unwind the tangled bedclothes from his legs.

Ren sprawled out on the floor in disgust. "To help me go to the bathroom, Mommy?" he said, making a face.

"To do anything," she said, intent on her task. She looked up at his silence, met his brown eyes with their sudden awareness and flushed hotly.

"Jennie, I—" he said awkwardly, and reached out his hand for her cheek. Hastily she pulled away, trying to laugh.

And through it all she heard the words she didn't even know if he realized he'd ever spoken: "I love you."

That night he watched her. She grew more nervous by the minute. As she sat beside him on his bed to pull up his sheets and to flip off his lamp, he said intently,

"Where'd you sleep last night? There's no bed in the other bedroom."

She flushed, but said in a matter-of-fact voice, looking down at him, "On your couch."

"My couch!" he exclaimed, then tried to push himself up. "Jennie."

"Ren, no."

"Why not? I'm not going to—to try anything. I couldn't if I wanted to. Just sleep here—" and he thumped the pillow beside his "—and we'll both be comfortable." His determination, his intensity, his serious, scratched face so close to hers made her waver.

In the darkness she lay down cautiously beside him on top of the bedclothes, then he slid his hand into hers.

"That medicine...makes me...too sleepy," he said, his words already slurring together. Jamie relaxed and squeezed his hand.

The next morning she was far too relaxed. She'd turned on her side during the night, and when she awoke, he was at her back. She looked down dazedly for a moment at the strong brown hand beneath her breasts that locked her tightly to the man beside her. They lay cocooned together in warmth, in the bed that smelled of his soap and his shampoo and just him.

Jamie had done a great many things in her life but awaking in a bed with a man's arms and legs and body imprisoning her was not one of them. Her only consolation was that Ren was still asleep, his face flushed and relaxed. She extricated herself before he awoke fully.

That day he wanted to touch her, and tormented by her own guilt, she kept stiffening away, afraid of how her heart had turned over when he'd smiled sleepily at her. He sensed her withdrawal, but said nothing. She drove him to the doctor's for a checkup that afternoon and kept herself busy cooking supper for him, frying chicken and making tea.

He walked slowly in on her while she worked, watched a minute, then kissed her cheek. "You're a good cook," he said, tasting the casserole on the counter.

Some devil rose in Jamie. "Better than Lucinda?" Then she could have kicked herself. He stood as if he'd been poleaxed, flushing.

"Is that what you're mad about?" he asked finally, almost in relief. "I told you I'd had a girlfriend, kind of, before you came. But, Jennie, I told you, too, that it wasn't like—like us. She just called me a lot, and I took her out—"

"Another woman chasing you?" Jamie said, and she tried to soften her words and tease. Why hadn't her wayward tongue stayed quiet?

"Only she never caught me," he flashed.

"Ren Garrett, I wonder about you," she answered dubiously.

That night he flatly refused his pain medicine, turning his head into the pillow mutinously until she finally put the bottle away in exasperation. And when she tried to make up the couch bed, he got up and took the pillows and sheets and hauled them to a closet and locked it. Then he stood before the doors looking down at her in her cotton gown.

"If you weren't already black and blue, I'd make you that way," she told him angrily.

"I told you before I wouldn't try anything," he said stubbornly. "Just go to bed."

She flounced into the bedroom, got into the bed and turned away from him in a huff. He was left to turn out the lights, and in the darkness she felt him ease gingerly into his pillow and give a long sigh of relief.

In the middle of the night, he pulled her to him. She said sleepily. "Ren?"

"Umm?"

"What's wrong?"

He whispered back. "I was just thinkin' I was glad I didn't take that medicine; I can't remember you at all last night."

She was lying curled back against him as closely as the previous night, but she was comfortable and sleepy. She'd move away sometime . . . maybe.

By Wednesday, Ren was a great deal better. Though the bruising looked worse, the soreness was lessening. Jamie knew with a sinking heart that she couldn't put it off any longer: She had to leave.

She had tried to repay Ren in some small coin, Todd was waiting for her and Jamie had a life to get back to. She didn't understand the melancholy that dogged her all day, the effort it took to hold back the tears. She was too quiet, too withdrawn.

Ren knew something was wrong. He watched her, circled around her mentally. Finally, he left her alone and went for a slow walk with King over the farm.

When he got back, she had an early supper fixed, and when they'd put away the dishes, she sucked in her breath, turned to look at his wary face and said in a rush, "I've got to go home, Ren. Tonight."

"Tonight! Why can't you wait and let me take you back in the morning?"

Because you don't know where home is for me, she wanted to say. "I have things I need to do. I can't—won't stay here again tonight."

Her words were too sharp, but she couldn't help it. The anguish in her soul made them that way.

Ren said slowly, "I don't know what's wrong. I can feel it, though. If it's your job, I understand. You gave up a lot to help me. I shouldn't ever have asked you. You saved my life, that was enough. Then you were good enough, kind enough, to help more."

Jamie said chokingly. "Please. No more. I'm not good or kind—"

"Yes, you are," he insisted stubbornly, "you're the best woman I've ever met."

For one ghastly minute, Jamie wondered if he were joking. "Ren," she said weakly. She walked away from him, into the living room, where she sat down on the couch. He followed, looking down at her. She started to cry. "I'm a terrible person. But p-please understand, I didn't mean to be. I never meant to hurt anybody. But my sister died, and I was the one hurting when I—" She stopped, choking on the tears, and hid her face in her hands.

He reached out and pulled her hands from her face.

"Jennie, don't go tonight." His voice was low and beseeching, its huskiness more pronounced than ever. He held her down against the couch, staring in the dim light at her face.

"I think I'd better," she said rubbing the tears off her cheeks. There was a danger here that made her forget her confession, made her look for escape. His face was intent, absorbed; his eyes held a look that troubled her.

"I want you to stay. Please. You're so upset over this thing with your sister. Let me make you feel better."

"Ren, I don't—Ren, no!" She pushed against his uninjured shoulder as he insistently drew near her lips, but he shifted one arm to pull her hand down to her side and locked it there.

Then his lips touched hers. He was surer now than he had been in the past, and the mouth he pressed determinedly to hers was warm and persuasive. He smelled good from his walk, like sun and fresh grass, and the brush of his body against hers was pleasurable. He broke off the kiss to spread others across her face, muttering broken phrases of praise and love between his caresses.

His hand pushed the one of hers that he held down between them and suddenly her palm brushed the skin of his stomach. She felt his muscles clench for an instant, and she started to pull away, but he made a protesting noise and pulled her body up into his. Her hand slid farther up his chest. He was gasping against her mouth, and the smooth skin under which she could feel hard bone and muscle was enticing and warm. She tentatively caressed him beneath the shirt. It was odd—she'd never dreamed he'd feel so good to the touch.

Then he did what he'd done before: he opened his mouth. And he insisted silently that she open hers as she had once before, forcing her lips back to his with his hand holding her chin when she tried to pull away.

"Jennie, you're killin' me," he gasped at last. "Oh, God, I love you!"

"Ren, no."

"Yes, yes—I can't stop, not now." His breath was hot against her face. He pulled her on top of him as he slid down on the couch. His arms were so strong, so safe, so—so exciting. Todd had never kissed like this, so hungry, so determined. So absorbed in her, in the person she was. Ren's face was blind as a child's with passion, completely immersed in her lips, her arms, her body. Maybe if his mouth had not wanted hers so badly, maybe if his hands had not caressed her so lovingly, maybe if his body had not arched so desperately into hers, Jamie might have come to her senses in time. But he gave of himself so completely, letting her see his need, his reaction. He hid nothing behind a sophisticated mask.

Suddenly something burst in her, a dam of passion that wanted to give this man more. She wanted that hot look in his eyes for her, wanted his feverish whispers of love on her mouth, her throat, her breasts; she wanted his arms around her and his body above her.

She had her eyes shut, her face buried in his brown throat when he half lifted her from the couch. He covered her so quickly when she fell against the bed that she never had a chance to swim out of the bursting, pounding emotions driving her. She opened her eyes to push his shirt off his shoulders, and all her dazed mind could register was that this man with his unattractive face had the most beautiful body she'd ever seen. His chest was broad and his shoulders brown and strong. The bandage against his shoulder shocked her; both of them had forgotten his injury. His stomach was muscled, flat and tight. And his big square hands that she had admired before—they were as gentle on her breasts as any calloused hands could ever be. He tugged the braid loose and made an appreciative sound in his throat as the beauty of her hair spread around them.

At last, he turned out the light beside the bed, and she was glad. In the cool darkness she could beat down the voice in her head that told her to stop now before it was too late, the voice that whispered she was going to hurt this man more than she'd ever dreamed possible instead of making it up to him. Too, she could yield to the devil in her that said no one expected virginity anymore—she might as well lose it now. To the voice that said none of her friends need ever know about this dark, tangled bed and the feel of this man against her.

But at the last minute when his naked legs brushed against hers, she made a feeble attempt to tell him.

"Ren, I don't want to hurt you. Ren, please, I've never done—"

But his mouth shut the words off. And Jamie, the good little girl who'd never allowed Todd more than a touch, let this man, the man who'd been the last choice in a cheap bet, have it all.

He was stunned at her virginity. She could tell by the jerk of his body, and then he whispered thickly against her face, "You sweet—sweet—I won't hurt you, baby."

But in spite of his tenderness, there was pain. She tried weakly to push him away when the pain came, but he stilled and soothed her again. "Shhh—easy. Easy. I love you." And he was easy, gentle until the very end, when his breath was harsh against her cheek and his movements uncontrolled and involuntary.

Jamie held him down to her, holding the thick mane of his hair with both hands. He had hurt her finally when he could no longer avoid it, but in spite of that, there had been a promise, an enticing hint of more. Something in her felt a rich, deep sense of satisfaction that she had given him such pleasure.

And it had been pleasure for him. He wept unashamedly against her face, hugging her to him, caressing her arms and her side, telling her in broken whispers just how beautiful she had been for him there in the darkness.

But when he slid sideways in sleep, she was the one who cried. She was weeping silently, but some sixth sense woke him. In the dark he moved, put his hand on her wet face.

"Jennie, baby, don't cry," he protested tenderly. "Why're you cryin'?"

"Oh, Ren, what have I done?" she choked out in despair.

"Nothing that wasn't good. Shhh. You and me—that's right. The way it's supposed to be. Jennie, I love you. I want to marry you."

"Ren, please..."

"I know I'm not doin' this the way I should. I'm not any good with words. But you know I've been lovin' you for almost as long as I've known you. Let's get a marriage licence tomorrow. Be my wife, Jennie."

"Ren, there are things about me you don't know... you wouldn't like."

He turned on his back a little stiffly now and pulled her head down on his warm, comforting shoulder. "Honey, the only thing a man worries about is who else has had his woman. And you just gave me an answer to that that's made me the—the happiest man in the world. But I would'a loved you anyway, even if there'd been somebody else. Don't you see, there's not anything that'll stop my lovin' you, not now. Jennie, this is the best night of my whole life. Now go to sleep." He gave a deep laugh as he shifted her against him. "You'd better get used to sleepin' like this. It's the way I want to sleep forever."

She lay there in the tangled warmth of his arms and legs, stroking his shoulder. Why was he so easy to touch, to caress? Even now her fingers kept returning to his skin. He fell asleep quickly, his face in the moonlight softer, handsomer than in the harsh light of day. He was a good man. That old-fashioned phrase said it all. If she had to lose her virginity, then it was right he was the one to take it. He deserved it for all she'd done to him and was going to do. She'd let him fall in love with her, playing on his niceness, his innocence. And now she was going to leave him.

How ironic. She'd planned on tricking him into letting her keep her own innocence so she could get the letter from Beth. Instead, when she no longer cared about the letter, she gave him her virginity and, in a way, took his. Or at least his trust. She didn't think he had been a virgin; she was beginning to wonder if he wasn't very experienced, indeed. He just seemed too good at this making love. He'd sure knocked one country-club, street-smart girl off her feet. Life was funny. Not funny ha-ha, but funny awful. The funniest part of all was that tonight Jennie Lynn would cease to be; she had to go back, wanted to go back, to the world of Jamie Logan. And when it was all said and done, this boy who'd once been a convenience, a shy, awkward means of success—he'd somehow touched her heart. Pierced it with a painful sweetness. She almost wished she were Jennie Lynn. For an hour or two longer, here in this bed, she'd pretend she was.

But it was Jamie Logan who kissed the sleeping Ren goodbye.

In the silvery darkness before the sunrise she looked down on his peaceful face, then slipped away, gathering up her few things silently. Like some lost wraith she slid out the door and into her truck, parked a good distance from the house.

Only King knew when she left. He followed her to the vehicle, whining anxiously. She looked down at the huge animal and whispered, "You take good care of him, King."

Then she was in the truck, putting it in neutral, letting it coast down the slight grade of the gravel road away from Ren's house. And away from Ren. She had to leave this way. She couldn't face him.

Back at the apartment she threw things into the truck, not even stopping to pack. Her clothes were dumped into the front seat, and everything that wouldn't blow away was tossed into the rear.

Just as she got ready to pull the door shut behind her for good, the telephone rang. It sounded like a pistol shot in the stillness, and she jumped in fright. But she wouldn't answer it. Not now.

By seven that morning she'd left a terse resignation letter for the Farmers' Association, effective immediately, citing family problems as her reason for quitting.

Then she was home. She stared down at the telephone as she stood in the morning shadows of her father's library. The hardest thing she'd ever had to do was dial Ren's number.

He picked it up on the first ring. His voice was so clear she thought he might be in the next room, and she tried to swallow the lump in her throat.

"Hello? Hello?" Then he said anxiously, "Jennie—"

"Ren," she finally got out on a harsh breath.

"Where in hell are you?" he burst out, and she felt his anger. "I woke up and you were gone, just like that."

"I . . . was scared, I guess, Ren," she faltered, and she was telling the truth.

"Scared! Of what?" he demanded.

"Of what happened between us last night."

There was a silence, and when he spoke again, his voice was gentle. "You don't have anything to be scared of. I love you. If I hurt you—"

Jamie's face went hot even on the phone. "No, you didn't. You're the most gentle man I know, Ren. But I—need to think. And there's a problem with, um, my family. I have to go back to see them. I'll call you when . . . when I—I get to Roswell again."

"Wait, Jennie—"

She hung up on his words, and the sick taste of guilt and lies was in her mouth.

At noon, Roberta ushered Sharon into the same quiet library and shut the door firmly behind her.

"I got your message, Jamie. What's wrong? Lord, you look awful!" Her worried voice took the sting out of her words, and Jamie made a face.

"Nothing like your relatives to tell you the truth," she said ironically. "I should have listened to you all along. I'd have saved myself a lot of grief."

"What's happened? Jamie, tell me!"

For answer, Jamie shoved an open envelope into her cousin's hand. Sharon stared at her an instant, then glanced down and pulled out the note.

"You do want me to read this?"

Jamie just nodded; she was having trouble speaking. Her voice kept getting caught in the tightness of her throat. She knew what the letter said. After all, she'd written it:

Beth -
I'll talk to Daddy about the job for you with Trevor and Harrison as soon as he returns from Europe.

Jamie Logan

Sharon closed her eyes a minute, then said in relief, "Thank goodness. This thing is over. You should be happy to lose a bet like this."

Jamie said nothing, just glanced away. The other girl watched her for a long, silent moment.

"Jamie." Sharon's voice was insistent, slow. "Look at me."

Jamie honestly tried to face her cousin, but something in that bright blue gaze locked on her face made her flinch and move away.

Sharon caught her by the arm. "You *did* lose this bet, didn't you?"

Jamie tried to answer her, to make a flip remark, but instead she stood flushing like some gauche schoolgirl struck dumb with embarrassment. "I—I—"

Sharon said incredulously, "You went to bed with the farmer, didn't you? Didn't you? Why would you do such a stupid thing?"

"Oh, Sharon." She hid her face in her hands. "I don't know what happened. He—he wasn't like I thought he would be. He was just plain nice. And real. He was a real person."

Sharon's face registered horror. "What do you mean, was? He's not dead or something, is he? He didn't die from that accident?"

"No. But he might as well be as far as I'm concerned. I've done something awful. Sharon, he asked me to marry him. He—he really loved me."

There was a long silence, then Jamie flung up her head defiantly and said to her cousin, "I wanted to make it up to him for using him. To somehow say I was sorry. So I went . . . I spent the night with him."

"There are other ways," Sharon said dryly, disbelievingly. "In fact, your apology is one of the dumbest things I ever heard of anybody doing."

"It wasn't an apology. Not really. And I—" she looked Sharon straight in the eye "—I'm not sorry for that, at least."

Sharon shook her head. "We are still talking about the same man, aren't we? The one named Ren Garrett?"

Jamie winced at the clear sound of his name on Sharon's lips. She pointed at the letter. "Please, would you take this to Beth? I just can't tell her myself. But it's important that she thinks she won. Don't look at me like that. It's not just for me, I swear. I've thought about this all morning. Tory's letter isn't worth it. Not now. And this way Ren doesn't—doesn't—"

"Look like an utter fool?" Sharon said helpfully, a little ironically.

Jamie nodded. "This way it looks like I either failed or just plain chickened out."

"There's nothing wrong with either on some occasions," Sharon said, folding up the letter. "Try it sometime." Then she relented and hugged her cousin. "It'll be all right. You didn't really mean to—"

But Jamie pushed her away. "Don't you dare forgive me, Sharon Logan. I don't think I could stand it. Not today."

PART TWO: The Payback

Chapter Nine

He was handsome. Oh, there was no doubt about that. Todd Jackson had well-cut black hair that lay sleekly against his nicely shaped head, brilliant blue eyes, a straight, elegant nose and lips that were made for sensual pursuits. He looked good in the silk suits and expensive sportswear he favored. There had not been a woman at the tennis courts on Saturday morning watching him play in his cool whites who had not been slightly envious of Jamie Logan, his partner.

They had soundly trounced Sharon and her companion, and Todd had been ebullient ever since. He was aggressive and competitive; he liked to win. Jamie had been in no mood to play and not much help, so she didn't point out to him that Sharon hated tennis. It didn't take a lot to beat Sharon's court act, certainly not Todd's hard-driving game. Sharon was sure death to whoever was unlucky enough to partner her in a doubles match.

But for all that, Jamie would rather have played tennis all day long and right on into the night than to be where she was now. It would have been easier than getting dressed in the tawny softness of her strapless gown and going to Claire's house, where a gala welcome-back party was being held on the huge lawn for Eli and Eve Logan. Tonight Jamie had to face everybody, especially Beth, and that was something she had avoided doing for weeks now, hanging close to home.

Not that she was sorry to have her parents back. For a twenty-two-year-old modern young woman, she supposed she had been unreasonably glad to see them return.

Her mother looked better than she had right after Tory's death. Eli was a little grayer. But he had hugged and kissed Jamie fiercely when they got home, just as he had when she was a child. Her father, especially, brought loud, noisy life back to the house. Their old housekeeper, Roberta, had not stopped smiling yet.

"Did you 'do' the Continent, Daddy?" Jamie teased.

"Something's been done to it. It'll never be the same," Eve put in, laughing. "You just don't know the atrocities this man has committed, enough to embarrass this whole generation of the family and the next, too. In Madrid he—"

"Give me a chance to breathe, Mama, before you start tellin' on me," Eli grumbled. "All I can say is, thank God for Kentucky. I'm back!"

Tonight it looked as if most of Kentucky knew it, or at least most of Claiborne County. Local people flocked to the festivities; tables scattered all around the well-lit lawn for the buffet supper were already full, laughter and talk mingled on the night air and the sound of a fiddler and his band wistfully playing "Fair and Tender Ladies" wafted in from far out under the trees.

Todd had been waiting for Jamie when she arrived with her parents. "Good evening, Mr. Logan, Mrs. Logan. You look gorgeous," he said to Eve, and she smiled up at him.

"You look very handsome, too, Todd, as usual," she replied.

"How was Europe, sir?" he asked Eli politely.

"It was there," Eli said shortly, in the edgy way he always responded to Todd. After a few minutes more of conversation, Todd, with a smoothness that told of years of experience, slid Jamie away from her family and out toward the band. Several couples were swaying to an old waltz tune, and he pulled her up against him as they joined the dancing.

His first words were abrupt. "So why couldn't you come with me tonight? What's the idea of letting me think you were going to? I'd already told everybody we'd be coming together. I spent a quarter of an hour after I got here explaining how you wanted to be with your daddy."

Jamie glanced up at his handsome, angry face. "I never let you think anything, Todd. You came up with it all by yourself. And there's nothing wrong with coming with Daddy and Mama. They did just get home a few days ago."

"What's wrong with you these days? You don't want to go out, half the time you don't want to kiss me. Don't tell me you're still sulking over that stupid quarrel we had more than two months ago. You can't treat me like this on and on. People know we're practically engaged."

Jamie took a deep breath. "About this engagement, Todd. We're not actually—I'm not your fiancée, you know."

He suddenly laughed. "Well, if all this standoffishness is to bring me up to scratch, we'll go get the ring tomorrow. I guess it is time I made it official. At least it'll stop Harry Sheffield from hanging around." He frowned.

Jamie looked at him, trying to see him clearly. All right, the man was handsome. No, he was perfect. Adonis. He was successful. He had confidence. And in a few years, he'd probably be extremely wealthy.

She clicked those facts through her head, adding them, and at last, she regretfully subtracted from them one thing: Jamie Lynn Logan. She and Todd were finished. There. She'd finally said it.

She had spent weeks now trying to work up her old attraction to him and his minty, sleek perfection, and the effort made her sick somewhere near her heart. It was ironic that at this closing moment, he'd finally made the proposal she'd thought would satisfy her yen for life. It had been tossed carelessly in her lap. But his nonchalance was a good thing, because it meant she could be just as casual when she gave him the answer she'd realized was the one she was going to make.

"To tell the truth, I have no intention of—"

"Todd, honey, there you are," interrupted the drawling voice of the wife of one of Todd's wealthiest clients. "Jamie, I hope you won't mind if I borrow your young man just a little while. For legal advice, you might say." Her false eyelashes fluttered as she smiled archly up at him.

Jamie stepped away. "He's all yours," she said, and this time the relief came through clearly in her tone. Todd shot an angry glance at her, but he dared not offend the older woman. She had him on her leash now, like some kind of trained dog, and he had to go with her, her prize until she decided otherwise.

Jamie watched them go, then started back to the buffet tables, but she saw Harry there, scanning the crowd. She had had a dinner date with him two weeks ago, and he had called her several times, sensing that something was going wrong between her and Todd. She had a good idea whom he was looking for, and she edged into the shadows, hoping that the warm glow of her dress wouldn't give her away.

In the darkness under a big oak tree, Jamie looked up at the white three-quarter moon. Though it had barely turned August, the air had an unusual coolness from the east in it. Grandpa Logan used to say that he wanted an east wind to be blowing when he died. Maybe he'd said it because there was something sad and poignant in that kind of breeze. Downright lonesome, that's how it felt.

She had once loved the night; now everything about it bothered her. Its very darkness, the brush of cool sheets against her skin. It all reminded her of one night weeks ago. One night in Ren Garrett's bed. Sometimes, she managed to fall asleep quickly, gratefully, only to wake up later, and in a sort of half dream, he'd be there. His hands would be touching her. She shivered and rubbed her arms.

Because what was worse was, she'd be reaching for him. Sometimes she wanted him so much she hurt.

She was an absolute fool. She knew she did not want Ren Garrett. He was hard to forget only because she'd gone to bed with him, for heaven's sake. What she was feeling was guilt. Or maybe it was frustration. She'd always heard that once Eve in the Garden had tasted the apple, she'd had to have another bite, so to speak.

Well, lovemaking ought to be easy enough to get. According to the movies, ninety-nine percent of the world was doing it ninety-nine percent of the time. Except that Jamie's own moral code did not allow casual sex. That code had stood her in good stead with every man except Ren, even Todd.

Not that Todd hadn't tried to persuade her numerous times. And it was Ren's fault that she couldn't respond to Todd in any way anymore. Regret and guilt were eating her alive; they must be what had canceled out any desire she might have felt for Todd. She had, after all, betrayed him with Ren. Why did Ren have to fall in love with her? Why couldn't he just have settled for the warmth of a friendship? She'd genuinely liked him, after all.

Jamie knew her reasoning had holes in it, but that didn't matter. It was the kind of reasoning that got her through nights like this one.

"Beautiful Dreamer." That was what the fiddle was pouring out now. She shut her eyes to listen to it, and instead, she heard over the music the clear, exasperated voice of Sharon, close at hand.

"Chopped duck liver," she was saying.

Her sixteen-year-old brother Beau answered in horror, "What did you say this stuff was?"

"Duck liver. Or goose liver. Or some kind of feathered fowl's little internal organs all ground up into pâté."

"And you nearly let me eat it?" Beau's tone was highly indignant.

"Let you eat it? You're the one that grabbed it up."

"It was on a Ritz. I never thought anybody would ruin a Ritz with a duck liver," he protested.

Laughing, Jamie went across the yard to where Sharon and Beau stood arguing. When she got close, Beau saw her coming and interrupted his sister's acid comments about his thinking abilities to say, "Here's Jamie. We've been looking all over for you."

Sharon turned and gave an exaggerated sigh of relief. "At last. Do you know how many places we've searched?"

In spite of the lightness of her tone, her eyes were panicky and her motions nervous.

"What's wrong?"

Beau answered, "Sharon got all bent out of shape because Beth Benton walked in a little while ago. She's got on a red dress and it's cut to *here*." Beau's face expressed his awed appreciation of Beth's neckline.

"Will you get lost?" Sharon snapped at him. "Go admire the view again, why don't you?" She pulled Jamie into the crowd, away from Beau. "The first thing Beth did was to ask me about you."

"Don't worry. I'm okay. I knew I'd have to see her tonight. She probably wants to know when she can move into her new law office." Jamie took a deep breath. "I want to get this over with. Where is she?"

"With Uncle Eli and Aunt Eve. Over there."

Jamie's parents stood at the edge of the patio. Beau had neglected to mention that Beth's dress sparkled with every move she made, and Jamie had to admit—with extreme reluctance—that she looked good.

"I heard she was in Richmond," Sharon muttered as they drew near the group. "I had hopes she'd stay there for the next decade. But she's home and she's brought some grumpy old lady with her."

Beth turned when Eli smiled over her shoulder at his daughter. "Hello, Jamie," she said, sipping her drink.

Beth might be beautiful, but there was such a pinched whiteness in her face that Jamie wondered if Beth had been sick. She was as nervous as Sharon.

Eve spoke, motioning toward a chair just behind the girl in red. "Come and meet Beth's great-aunt, dear. This is our daughter, Miss Hill. Jamie, this is Miss Sidney Hill from Roswell. She's never—"

Jamie didn't hear what it was Sidney had never. She couldn't hear anything over the deafening roar in her ears. All she could see in front of her eyes was—Sidney Hill.

Ren's Sidney Hill.

She painfully sucked in a breath of needled air. Her face and fingers felt numb. And she couldn't think at all. She just stood there, gasping, white-faced, suspended in some kind of vacuum for a timeless eternity.

But when something snapped inside her and her senses suddenly flipped on again, nobody had noticed anything. Except Beth. Her brilliant gaze was trained intently on Jamie's face.

I'm going to wring your cheating neck, Elizabeth Benton. You can count on it, Jamie promised to herself.

"—knew your Grandpa Logan when he was sharecroppin' a farm on the edge of Claiborne County," Sidney was saying. Jamie, still trembling from reaction, tried to concentrate on her words. "But I never met your daddy till tonight. I remember hearin' when he was a boy that he was good-lookin' as sin." The old lady eyed Jamie. "It appears you've inherited a lot from him."

"Handsome is as handsome does," Jamie murmured inanely.

"So they tell me," Sidney said, and looked sharply at her.

Somebody made a comment, Jamie didn't know what. She edged away from the conversation, trying to hide behind her father's big bulk.

There had not been a flicker of recognition on the old lady's face. Was it possible Sidney didn't know her? That Beth hadn't told? Anyway, Jamie reminded herself, there was nothing to tell. Beth thought she'd lost the bet. Or maybe Sidney had never mentioned Ren to her great-niece. And maybe dogs fly.

Jamie twisted around her father to look at Sidney, and suddenly the strangest thing happened inside her: all her days of being Jennie seemed real again, part of her, as if two halves of a whole had abruptly melded together. The sharp pain that shot through her felt like a piercing regret, not for what she'd done, but for what she'd left behind.

She didn't know what she said when she took her seat at the table. She just smiled at everything, even at Harry when he somehow wound up beside her. At Todd's angry face. At her father's story of an escapade in France.

And she ate whatever it was in front of her. Chopped duck liver. Was that what somebody said?

At last Sidney, who'd been watching her like a pinned insect, put her out of her doubt and misery.

As Jamie stood with Sharon later, wondering how on earth she could get out of here and go home, Sidney hobbled up and poked her sharply with her cane. "Ever been to Roswell, girl?" she asked abruptly.

Be careful, Jamie cautioned herself. "Y-yes, I have. Several times."

"I thought so. You know something? I believed in you, too. Like he did."

Oh, yes. Sidney knew.

Sharon looked in bewilderment from one to the other, then said on a note of confused laughter, "What does that mean?"

Sidney said pointedly, "She knows what I mean. And I know her. I just don't like her."

"What in the world is she talking about?" Sharon burst out, and got violently motioned into silence by the other two.

"I'm going to interfere in your life one time, Jamie Logan, or Jennifer Lynn, or whoever you're pretendin' to be now. I wouldn't do it except for the boy who's grievin' himself to death. I'm not doin' it for you, that's for sure."

Chapter Ten

"You'll just have to leave town for a few weeks. That's all there is to it," Sharon concluded once again, pulling nervously at the curly hair over one ear.

Jamie turned from the mirror to say in exasperation, "How am I supposed to vanish from my own home with my parents just back and stay gone for weeks? They'll think I've lost my mind. I've told you and told you, I'll just have to wait and see what Sidney meant last night. Half the time she's just talking."

"I can't believe you're so...so cool," Sharon burst out angrily. "I'm coming apart at the seams, and you're the one in trouble. Jamie, I'll bet that old woman went straight back to Roswell last night, hunted up Ren Garrett and told him everything. You're calmly getting ready for church and he's probably headed here with a shotgun."

Jamie's hand, which was applying lipstick, shook for a second so badly that she had to put the brush down. Then she took a deep breath and looked in the mirror to catch her cousin's gaze. It was then that Sharon saw her worry and fear.

Jamie spoke to the reflection. "I can't run every time somebody says he's coming. Anyway, why would he? If he even believes Sidney, he'll only be hurt at what she tells him. And Ren's not the kind to come charging in, demanding explanations. Besides, Sharon—" she glanced away to reach carefully for her perfume "—maybe he doesn't care anymore." The bottles jarred against one another as she tried to choose one. "It's been six or seven weeks now. He's forgotten."

"You heard what the Hill woman said. Just look in the mirror at yourself, Jamie Logan," Sharon answered sharply.

Her cousin did as she was bidden, taking in the full, soft waves of tawny blond hair that lay on her shoulders and down her back, the worried green eyes, the straight nose, the fullness of the pink lips that she was biting nervously, the delicate blue-green of the blouse with its scooped neck and its tiny row of buttons down the front.

"So? What am I supposed to see? That I have my lipstick smudged?"

"Do you honestly think a girl who looks like that one would have an easy time of getting away from any man? Especially one she's chased and dazzled and given her virginity to?"

Jamie flushed and tried to turn away, "Stop it, Sharon."

But Sharon said insistently, "He hasn't forgotten. He's probably trying to understand what hit him."

"I didn't mean to hurt Ren!"

"I may be the only person in the world who ever believes you. But I know how naive you are, no matter what you look like. Your father's protected you all your life. Even Tory made it clear to men that they'd better toe the mark with you." Sharon turned away, saying slowly, "Sometimes I think she did it because she knew how much her own behavior hurt Eli, and keeping you innocent was her way of making it up to him."

"Don't psychoanalyze Tory or judge her now, Sharon," Jamie said sharply. "It won't do her any good."

They looked at each other, as close to an argument as they had been in years. Then Eve knocked on the door, and they were forced to smile and leave for church as though it were a normal summer Sunday. But Jamie forgave her cousin as Sharon said under her breath when they brushed past each other, "If Beth comes to church today, lightning had better strike Reverend Addison's sermon right out of his hand."

Reverend Addison had no problem with his sermon. It was long and scholarly, and Jamie heard all of three minutes of it. She sat going through everything in her mind. By the time she and Sharon had climbed in the car with their mothers and started home, she'd reached one sure conclusion: Ren would never come after Jamie Logan, not once he knew the truth. She understood him that well, at least.

There was the usual line of vehicles parked in the circular drive under the shade trees at home. Sunday dinners and Sunday afternoons were a tradition at Eli's. Most of the sprawling Logan family would be here. They started drifting in early on Sundays, knowing that Eli didn't go to church. By noon, there was always a house filled with laughter and people.

"Lord, Beau's got his motorcycle out of the shop," Sharon moaned, pointing to the vehicle parked on the edge of the lawn. "One more wreck or one more ticket—that's all the word *Honda* means around our house."

Smiling, Eve nodded toward one of the cars and said, "Todd is here, Jamie. How nice for you."

The housekeeper met them as she crossed the foyer with a tray filled with glasses. "Everybody's in the back, tearin' up perfectly good grass."

In the backyard, several cousins were involved in some wild, shouting sort of keepaway game over a ball. Mostly they were aggravating Beau, the youngest. He was laughing too hard to do much protesting, but he kept brandishing a heavy stick threateningly.

Todd was watching from the side with two of Eli's brothers, but he saw Jamie after a few minutes and crossed to her. His hair gleamed raven-black in the sun, and his pastel polo shirt looked as crisply fresh as if he were in the courtroom.

He had barely reached her when Roberta called from the wide back porch, "Somebody at the door to see you, Miss Jamie."

"Are you expecting someone else?" Todd frowned and Jamie shrugged and turned to follow Roberta. Todd waited a few seconds, then started after her. "Jamie!" he called impatiently.

Her mother and father stood talking in the study just off the entrance area, and Eli winked at her as she passed in the shadows of the cool foyer. There was a tall man standing sideways against the doorframe, looking out over her front lawn.

She froze.

She should have been prepared. Sidney had warned her, after all. But the sight of Ren standing in her own home was not something she could have planned for.

It really was Ren. In the flesh. Jeans and T-shirt. His shoulders were still as broad, his hair as rich and thick. After the first hot flush of recognition faded, a sick relief chased through Jamie. Whatever happened, it was all going to be over.

He had a paper in his hand. Ren's hands, still big-knuckled and square and strong. Hands that once had touched her. She trembled away from that thought.

Go on. Look up. Look at me.

Something alerted him to her presence and he glanced around. His eyes were as warmly brown as they had been before.

He couldn't really see her standing there in the shadowy foyer; his eyes were still full of bright sunshine. He said uncertainly, "If you're Jamie Logan, I'm supposed to give this letter to you. Sidney Hill sent it."

He straightened with his easy, long-limbed grace and hesitantly held out an envelope.

Gasping at breath, she took a step toward him. Then another. She was supposed to look at the letter, but her world was a pair of brown eyes.

At her third step, when he got his first good look at her, his blank face changed drastically. He sucked in his breath harshly, staring.

"You're—Jennie! My God, Jennie!"

He dropped the letter and reached for her with his usual straight-to-the-point style. His hands crushed her clothes and hurt her ribs and tangled in her hair.

Then he kissed her.

It was not a sweet, gentle Ren kiss. It was hot and passionate and dark; it opened her mouth; it set her on fire.

She knew nothing except her exploding heart and the thick, welcoming pleasure that rushed through her. For her, there was total silence, a rich oblivion for only the two of them. She wanted to pull him to her, but his hard arms locked her still. She didn't care; she would drown right here, in this kiss.

Then Todd's voice was raised angrily, shouting something, and he was yanking her away from Ren. She felt light and disoriented, and Ren's bewildered face registered the same surprise as he caught sight of Todd.

"You damned lunatic! Get your hands off her," Todd spit angrily.

Ren looked at Jamie, who was still staring at him, and there was a flash of temper on his face. He reached for her hand and took it. "Jennie, I—"

"No, please." In confusion and panic, she tried to pull away.

"She said no and I told you to turn loose," Todd shouted, and in a culmination of all the past month's anger, he gave a wild punch that landed on Ren's chin and made him stumble into a table beside the door. It turned over, and there was the loud sound of breaking glass.

Jamie heard exclamations and footsteps behind them. Her parents.

Ren straightened, one hand on his mouth. And Todd suddenly shoved away from Jamie and went after him, punching at his face again, throwing himself at Ren's stomach. They knocked over a plant and both fell heavily, jarring on the floor. Then they were struggling, panting, rolling over and over.

Eve screamed when their heavy bodies rolled into her feet and legs. Jamie finally got enough breath back to cry, "Todd! Stop it!" and Eli roared, "Call Cody!"

Eli's motionless, staring wife started violently and ran for the phone.

"No! Mama, not the sheriff's office!" But another pot of flowers crashed to the floor over Jamie's voice, and Beau, Roberta and others came pouring into the foyer at the sounds.

"It's Todd!" Beau announced in shocked amazement to his equally stunned relatives.

Then Ren shoved Todd off at last and rolled to his feet to stand, a disheveled stranger in the midst of the family. He turned, looked for Jamie, came for her and grabbed her arm.

"I just want to talk to you, Jennie. I don't—"

Todd slammed into Ren from the back just above his kidneys. Ren, finally angry, turned his full attention to him. He gave Todd a good, hard shove that sent him stumbling. "Now you back off," he said warningly. "Just let me have my say."

Todd righted himself, and instead, hit Ren in the mouth.

"Stop it!" Jamie cried again, backed up against the wall by their painful struggles.

But Ren had already retaliated. He swung a fist that cracked open Todd's lip and sent blood flying. Then he simply and efficiently punched him once, twice in the stomach. Todd made a strangling sound, doubled up and crumpled in a heap against the stairs beside the wide-eyed Sharon.

There was a thick, shocked silence from the gathered people. Ren shook his head to clear it, and breathing hard, turned straight to Jamie. "Jennie," he said pleadingly. "I don't understand any of this."

"Her name's not Jennie," Eli interrupted harshly, holding out his arm to shield his daughter and keep this wild man from her.

"What? But—" Ren made a passionate, powerful gesture. "I know she's Jennifer Lynn. Nobody kisses me like that except Jennie." His face softened and he reached for her again.

Eli swore. Jamie saw Beau, behind Ren, glance quickly down at the stick in his hand and read his intentions.

"Beau! Don't!" And she sprang forward, just an instant too late. Beau hit the unsuspecting Ren across the side of the skull. He fell heavily at Jamie's feet.

This time in the silence, Sharon looked up from the sprawled bodies and said with a hysterical giggle, "Strike two."

"Now, young lady, you can just explain to me what's going on here," Eli said sternly, as he closed the library doors behind him. "You better hurry. Cody Nichols is waitin' out there to haul that maniac off to jail, if the paramedics ever bring him around."

"Beau shouldn't have hit him!" Jamie protested.

Eli snorted. "If this is not just like a woman. Some schizo comes in here callin' you 'Jennie,' grabs you up and tries to eat you alive, and you're worried we hit him too hard. You're upset because he's going to jail."

Jamie turned a bright red. "All he did was kiss me once. You can't lock a man up for that."

"Kiss you once, my eye. I saw that kiss from the library. If Todd hadn't hit him, I would've. There's hope for that lawyer yet. Nobody kisses my baby that way. Not unless you've got his ring on your finger and you're both in your own bedroom."

"I'm twenty-two, Daddy, not ten."

Eli looked at her guilty face, and his anger slowly shifted to wariness. "Do you know that man out there?"

It hurt to fling up her head and look with embarrassed eyes at Eli, but she did it. "His name is Wrendon Garrett. His friends call him Ren. I can't let you put him in jail. He hasn't done anything."

"And...does he have the...the right to kiss you like he did?" Eli asked slowly, painfully.

"He...he might think he does," she choked out. "Just like he thinks my name is Jennie."

She tried to tell the complete truth. Sometimes she told it to the oriental rug because it hurt her too much to see the grayness creep into her father's face. About her grief over Tory, her anger with Todd, her need to see the letter. About how she chose Ren, how he'd loved her and how she'd finally gone to his house and to his—

"No more. God, no more. I don't want to hear it," her father gasped out at last, turning from her. He was shaking, sweating. There was complete silence in the library for minutes on end, except for his heavy breathing. Then he spoke from his hunched position.

"Hearin' you is nearly as bad as buryin' Tory. You're both lost from me. Strangers. I thought you were mine, Jamie. Tory was always like some of your mama's people, right and rich. I loved her anyway, but you made things fair. Tory for Eve, and you for me."

He turned to his daughter, his face full of shattered hopes.

"Please, Daddy—"

"It wasn't right of me to think that way. This is punishment. It's not even really what you've done with this man that's hurting me so bad. I don't like it, understand that. I hate it like hell. But it's how hard on others you've been, Jamie.

"You can't use people like they've got no feelings or like they're just things. How can you be mine and not understand that?"

She could say nothing to help him or her, just take the hurt and keep looking at him. Finally, he walked to the door, old and slow. "I'll get over it. Give me time. I . . . I expected too much from you."

She nodded once. What else was there?

"Don't say anything to your mother. Let her go on thinkin' he mistook you for somebody else. The truth would hurt her too bad. I'll send this Ren packin' back to Roswell."

"I want to see him."

Eli turned sharply at her low words. "You're out of your mind. There's no tellin' what he'll do to you if you try to explain."

"I will see him. If not here, I'll go to Roswell. I want it to end tonight."

Her determination swayed Eli, and reluctantly, finally he said, "All right. After I talk to him to see what he's like. Maybe it's better to get it over with here where you've got people to come runnin' if you need them."

She watched the sheriff's car pull away with only Cody in it. One by one her relatives had left, faded away into the hot Kentucky afternoon. No dinner at Eli's today. Just a fistfight or two. A shoddy little deception revealed. A father's dreams destroyed.

When she heard footsteps approach the library door, she stiffened and then panicked. She had a wild thought that she'd better get behind Eli's desk and she twisted to run for it. Then the handle turned and the door opened. She stopped short, caught halfway across the room. Her heart began to race.

Ren Garrett stood framed in the doorway. He stared at her a minute, and she felt a stab of remorse when she saw the bruising on his temple. He'd just had a concussion six weeks ago.

They said nothing, then he shoved the door shut behind him. His face was stern and harsh, hers white and frightened. She was scared of this stranger who resembled the quiet, unassuming boy she'd known but whose features were somehow shockingly unfamiliar and threatening.

"So you want to talk to me," he said at last and his voice was low and flat.

He came toward her, and she said, "Stop. That's close enough."

He just looked at her and kept coming. She suddenly realized how angry and uncontrolled he was. In a surge of fear, she backed into the desk and knocked over a gold-framed picture.

Daddy was right. This man was dangerous, someone who might hurt her.

He caught one arm above the elbow and pulled her up against him hard.

"I'll scream," she gasped in childish panic, and tried to twist away.

"For your daddy? Or for your boyfriend?" he said bitterly. "Go ahead. I don't give a damn anymore." And he reached to touch her hair on her shoulder, to watch the golden strands glitter through his fingers slowly. Then he looked down into her face, frowning.

Her heart nearly stopped. She was within inches of his lips, his own heart was beating furiously against her, his body was heavy and his hands hard on her.

Surely he felt how she shook against him, but he only scanned her face, and then, letting out the breath he'd held, he said in defeat, "You really are Jennie."

"I'm not Jennie Lynn," she burst out. Couldn't he let go of that name? She was real only as Jamie. Didn't—

But that hot, flaring temper shot up in his eyes again. His face itself was weirdly still as he suddenly put his hand on her shirtfront, between her breasts, and ripped the cloth. She gasped in shock, buttons flew and the delicate blue-green fabric tore all the way down to her skirtband.

She cried, "No!" and hit at him with her free hand. His stone face, his silent determination, the physical contact drove her wild with fear. Then his hand was under her silk camisole and his fingers were on the skin just under her breast.

She stilled instantly at the touch of his hand, shocked into breathless immobility as she stared up at him. She felt his fingers tracing the tiny thin line of the scar that ran under her left breast. She remembered with a quick blinding intensity the way he'd found the scar that day in the sunlit field by the creek, the way he'd traced it with his lips. The day he'd asked her if they were "all right together."

They stared at each other while his hand traced the scar a second time. "I don't even know why I had to find out if this was here. I already knew it would be. So don't lie to me. Not anymore. Stop pretending and tell me the truth, Jen—no, what's your name? Jamie?"

The tears that had risen in her throat as she looked up at his set face and remembered that day by the creek kept her from speaking.

"You don't know your own name? By God, you know mine. Don't you?" He shook her, hard. "Say it. Damn you, tell me who I am."

His willpower pulled the name from her at last. She choked out in a half whisper, "Ren. *Ren*."

He let out all his breath, shut his eyes a minute, then said, "That's right. Ren. The biggest fool ever born."

Then he abruptly turned loose of her, pushed away, turned his back. She was shaking, but she sensed that the worst was over; Ren was not going to hurt her. She let her head drop forward just a second in relief, then rubbed the numbed arm where he'd held her so tightly. She tried to fix her blouse, pulling the torn pieces together. All the while she warily watched the broad back of the man before her. He pushed one hand through his hair to smooth it down, then turned back to her as she stood cornered at the desk. His face was granite, his brown eyes dead.

"I want to know why. That's all. I sat out there in a room with the sheriff and I had time to think—to see you'd lied to me. Now I want the truth, if you know what that is."

Jamie swallowed convulsively, but she rushed into words when he took a threatening step toward her. "It was—it was a bet," she said quickly. There was no time to think of a subtle, nicer way to say it, and besides, it was too late for glib phrases.

"A *bet*?" he repeated incredulously, and his face flushed darkly. "You—you bet what? That I'd fall like a ton of bricks for you?"

Shamed into looking away, she pushed the words out as fast as she could, trying to get rid of their taste in her mouth. "I had an argument with a woman I don't like very much. I was lonely, hurting. I'd—I'd had something to drink and I wasn't used to it."

"I don't want the excuses," he cut in, impatiently.

She stared at him. She couldn't reconcile this hard, bitter, demanding man with the boy who'd teased her, loved her, been seduced by her.

"Beth said I couldn't get an ordinary man, one without... without an interest in my father's money, to go out with me. She said I didn't have the... the nerve to—" Her face burning, she turned away to finish. "The nerve to go to bed with a man like that, one who didn't know who I was or who Daddy was."

In the long silence, he finally asked in shocked disbelief, "You made a cheap bet like that?"

She flushed at the contempt in his voice and said defensively, "She had something I wanted. A letter from my sister. I thought I had to have it."

"But why *me*? Out of all the unlucky bastards in this corner of Kentucky, how'd you decide on me?" he asked bitterly.

She looked at him and tried to explain. "You—you met all the... the requirements. You were a stranger, you were from out of the county, you didn't seem to have any ties—"

He cut in. "And I'm ordinary. Yeah, I'm about as ordinary as anybody around." His voice held a self-derision that cut her to the heart.

She stepped toward him. "Beth—put you on a list she'd made. Just chose you at random, I guess."

"Beth Benton? Sidney's niece?" he said. "I don't even know her except to see her."

"There were others. All of you from Calhoun County. I thought you—were nice. Decent."

"Decent! Well, that sure as hell got me a lot, now, didn't it? Don't give me this line, Jen—Jamie. You picked on me because you thought I'd be the easiest, the one who'd fall for you without any effort. And I guess I was." He made a gesture of weary repugnance. "This whole thing makes me feel dirty. It was all a lie. You *used* me, but it's my own fault. I was stupid fool enough to think that a girl like you was real. Dumb and blind enough to fall in love with a fake like you."

Scalded by his words and the way he verbalized her own torment, she snapped back defiantly, "I didn't ask you to fall in love with me. Or try to find me. We had a good time together—I gave you a solid month of good times. And I gave you—" She cut herself short, cheeks burning. "You got what every man I know is after. And there were no strings. Now it's over. What d'you want? What more is there?"

He stared at her, then he swallowed hard. "You make me sick, Jamie Logan." He turned to the door, and grasped the knob.

She was hurting, stinging from his words. But she had to hold him just one more minute; she had to have something from him besides his contempt. Now, when it was too late, she cared for his opinion. Something in her was breaking apart.

"Ren, I'm...I'm sorry. I meant it to be a fling, that was all. I didn't mean for it to—to go so far. For you to be hurt." Her voice broke, then she said on a sob that she stubbornly held back, "If it means anything to you, I've lain awake nearly every night since, feeling ashamed and regretting what I did."

He stood stock-still with his back to her while she spoke.

"I wanted to tell you myself. To let you know that I'd give anything to go back and undo all the wrong I've done to you. And I'm glad you know the truth. I've been running and hiding from it ever since I left."

"You mean since the night I asked you to marry me? God!" He rubbed his hands over his face.

"At least this way it's finished. And maybe someday you'll forgive me."

He gave a half laugh. "Yeah."

This time when he reached for the door, she let him go.

Chapter Eleven

Jamie made it up the stairs to her room without seeing anyone, feverishly tearing off her torn clothes, reaching for others. She caught sight of herself in the mirror as she pulled on a shirt. Her face was hot, her eyes glittering with hurt. And like a brand, there was the scar, the tiny line that had always seemed so unnoticeable until a few minutes ago.

There was a tap at the door. She wanted to scream. No more. She couldn't handle any more.

Then Sharon's voice, hesitant and worried, "Jamie?"

Taking a deep breath, she flung open the door. Sharon saw her, the half buttoned shirt, the scattered clothes, in a wide-eyed glance before she came in.

"Are you all right?"

Jamie nodded and went back to buttoning the shirt.

"I'll leave you alone. I can see you want to be by yourself. But I picked this up from the floor and thought you'd better see it." She held out the letter Ren had been carrying.

Jamie stared at it, then reached for it with shaking fingers. Sharon started to leave, but Jamie said desperately, "No—no, wait."

This letter was going to hurt. When she opened the envelope, there were two separately folded sheets in it.

The first was in a spidery, crawling hand that was Sidney's:

> I'm sending him to you. One way or another, it'll settle things for him. As for you, it's your second chance. A piece of advice, girl—don't throw away something good. Years get long when you let pride rule.
>
> My niece says she thinks this other letter belongs to you.

Too late. Sidney's letter had been too late before it was written.

Jamie's hands were clammy as they held the second piece of paper. She recognized it. This delicate, creamy sheet of folded stationery was what she hurt Ren for. Her last link to Tory.

She opened it quickly, before her nerve ran out, and sucked in her breath at sight of her sister's writing. The choppy penmanship, the looped flamboyant *T* in her signature. It felt as if Tory were here, whispering from the shadows.

> Beth,
>
> I know about you and Todd, and I know why. I won't let you hurt Jamie just to get back at me

because you think I took Adam Ralston from you. I'll be there tomorrow night at eight. You'd better see me.

Don't you understand? Jamie really loves him.

Tory Logan

"Oh. Oh." The quick blows to her heart were over now. Everything was crystal clear, as if a great light had snapped on.

For a minute she felt numb, then it was almost funny. All of this agony to find out that Todd was unfaithful. The one she didn't give a damn about. Tory had died trying to salvage Todd for her.

And Beth had set Jamie up, used her just as she had used Ren. Well, for all her hard work she could have Todd on a silver platter.

Stone-faced, she handed the letter to Sharon. She heard the quick intake of her breath as she read it.

"Why, that scheming, conniving— Why did she do this? Why didn't she just tell you?"

Jamie shrugged. "It doesn't matter anymore. I know now. I understand."

"Understand! Well, that's good of you!" Sharon took her cousin's arm, shook her. "Todd has lied to you, gone out on you. But maybe it was a one-time thing. Men do things like this when they're not married or engaged. But Beth. She's plotted and connived. Stop understanding!"

Jamie faced Sharon. "Beth's right about me. I've only ever gone out with men who wanted Daddy's money. I don't know how many of them wanted me for *me*. And Tory was wrong. I don't love Todd. He doesn't love me. He didn't want to be my husband—he wanted to be Eli Logan's son-in-law."

"You don't know that. You haven't even asked him for his side of it."

"I don't have to. When a man loves you, he watches you with a special look. He wants to touch you. He kisses you like he can't get close enough." The stone mask that was her face felt wet. Tears were sliding down her cheeks, and she didn't even know when they'd begun. "I know. Other men—a different sort—act like that. Not Todd. Not with me. I'm just the prize."

Sharon watched her, then said uneasily, "This conversation's not about that farmer, is it? He was the man who brought the letter, wasn't he?"

Jamie turned away to the window and wiped the wetness from her face. "That was Ren. Everything's settled between us. I can put it all behind me and get back to living again."

The sun was still shining. She glanced in surprise at the clock. It was only three-thirty on a hot Sunday afternoon.

Jamie went to see Todd early the next morning, determined to control her own fate from now on. He'd been in the emergency room last night, under sedation while his lip was being stitched up from the blow Ren had administered.

He wasn't particularly happy to see her standing at his apartment door, but he let her in. His hand went up to try to hide the ugly swelling on his lip. There was a bruise on his cheek.

It was the first time she'd ever seen him look so disheveled, and he was plainly put out with her. Jamie gathered quickly that in his eyes she was somehow to blame for all his woes, so she went straight to the point.

"I think you already know this, but I'll tell you anyway, Todd. We're through. I don't love you, you don't love me."

He gaped at her, then protested. "You don't know what you're saying. Of course I love you. What do you think these bruises and this cut lip are all about? I'm even willing to forgive you for letting that fiasco happen yesterday."

"Letting—" Jamie broke off. "That's good of you, Todd. Big. But it's still over. I don't want to see you anymore." She turned away, and he caught at her angrily.

"You can't do this to me. I've hung around this little town for months just for you, instead of moving to the city where I wanted to live. I never laid a finger on you because you didn't want it. Yesterday some stranger walked in and you melted all over him. How was I supposed to act? Look what this has done to me. My face is ruined. I can't even go to the office."

"I'm sorry you got hurt. But so did he. And this is not about yesterday." She wanted to throw his affair with Beth up to him, but since her own conduct had been somewhat less than sterling, she bit her tongue. Beth could fight her own war with Todd, anyway. "This is because I don't love you. I don't want to marry you. Do you hear me?"

"And what about me? What do I tell my friends? How am I going to look?" he said furiously.

Self-centered. That was the word she'd searched for when she'd tried to tell Sharon how she knew Todd didn't love her. Todd was concerned with Todd. He could never love any woman the way Ren could.

"I imagine that when the swelling goes down, you'll look like a Greek god. Just like normal for you," Jamie said calmly.

Todd heard the sarcasm. It stunned him, and he said in disbelief, "You're breaking it off with me."

Jamie said nothing.

"You're involved with that guy, aren't you? The one who did this to my face!"

She turned and walked out the door, leaving him swearing behind her.

A few days later, she broke and ran. Her mother was going to Paducah for a short visit with two spinster cousins and out of desperation Jamie went with her. She had to get away from her curious relatives, from the memories of a man she couldn't have and from the anger of another that she didn't want anymore. She had to escape her father.

On the morning she left, Eli abruptly spoke to her. "You talked to Todd?" He was rolling up his shirtsleeves as he and Jamie met in the kitchen.

"Yes."

"So both of them know where they stand with you now."

It was a statement, so Jamie made no answer.

Eli eyed her a minute, then asked, "Took it pretty hard, did he?"

"No. Todd will have another girl on his arm before the month is out."

Eli finished with his sleeves, then looked squarely at her. "I wasn't talkin' about Todd."

Yes, she had to get away. If her innocent mother was surprised at Jamie's sudden fervent desire to visit

Cousins Olivia and May, she was so pleased to have her daughter come with her that she said little about it.

Chapter Twelve

But there was no escape from Eli. When Jamie and Eve returned five days later, he was waiting for his daughter. After supper, he called her out to the patio.

"I've been thinkin' about you this week," he announced with the air of a man who'd burned all his bridges. "And you know what I've decided? That you need something to keep you out of trouble."

"Daddy, you sound like something out of the Dark Ages," Jamie protested.

"No, I don't. I sound like a worried father who's lost one daughter and doesn't plan on losin' the other. Now, Jamie, tell me—do you plan on ever usin' that management degree you somehow earned at college in between those doses of culture they spoon-fed you?"

"What?" she exclaimed, half amused and half puzzled.

He slid his hands in his pockets and spoke calmly. "You know I always meant for you and Tory to run the Logan Corporation. Well, now it's up to you, and maybe someday your husband, too. You've been driftin' long enough, Jamie, and it's time for me to be blunt. You're not goin' to inherit from me unless you're willin' to get in the middle of the business and learn how it's all done."

Jamie asked slowly, "What does that mean?"

"It means that a woman could run all of my affairs, but only if she had experience and training. You could, Jamie. I want you to be the one. I'm ready to put you to work Monday morning. But if you're not interested I'm goin' to train Beau to take over the whole shebang instead of just his daddy's share. And I'm goin' to will him what would have been Tory's half of my estate."

"You don't have to blackmail me, Daddy," Jamie said sharply. "I want to learn. I always intended to. Leave Beau what you want to leave him. I'll still go to work for you."

Her father finally smiled, a smile so huge it covered his face, "Good. Good." Then he reached out to hug her, and Jamie felt relief and a small measure of joy creep back into her heart. Eli was really going to forgive her. Tentatively she slid her arm around his waist.

He stood with his cheek on her hair a minute, then he lifted his head. "The first thing I want you to do is to hire me a farm manager."

Jamie looked up at him in surprise. "But Daddy, you've always held on to the farm. You said you'd never let strangers handle it, that it was the family's."

"I know. But I need spare time right now if I'm goin' to be givin' on-the-job-trainin' to my newest employee. Besides, I've already got the man for the job picked out. I did some checkin' on him this week, so I just need you to go hire him." He was casual, too casual.

Jamie watched him suspiciously. "What's going on?"

He looked her straight in the eye. "You won't like it. I want to hire your Wrendon Garrett."

She just stared at him for a minute, gasping, then she got enough breath back to protest, "No! Not Ren. How d'you think I'd feel seeing him all the time? How about his feelings? He won't do it. I don't want him to!"

Eli had the stubborn look that her own face wore all too often. "He's perfect for the job. I'm goin' to go see him about it. But I'd rather you go. Make him understand that it's all right with you."

"But it's not!"

"Why? You won't have to see him. He'll be out on the farm, you'll be at the office."

"Daddy, why are you doing this?" Jamie asked in despair.

"Because you owe him," her daddy said bluntly. "He's right for the job. And because I think he might be havin' a hard time of it in Roswell."

"What hard time?" she asked, puzzled.

"His pride's got to be takin' a beatin'. He had some Dalton man with him, waitin' for him when he came to give you that letter. Somehow he got part of the story, and it's all over the town," Eli answered.

"Oh," she whispered in dismay. "What are they saying?"

Eli shrugged. "I don't like what's goin' around about you, but I can't do anything. Accordin' to them, you're the spoiled little rich girl who made him your summer fling. That's hard for a daddy to take, Jamie."

She swallowed. "And Ren?"

"They're about to smother him to death with sympathy. And under the circumstances, that's hard for any man to take. Give him an out if he wants it, Jamie. Offer him the job."

She stood there indecisively, torn. Part of her wanted to hide, never to have to face Ren again; but another part of her had suddenly felt a fierce excitement.

"All right," she said at last. "I'll—I'll ask him."

She'd thought it all through carefully. She would have to see Ren just as he left work on Friday night. There were few people around then, and it would mean that she wouldn't have to go to his house. She couldn't stand the thought of going there. She'd go as Jamie Logan, well dressed and uptown, so that he'd understand that this was strictly a business offer, that she wasn't trying to trick him or lure him again.

If she hadn't been so nervous and hot, she might have enjoyed the slow ride in the convertible. There had been an afternoon shower, and the early dusk of the summer night was cool and fragrant.

It felt funny to be back in Roswell. Somehow she'd thought it might have vanished when she left, like Brigadoon into the mist. She got out in front of the feed store, her heart tripping rapidly. There was Ren's truck. Enoch Johnson's old car. That was all. She was lucky.

Enoch was emptying the cash register when she went in. Ren was doing something at a counter behind him.

Both glanced up. Ren froze in instant recognition while Enoch said politely, "Can I help you, ma'am?"

Her cool navy suit, her controlled chignon, her heels and big earrings did their work only momentarily, because by the time she managed to get out, "I want to see Ren," Enoch knew who she was and was frowning in anger.

"What d'you want?" Ren asked brusquely, rudely, moving up beside the old man. "And what are you doin' back in Roswell? Why don't you just stay where you belong?"

Sensing trouble, Enoch said hastily, "You came to see Ren, did you? Well, if he's willin' to speak to you, I'll leave y'all alone. Lock up for me, son, when you leave." And he stumped out of the store and then pulled off in his car.

That left them staring at each other.

"Ren." She got out his name at last. "I've come to...to ask a favor of you."

He laughed in disbelief. "You gotta be kiddin'. What d'you need this time? Another boyfriend punched out? Or is it another bet you want to win? Sure. Just come runnin' to me and I'll do it."

"There aren't any bets. And I broke up with Todd, so he isn't my boyfriend anymore either."

He stood there watching her. She was trying hard to remember that this was business, trying not to notice the pulse beating in his throat, just where her lips had once touched him.

"Daddy wants you to consider a—a job. He wants to hire you as manager of Logan Farms. Your salary would be a good one. The position is—"

He interrupted her. "You came here to offer me a job? You want me to *work* for you?"

"For—for Daddy. Please, Ren, it's not what it sounds like." Her cool facade fell apart and she tried to explain. "I work for him, too. I don't want to sound patronizing. And I don't want you to think I'm chasing you again."

He laughed, but it was not the teasing laugh she remembered. It was unpleasant. "Don't worry. I'm not as big a fool as I acted before."

She made one last desperate attempt. For Eli's sake. "If you want the job, it's yours. You won't have to see me if you don't want to. I just came to tell you that it's all right with me if you decide to say yes."

He looked at her, the incongruous picture her elegance made against the feed sacks and the hay rakes. His face was anguished for just a minute and he said, "Why couldn't you have been real?"

Her heart twisted and she made an involuntary movement toward him. "Ren, it wasn't all a lie. I never—" Just then a truck pulled into the parking area. Ren glanced away, and she moved too, as laughter and voices spilled onto the air.

A girl in jeans left the others and climbed the steps. She came through the door smiling. "C'mon, Ren, you slowpoke. The movie's—"

Then she caught sight of the other figure. They recognized each other immediately, Lucinda and Jamie. "What's she doin' here, Ren?" Lucinda asked accusingly, her eyes full of fear and dislike. "Why doesn't she leave you alone?"

"It's nothin'. She was leavin'."

There wasn't anything left for Jamie to do but force herself to walk out the door. Ren had practically thrown her out. She was stiff with pride when she went past Lucinda.

It was anger that made her hot on the way back to Claiborne County. He had a date. He was going to the movies with Lucinda. Just as they had once done. And when it was over, he'd probably sit in that damned truck of his and kiss her senseless, too.

She had been tearing herself apart, worrying about his broken heart and his shattered pride. So much for that. She was through.

The long, hot summer dragged on in Claiborne County. The only relief came from the rain that now fell regularly, usually at night, and though the fields became richly blue-green and the mists rose like a blessing out of the hollows every morning, the old-timers shook their heads. Such regular rain during the sizzling month of August and on into September wasn't normal or right; it was as eerie as the sporadic hard rain of June and the scorching drought in July had been.

Jamie looked upon the strangeness as just an echo of her own mixed-up life. She swung from depression to fury to resignation. Sometimes she'd think of Ren and drown in the sudden heat that flooded her heart. To escape, she threw herself into her new job with a fervor that pleased Eli vastly. She went over plans to update offices, she studied budgets, she took on a public relations job for the Logan Corporation.

Still she was empty and unhappy, so she made it a point to stay out so late she had to fall asleep when she wearily climbed in bed. Sometimes she was with Harry, sometimes with somebody else. And she was so miserable with them, so tired of the game, that she wanted to be sick.

Then one day Eli handed her a folder full of paperwork from the farm, and as she went through it, a name leaped out at her. It was Ren's signature, scrawled across a bill, where he'd signed for supplies. Frantically she flipped through the rest. His signature was on all of them after the tenth of the month.

Ren Garrett was officially the new farm manager, the first one Logan Farms had ever had.

A few days later she got confirmation of that fact in the flesh. It was barely seven in the morning when she wandered, yawning, into Roberta's kitchen in a dainty cotton gown, and ran right into Ren and Eli, sitting at the kitchen table.

She jumped, and flushed and stammered in her surprised embarrassment, but Ren slowly got to his feet and turned away. Eli was brusque when he called after her defensively that he hadn't expected her to be up since she hadn't gotten home that morning until after two. She didn't answer, just let the swinging door go with a great deal of vigor.

After that, an awareness of Ren's presence was always in her. He was on the farm every day. She saw—no, she looked for his truck, and sometimes she saw him. But he never spoke, never glanced in her direction. And the wild idea that he might have come to this job because of her slowly died a bitter death.

Then one night he unwittingly jolted her into a longing that she hadn't known she could ever feel for any man.

He worked long hours some days; she knew that. But since she stayed out late nearly every night and even spent several nights at Sharon's, she didn't know just how much at home he was at her father's.

On this particular hot Friday night, she'd gone out to eat with several friends, Claire and Sharon among them. When they piled into her convertible, Sharon had said, "Let's go for a swim in your pool, Jamie. It's hot, and there won't be many more nights like this before fall."

The soft laughter, the talk and the scent of rich perfume that clung to the four women depressed Jamie, reminding her unpleasantly of the time they'd all been together last spring at Claire's cabin on the lake, when she'd made that desperate wager. To escape the feeling, she agreed with a bright determination to Sharon's plans.

They spilled into her bedroom, exclaiming over the swimsuits she tossed at them. Once dressed and past Sharon's protests over being assigned a polka-dot two-piece that made her look as if she were wearing "two Band-aids with measles," they tumbled down the stairs and out to the shadowy pool. Its lights were not on and only those around the patio relieved the darkness of the yard.

Claire was shrieking in protest when they shoved her in, but when her head came up from the water, she was shrieking in fright. "There's something in here—oh!" she spluttered, swimming for the side.

They fell silent as somebody in the pool with her broke the surface and swam strongly for the opposite side.

"Who is it?" Jamie called sharply, and the voice that answered was a shock.

"Me," Ren said. "Ren."

"Ren!" she gasped. She could see his outline now, the wide shoulders and strong arms pulling him out of the water. "What are you doing here?" Her voice was angry and peremptory.

"I worked late gettin' the cattle loaded for the sale. Eli said I could use the pool," he answered, his voice absolutely emotionless.

Eli! He called her own father "Eli."

He twisted to sit on the edge, and finally said into the silence, "My—my clothes—the towel. They're over there with you. Would you...I mean, I need you to throw them to me."

He was embarrassed before the five of them. Jamie could picture the red flush on his cheeks even now.

Claire found them, reached for them. She said with a laugh in her voice, "Maybe we should make him come after them."

Jamie angrily jerked them away from the other woman's hand and walked around the pool. Nobody but her was going to deliver those clothes to Ren Garrett.

"Here," she said shortly, trying to hand them to him and look away at the same time. "Don't you know better than to go skinny-dipping here? This isn't the creek."

"I'm not skinny-dippin'," he returned and pushed himself up from the pool's edge. Her head snapped around. Standing this close she could see the wet cutoffs he was wearing. "I just wanted my clothes and Sharon was standin' on 'em."

Sharon. He called her own cousin "Sharon."

He turned to the light to see how to straighten the T-shirt he was holding, and suddenly Jamie felt as if she'd received a quick sharp blow. Naked skin gleaming like wet bronze from his shoulder to his stomach muscles only emphasized the unexpected grace of his body.

And then Jamie got a hard jolt. Claire, teasing and provocative, called out, "Hey, Jamie. Who's your friend, the hunk?"

Ren, startled, glanced up as he hastily pulled the shirt down around his waist. His skin was still wet in places, and the cotton clung to him tantalizingly. That and his confusion at Claire's words, as well as her words themselves, made Jamie suddenly furious.

"He's Daddy's farm manager," she snapped, hoping that the knowledge would turn Claire's attention away from him. Too late she realized how she must have sounded, how snobbish and condescending.

"Jamie!" Sharon said, in warning and protest, but Ren had already turned away wordlessly, striding back toward the garage where his truck must have been parked.

Jamie stood motionless a second, then ran after him.

"Ren, wait." She caught up with him in the dark shadows at the truck. "I'm sorry. I didn't mean it the way it sounded."

"It doesn't matter," he said shortly, and opened the truck door to slide in. In the dim light she could see his face, could tell how tired he was. He said he'd been getting cattle loaded for the sale. He'd had a hard day, and a long one.

"Why don't you go in the kitchen and let me get you something to eat?"

He looked up at her in angry puzzlement as he leaned out to close the door. "I gotta go. I've got a date and she's got supper waitin'."

She stepped back as if she'd been stung, and he pulled away. Slowly, she walked over to the others. It didn't help when Sharon's first words were accusing.

"Why do you have to be so hateful to him, Jamie?"

Jamie stared. "When did you get so chummy with him? You used to call him names and worry that he was 'mean and crude.'"

Sharon answered defensively. "I was wrong. You were right. Remember when you said he was nice?"

Jamie's mouth fell open. Her own cousin had gone over to the enemy?

"He's also a hard worker. Daddy and Uncle Eli say he's great at his job, and Beau's crazy about him. He's going with him to the sale tomorrow. Beau's even quit riding his dumb motorcycle so he can run around with Ren," Sharon persisted uncomfortably.

Claire gave a husky laugh. "If you don't want him around, Jamie, tell Eli and get him fired. Then I might have a job for him. If you know what I mean."

Jamie didn't like Claire much, she suddenly discovered. And she got her meaning, all right. Even though she knew she was being ridiculous to react to Claire's teasing, she muttered, "You didn't even see his face."

Claire shrugged. "Who needs to? I saw enough."

Sharon hastily changed the subject, but Jamie didn't forget. That night in her room she was tormented by thoughts of his "date." It had to be the next best thing to Betty Crocker, Lucinda Travers herself. Jamie tossed restlessly, thinking in pain of the love on the other girl's face as she bent over Ren in the hospital. She was pretty sure that if Ren wanted somebody beside him in bed tonight, Lucinda would be willing. Before long, Ren would be married. He wasn't the type to use a girl, especially not one as wild about him as the Travers girl had been. And then he would be out of Jamie's reach forever.

Jamie's mind wandered off into imagining Ren's face as he bent over a wife, the bright brown of his eyes, his intent, intoxicating, absorbing kisses. She could feel his hands sliding down her, caressing, cuddling. And she was reaching out to hold the strong ribs she'd seen tonight, to slide her hands up under his shirt, to pull his mouth to hers and his long body down against hers.

She tried to escape that horrible-delicious scene by thinking of something else, but then the image of Claire rose up before her. Claire, who was no fool and whom Jamie could see reaching for Ren, too. Jamie swore and pulled her pillow over her head.

Jamie's work at the office took her down to the red brick courthouse a few days later. Several of the old men on the bench outside the door had been Grandpa Logan's friends, and they spoke to her just as they had for twenty-two years.

Inside, court was in session and the hall was full. Everybody seemed busy, but she was so well-known to most of the people in the assessor's office that when she needed to look up property information, they sent her back to the file room alone. She had been there only a few minutes in the dust and quiet gloom when a voice spoke behind her, making her jump.

"Hello, Jamie," Beth Benton said quietly, "I saw you come in here. I want to talk to you."

Jamie laid down her pen and reluctantly turned to face Beth. "We don't have anything to say to each other. I did something stupid, and you made sure I paid for it. That's all."

Beth twisted her hands together. "All of that's true. Except I want you to know why. I first met Todd when he came to Kentucky to go to law school. He was in Claiborne County a lot, visiting some of his family who live here. We were at the university together and we dated for a while. Then we broke up. But last year when he came back here to join Martin Trevor's firm, I thought it was because of me." She looked at Jamie and grimaced. "Instead he met Jamie Logan. He was impressed with your looks, Eli's money and most of all your reputation as the snow-white goddess. I don't have to tell you that I was jealous."

"Why didn't you just come out and say you were having an affair with him?" Jamie burst out in frustration.

"Because Todd would have been furious with me if I'd told. It wasn't even an affair. We just wound up together again one night a few months ago, and then it kept happening. I never meant for the bet to go through to its finish. I thought you'd choose Todd's cousin. The banker on the list. He's handsome, and he goes for anything in skirts. I hoped Todd would find out right away that his good little girlfriend was chasing his cousin, and that might have been enough to split you two up."

Beth frowned. "I never counted on your choosing Garrett. I just needed a fourth man, and I'd seen him at Aunt Sidney's."

Jamie turned abruptly away. "All right. You've explained. Now I need to finish this work."

"Jamie, I'm pregnant."

Startled, Jamie dropped the pen and stared in disbelief at the flushed face of the other girl.

"It happened right after he came back from Alaska, while you were in Roswell. That's why I had to push the issue and tell Sidney I knew the girl Garrett had been involved with. He was hurt so much when you left, I half suspected that you'd gone through with the bet after all."

"You're really pregnant? You?" Jamie asked slowly.

Beth laughed, but there were sudden tears in her eyes. "I can't believe it, either. Me, the original modern female. I went to Richmond to have an abortion, but I just couldn't do it. Even if Todd never looks at me again, I want this baby."

"Does he know?" Jamie couldn't imagine Todd as a father.

"He does now. I told him last week. He—he turned white as a ghost and slammed out." Beth made a wry face. "Maybe he'll come back in time to see it born. I don't care so much anymore. I'm moving to Atlanta next month, with or without him."

"I'm sorry."

"Don't be. Not for me," Beth said with a touch of her old imperiousness. "But you did me a favor. You didn't tell Todd about any of this bet. So I want to return it, to help if I can."

"I don't need help." Jamie couldn't like or trust Beth, and she didn't want to get any closer to her.

"You want to know about Tory's death. Sharon let something slip that made me think you suspected suicide."

Here it was at last. The answer. But now did she really want to know?

Beth continued. "There was no suicide. And our quarrel wasn't about Adam. I don't know why she broke it off with him. She came to see me because she'd found out about Todd, and she threatened to cost me everything, including my law practice, if I didn't give him up. Knowing Tory, she probably would have taken every action she mentioned."

Jamie looked down at her hands. They were trembling, so she put them behind her.

"Anyway, I tried to make her understand that I really loved him, that I couldn't just hand him over to you without a fight. Then she left the house, but she was in a rage, driving so fast she barely made the turn out of the drive. I knew she'd wrecked as soon as I heard the sirens go past out on the highway, and I knew why. She was going too fast down a dangerous road."

It should have been Tory's epitaph, Jamie thought painfully, turning away to hide her emotions.

Beth waited a few minutes in silence, then she said hesitantly, "Well, that's all I wanted to say. Except—I'm not the one who told any of this in Calhoun County. The town's really put out with you. Sidney, now, she knows more than the rest of them do, and so I'm the one she's not speaking to."

Jamie had to laugh a little. She could imagine Sidney's reactions.

"Garrett told Sidney he didn't want anything to do with you, but when she advised him to take Eli's job if he ever hoped to see you again, he did. Everybody in Roswell thinks he's nuts, but Sidney says he loves you." Beth turned to leave, then she smiled a little at Jamie over her shoulder. "She says you love him, too. And I've discovered that Sidney's generally right."

Jamie didn't move as Beth left. She just sat like a statue looking out the one window that this little cubbyhole of a room had. It was narrow and long, reaching into the shadows near the tip of the twelve-foot ceiling. Through its dusty panes she could see Main Street. Cody was out at the edge of the shady courthouse lawn, apparently trying to explain to deaf old Mr. Thomas why he had to put money in the parking meter in front of his beat-up Ford truck. Things were normal at the county seat.

Except that this was not the sort of place she was supposed to be struck nearly senseless with the realization that she had fallen in love. Nobody was supposed to have to take such a heady strike to the heart in the back room of the tax assessor's office.

She loved Ren. She was in love with him. That was what all the agony had been about, and she'd had to hear it from Sidney. No matter what he was or who he was or how they'd met, she loved Ren.

There was satisfied warmth seeping through the raging excitement inside her. A glow. She knew now, and she wasn't going to deny it or walk away from it ever again.

It wasn't a game anymore, as it was supposed to have been. She'd tried to end her emotions and forget when the bet was over. She had tried to play by the established rules. But Wrendon Garrett did not play games, and now she discovered she didn't want to, either. Forget how it started; somehow it had become love.

Maybe it was just that, his very lack of sophisticated lines and come-ons and suggestive sexual teasing, his very inability to participate in that kind of setup, that had attracted her. She'd been wooed and wined and dined and cajoled for years, and she'd come to despise the way men came after her as if she were a way to score, some sort of high-stakes gamble herself.

Or perhaps it was the way he had cared, the time he had given up for her. Like fixing her radiator hose, or driving her into town after dark when he was tired himself, or coming to the farm office to punch Jason Barnes out cold if he had to. Those things made her feel more loved than any compliment Todd had ever given her, more loved than the two dozen roses Harry had sent a week or so ago.

Or maybe it was just because he was Ren, who had made her feel as if she'd come home when he held her, as if they belonged to each other.

But they didn't. That was the problem, because they should. Ren Garrett ought to be hers; he *was* hers. She could feel it, she knew it. That was why she'd felt so betrayed and hurt when he'd been with Lucinda. The awareness was there. She could feel it beating between them when they were together. Ren never gave a clue these days, but she knew it was not just on her part.

Jamie thought Sidney might be right. Ren's heart still cared, but it was an unwilling and reluctant caring. He had closed up to her. How could she break through his barriers to get to him? He would never approach her, and she was afraid to chase him again. He certainly wouldn't trust her, not this time. Anyway, love made her shy. Now nothing was easy.

Don't play games. That was the trick to it. If she wanted Ren, she had to be straightforward. She had to drop the other men, drop the acts. And take it slow and easy.

Jamie sat there up to her elbows in old tax papers, vowing to herself that she'd give it all she had, just one more time.

The next morning she was a nervous wreck. Then at breakfast she noticed a stack of papers at Eli's elbow that he'd been looking at. The ones on top looked like— "Are those stock lists, Daddy?" she asked tentatively.

In surprise, Eli answered, "Yeah. Ren brought them to me so I could see the bloodlines of the cattle he bought Saturday."

"Are you through with them?" she asked casually. "I'm going by the farm office on my way to work. I'll drop them by."

Eli stared at her openmouthed, but he handed over the papers. She felt armed when she had them, so it was easier to drive straight through the gate to the office, which was just down the road from the house.

She spoke to the two or three men present, but she kept walking, right up to the tall one, who backed away a little in suspicion at her approach.

"I'm returning these to you, Ren." She smiled. "Daddy had them thrown all over the breakfast table this morning. He said you'd bought blooded stock Saturday."

He had little to say. She could almost feel his wariness. But she wrung a few minutes of civility out of him before she left to go to work.

As she started out, she looked up at him and smiled again, letting all the warmth in her heart show, and she said, "You're doing a really good job here, Ren."

That afternoon she came home early, put on her most comfortable jeans and walked down to the barns. Beau was there with two new horses, and she let him show them to her with his usual eager enthusiasm. Ren did not turn up until she and Beau were both involved in putting the horses through their paces in the side pasture.

He frowned at her, but he didn't leave. There was a strain in the atmosphere as they groomed the horses and put them up for the night.

"You ought to ride again, Jamie," Beau told her. "You used to be really good before you went off to that fancy college of yours."

"You sound like Daddy," Jamie teased. "And that's not a compliment."

Ren heard their exchanges, but said nothing. As she started to go, following Beau out the door into the twilight, she said, "Good night, Ren." And after a moment's silence, she walked away.

She'd never thought before about how difficult it was to undo damage to a heart. Now she wondered if it was impossible. Because although she repeated her afternoon visits for the rest of the week, they got harder, not easier. Ren withdrew into a shell, pulling away a little more every time. Even Beau's presence failed to do any good toward breaking past Ren's silent exterior, and the teenager himself began to squirm uneasily whenever the three of them were together.

On the fifth day of her visits, Ren did not come at all, and Jamie, heartsick and bruised, let Beau go home early so he could get ready for some date he had. Then she moodily went about grooming their horses and putting away equipment.

It was a sticky, sultry afternoon, so she rolled up the hot jeans she'd worn to ride in, and finally, in exasperation, pulled her hair back from her face in a sort of knotted loop to keep it out of the way. When she finished the chores, she washed her hands at the pump, splashing the water on her face and throat. And when she turned, shaking the water off her hands, Ren was there, standing not four feet from her, watching her somberly.

She was so surprised she could say nothing, finally rubbing her wet hands nervously down the sides of her loose, cool top.

Ren spoke abruptly. "You look like Jennie. You even act like her right now, so much I almost... almost believe she's here again."

So the long silence was over. Now she was no longer somehow forbidden to speak of their past.

Jamie made herself swallow the lump in her throat, and she said slowly, "I don't know what you mean. Just because my name is different from what I once told you, that doesn't change who I am. Everything that was Jennie is me. I'm the same girl who was in Roswell. With you."

Her answer darkened his face, and he said in rising anger, "You mean the one who pretended her truck broke down in front of my house? And who lied about needin' a job? And havin' a family in Tennessee?" He took a step closer to her. "The one that just walked right in the middle of my life and tore it all apart and never thought once about it?" he demanded furiously.

Jamie whispered at last, "Yes."

She'd barely spoken the word when he made a sudden violent motion and threw the metal bucket he had in his hand across the barn at an empty stall, where it made a loud clanging noise against the wooden slats.

In the stillness after the echo died away, after his ragged breathing calmed a little, he turned from her and said more quietly, "Then you're not Jennie. She cries for people when they're hurt. She cares about an old lady who needs friends." He added painfully, "She even cared about me. When she kissed me, it was—" He broke off, then moved decisively away, crossing to pick up the bucket he'd thrown and hang it over a post.

At last he turned around to the stricken girl, his face shadowed and drawn. "I made up that girl in my mind. I just thought Jennie was real. I was wrong."

He took several steps that were vaguely threatening, stopping within inches of her and staring down into her face. "And one of these days, I'm gonna be able to look at you and not see anybody but some spoiled beauty queen named Jamie Logan. No more Jennie. Then I'll be free."

His words hurt, but it was not that that stunned her so. What shocked her was the rush of emotion she felt emanating from him. He'd held himself and his feelings so severely in check around her that she'd begun to believe he had none where she was concerned. She was unprepared for this sudden release, the force of the emotions she could see clearly on his angry face and in the fast rise and fall of his chest. There was nothing still and withdrawn about him at this moment. She'd found the real Ren Garrett again, with a vengeance, and at last, in spite of his anger, he was touchable.

So touchable.

Blindly, she rose a little toward his mouth. It was such a timid gesture, such a small invitation. But Ren caught it, and somehow, he was kissing her. Her hands clutched at his shirt. She had to pour her heart out to him with this one kiss in case she never got another.

She had to make him understand. Never mind that there was temper and hurt and resentment on his lips. There was a desperate need there, as well, one that made him wrap his arms around her and strain her to him.

For a minute they stood like that, bound together in a churning caldron of feeling. Her hands knew him so well, and her heart plunged into its old trip-hammer action.

Then, rudely, with hard hands, he was pushing her away. "No," he gasped out. "You won't do this to me again."

Hurt and angry, Jamie panted. "What's the matter? Wasn't that real enough for you, Wrendon Garrett? You weren't kissing any imaginary Jennifer Lynn. That was me. Me. Jamie Logan."

She paused to breathe a second, to stop her voice from cracking under the strain of her swirling emotions. "And . . . and I liked it."

Then she turned and fled before she fell in a heap at his feet.

She couldn't face him for a few days after that. In fact, she almost hid in the house to avoid seeing him. Then she began to remember his words instead of her own rash ones. He'd said that he'd be free of her. Did that mean he'd thought about leaving?

That brought her up short and sent her back out to the stables the next day. She made sure Beau was with her, though, and when Ren finally arrived, she managed to be so busy with her cousin that they said little to each other.

There was one comfort: Ren watched her. She ran into his brown gaze everywhere she turned, and when she accidentally looked right into his eyes, she grew flushed and confused.

One night she lay in her bed thinking with bitter irony of how things had come full circle. Once it had seemed easy to get his attention; once he had been the one who blushed and stammered; once she had thought him unattractive.

It almost made her angry to think of how stupid and how unsophisticated she was in her response to him. Where was Jamie, the old Jamie, who'd been assured and unruffled around all those men who sent her friends into raptures?

Those thoughts stayed with her all the next day. They were what made her finally walk down the road Wednesday afternoon to the barn alone. They were what stiffened her back even when Ren saw her coming and leaned on the gate, waiting for her.

At least she didn't have to think of things to say. He was speaking even before she got to him.

"Look, Jamie, I don't know what your game is this time, but I'm not goin' to play. And I don't think I can stand much more of this, so quit comin' out here. Go find somebody else to dangle on your string. Not me."

"I don't want to dangle you on—"

"Don't lie. You're here because you want somethin' from me again. I knew that the other day when you kissed me like you did."

She was stunned by his bitter attack. The kiss that she had pinned such hopes on, he had thought was a trick. "I'm coming because I...I want to see you. I'm willing to admit that. I don't like chasing after you like this. I'd rather you'd—you'd come for me. But you won't. Maybe after Roswell, you can't. So...here I am. No more tricks, Ren."

There was a long, choked silence. Then he made a movement as if to push her out of his sight. "No. No. I don't believe you."

"I've told you I'm sorry, Ren," she cried, grabbing his arm. He flinched, then jerked away. "Can't you believe that, at least?"

He shook his head slowly. "I swear to God I don't understand you. I've listened to all these people around here talk about you, how sweet and wonderful you are. And Beau, he thinks you're an angel. He wants to protect you. That's a laugh. If he only knew. He's the one who needs protectin'. They all must be blind and dumb to think you're innocent."

His words hurt her like so many blows, and she answered him passionately. "You of all people ought to know whether I was innocent or not."

Her meaning hit him hard. He turned pale and his face twisted. "I don't understand that, either. Why you'd let *me* go all the way, when you'd never had another man. You let me make love to you for such a—a damn fool reason. I've wondered and thought about it, drivin' myself crazy. But no more."

"I never meant to do it, Ren, before I knew you. I was going to trick Beth, just let her think I'd stayed all night with you. But I—I hadn't counted on what you'd be like. That night wasn't planned or part of the bet. It was just—me and you."

He turned to look at her, his face disbelieving. She burst out, "It's the truth. But how can I prove it to you?" She reached out, caught his thin shirt, held him because he let himself be held. "I could have had the letter after the first night I stayed. The night you were knocked out with that shot they gave you at the clinic. But I didn't take it, not then or later, and I let Beth think I'd lost the bet. I never saw that letter until Sidney sent you to the house with it."

Something struggled to come to life in his face, a remnant of the laughing, gentle boy he'd been. She longed to see that boy again, to kiss him in tenderness. She bit her lip and said softly, "Give me another chance, Ren. Try again."

But the harshness in him won, and he shrugged away from her. "What do you want me to do? Join your fancy lawyer and your stockbroker and all those others who stand around in line for you? The ones that keep you out till three in the morning? Or d'you want me to do like before? Hide somewhere in Calhoun County till you feel like sleepin' with me, and nobody will be any wiser? No. Just leave me alone."

He stalked off.

She called "Ren!" but he just kept going. She pushed away from the gate and ran after him, running in front and forcing him to stop.

"There won't be any more boyfriends, no more lawyers or stockbrokers or anything else. Just one farmer. If you'll only try again with me, I'll get rid of them all." She looked down at her feet and muttered, flushing, "And I'm not particularly crazy about Lucinda, either."

He made a sudden sound of comprehension. "So that's what this is about. Lucinda."

That anger that had been in Jamie the night before came surging up again. She threw up her head and said defiantly, "No, it's got nothing to do with her. Because you don't want Lucinda, Ren. You want me, whatever my name is. She can't have you, anyway. I won't let her."

Before she'd even finished speaking, she was blushing a brilliant red, realizing too late exactly what she'd said. There was more of Tory in her than she'd ever suspected. Those words sounded as if her headstrong, imperious sister had spoken them.

Ren stood stock-still, staring at her. Emotions played across his face, surprise, amazement.

"You won't let her! You don't have anything to say about it. Not anymore. I offered you everything. Hell, I wanted to marry you, and it was all a big joke. If I ever think—think—about wantin' you again, it'll be on my terms. My way."

Hope sprang up in Jamie's heart. He'd stopped saying no. So she said yes. "All right. Yes."

"Yes to what?" he asked in shocked confusion.

"To your terms."

"But you don't even know what they are."

"I don't care."

He laughed finally, disbelievingly, and looked into her face for a long moment. And in his own eyes, maybe, just maybe, there was hope, too. Then he took off around her toward the barn, settling into the long, easy, relaxed stride she remembered from Roswell. She watched him go with a rapid, warm heartbeat.

Chapter Thirteen

On the following Friday night, everybody got ready to attend the Fall Festival down on the town square. It was held every year around the first of October and was the biggest event in the county. There would be booth after booth of food, square dancing, bluegrass bands, games, livestock shows and horse races.

Jamie had halfway agreed to go with Harry several weeks before. Now, even though one certain man did not even hint that he had other plans for her, she decided she'd just have to disappoint Harry. But when she called Thursday morning to break the date, no one was home. Then she phoned his office and told his answering machine that she could not go out with him. That would probably put paid to Harry's courtship, Jamie thought as she hung up. No man liked being stood up by way of machine, especially a machine that his receptionist might hear. Now Harry had no date, and for that matter, neither did Jamie. But she had hopes.

At last, however, she faced the fact that Ren was not going to call. She reluctantly put on the peachy soft dress and fixed her hair in the exotic tangle of tawny curls she usually wore on special occasions. Then she fastened on her earrings, sprayed herself with a delicate perfume and went downstairs to find Eli to tell him that he had one more female besides her mother to escort tonight.

Instead, she found Beau, sitting slumped in a chair in the foyer alone.

He grinned up at Jamie as she came down the steps. "Gosh, Jamie," he said admiringly. "You look like one of those pictures you see at Halloween."

Jamie laughed, and he began belatedly to protest. "No, I didn't mean witches and stuff. I meant like haystacks and blue skies and pumpkins."

"Thank you, Beau," said Jamie gravely. "I've never been compared to a pumpkin, but I know exactly the kind of scene you're talking about."

"I meant you look nice," he said resignedly.

She looked him over as he stood. "Well, I have to say that you do, too, Beau. What are you doing here? I thought you had a date."

He made a face. "I asked, but she said no."

Jamie said sympathetically, "Sorry, Beau." Then she teased, "Maybe it's your way with words."

"Maybe. Sharon said I could go with her, but she was with David Talbert, and I could tell he wasn't too happy about havin' me tag along. So here I am, with Pop. I tell you, Jamie, bein' sixteen is not what it's cracked up to be."

"Neither is twenty-two. I don't have a date, either, so maybe we could keep each other company. Otherwise, there'll be two of us with our pops," Jamie said consolingly.

At that moment Eli and Beau's father emerged from the study, and Eli was speaking worriedly to someone behind them. "So you think it'll be all right to show the mare tonight? You'll be there to make sure she's not too upset?"

"She'll be okay as long as—" Ren broke off his sentence as he stepped into the doorway and caught sight of Jamie standing there. As he looked at her, she suddenly felt a hot, unexpected wave of exultation. He liked her. He liked the way she looked. It was the first time he'd ever revealed that flash of emotion for her as sophisticated, well-dressed Jamie Logan. She'd never felt more beautiful than the way she saw herself reflected in his brown eyes, eyes that for a second held a yearning question in them.

Then the moment was over. He turned away, going out through the door and onto the long front porch.

No. No. Ask me.

She went after him, and stopped short just outside the door. He was standing on the porch, as if he were...waiting. He stood just a second, caught in profile. Then he turned to her, his gaze dark and intent.

There was silence between them, silence and that forever beating pulse.

At last she spoke, her voice so low the breeze nearly carried it away. "All you have to do is ask me, Ren."

He took a deep breath and said with a struggle, "Will you..." Then he held out his hand. "I'd like it if you'd go with me tonight, Jamie."

Bells must be ringing somewhere, because she could hear them past the roaring in her ears. She put out her hand. It was shaking. She laid it in his, in Ren's warm, capable grasp.

He was just beginning to smile at her, pulling her toward him when Harry's red car roared up the drive. He swung out of it, waving at her.

"Sorry I'm late, darling," he called, bounding up the long shallow steps. Then he saw her hand caught in Ren's.

"Who's this guy?" he demanded. He looked at Ren, still in the T-shirt and jeans he'd spent the day working in, at the suddenly dark, forbidding expression on his face, and apparently leaped to horrible conclusions. "Here, you, turn loose of her," he demanded, almost as an afterthought.

Behind her somewhere, her uncle's voice said bemusedly, "Have we done this before?"

Ren dropped Jamie's hand and looked at her in accusation. But she wouldn't let this misunderstanding go on, not tonight. She spoke quickly. "I'm going with Ren to the festival. I'm sorry."

"What?" Harry asked incredulously. "Who's Ren? This guy?"

"Yes. I said I was sorry, Harry, and I don't want to hurt your feelings, but I want to go with him. I left a message on your machine to tell you that I wasn't going with you. Didn't you get it?"

"No. I've been out of the office. So it did me a lot of good, didn't it?" he snapped. "You changed our plans so you could go with this—this redneck?" Harry broke off to punch at Ren with his finger and say angrily, "You're going to be sorry for this." Then he turned back to Jamie. "As for you, you little—"

"No," Ren said suddenly. "No more."

Jamie's heart jumped when she looked up at his face. Ren was mad, in a temper nearly as strong as the one he'd shown when he ripped her blouse.

He put his spread hand on Harry's chest, pushing him back. "I don't know if you know what a two-by-four is or not, but you better find out, because if you ever do come after me, I'm goin' to get one and use it on you. To tell the truth, I'm thinkin' about knockin' you flat with it if I even see you at this door again."

Harry, gasping, stumbled backward down the steps with the help of the shoving hand on his chest. He saw something in Ren's face that must have told him the other man was deadly serious, because after a minute, he shut his dropped mouth, turned and fled to his car. They watched him go, standing like statues until the sound of his motor died away.

Jamie was staring at Ren much as Harry had. His voice had been so—so authoritative. Where had he learned that? Only a fool would ignore this side of Ren Garrett. No wonder he was good at his job, and no wonder Eli thought he was the biggest marvel since sliced bread.

Ren turned back to Jamie. "I'm not goin' to be beat up and knocked around and threatened for you anymore. This time it's my way. And while I'm talkin' and since you let me know how you feel about Lucinda, I'll tell you this: I'm sick to death of Harry Sheffield."

He went down the steps and out to his truck. Then he stood waiting until she followed.

"I told Eli I'd help with the horses at the show. I don't know if there'll be much time for fun tonight.

And I reckon everybody will be like Harry and wonder what you're doin' with me. But I'm goin' to get cleaned up, and I'll be back in a little while."

"I'll be here," she said simply.

Just then her mother's voice floated down the stairs from the floor above and out onto the porch. "Eli, good heavens. What are all of you doing crowded in the doorway?"

When Ren got back to the house, everybody else had gone and Jamie was sitting on the long shallow steps waiting for him.

He looked good in the pale blue shirt. She started at his tennis shoes and went up, admiring him as he stood over her. He looked at her, too. Then, slowly, he sank down on the steps beside her. The stars above them twinkled merrily.

"The last time I was with you on a porch," she said, trying for a smile and normality, "King was sprawled all over my feet."

"He's at Dan's. I worked so late this week that I asked Dan to keep him so he wouldn't be by himself."

"Does Dan know... where you are tonight?"

"You mean does he know that I'm with you. Yeah."

Jamie didn't want to pursue that avenue of thought at all, so she asked nervously, "And the job? You're liking it?"

He shrugged. "Sure. Who wouldn't? Eli's got everything a farmer ever dreams of havin', and some things most of us have never heard of. And he's got a feel for land. It makes him easy to talk to, to work for."

Jamie made a face. "Try being his daughter while you're working for him. Some days I can't do anything right, and Mama has to separate us at supper to keep us from killing each other."

"He loves you."

"He likes you," she returned. "With Daddy, it's easier to be liked. I hear about how wonderful you are all the time. Did you know..." She hesitated a minute, then laughed. "After I told him about Roswell, and right after you came here, when Daddy was barely speaking to me, I was almost jealous of you."

Ren looked at her one long minute. "You don't have any reason to be. He's makin' an effort with me because of...of what we did."

There was a loaded silence. The man beside Jamie was suddenly too threatening, too close. "I guess we'd better go," she said haltingly. "Sharon's expecting to meet us at the music show."

"You and Harry?" he asked flatly.

"No!"

Ren helped her up, then spoke once more. "Why do you want me to try again, Jamie?"

It was such an intent, unexpected question that she flushed and her voice wouldn't work. There was only one good answer, the truth. But somehow, looking at his set face, she couldn't get the words out, couldn't whisper three simple words.

He waited, and at last she answered with her own question. "Why did you take the job with Daddy?"

"Because Sidney Hill told me to."

"Oh."

Then the moment was over and it was too late. And somehow that unanswered question changed Ren and spoiled the night. He gave her no chance, no opening, to correct her mistake.

Jamie wavered between delight and despair. She loved it when he locked his hand into hers as they walked through the booths, and when, in the darkness during a bluegrass show, he caught her foot between his and sat like that. But she did not like the proprietorial way he pulled her up against him when they met the angry Harry, and sometimes she wondered if it was actually dread or fright she was feeling. That was when Ren was deadly silent and preoccupied. If he had been anybody but Ren, she would have called him moody.

He was silent even around Sharon. The only time he really relaxed was with Beau, when they met him at the arena with the mare. Beau apparently saw nothing wrong, even going so far as to tease Ren about his threat to Harry.

"I got the idea from you," Ren answered, laughing, and rubbed his temple suggestively.

Beau protested, "Aw, Ren, come on. I didn't know you then. Anyway, we're even now. You took my date for the night. She just walked off with you." He grinned and nodded at Jamie.

Ren glanced down at her in surprise, and for once, Jamie blessed Beau and the way he always told everything he knew. But after Beau left, Ren retreated once more into himself, and he took Jamie home early, before anybody else got back.

He refused her tentative invitation into the house, but when she reached in defeat for the door handle of the truck, he caught her and pulled her to him fiercely. His hands tangled in her hair when he held her head still to kiss her, and his lips were hot and hard. Then he kissed her cheeks, her ears and her throat as though he wanted to devour her. When he got to the neckline of her blouse, he paused only long enough to pull it loose from her skirt. Then he pushed it up and bent her back over his arm. His tongue and mouth were like hot brands on her skin, his hands everywhere. When he lifted his face to hers again, he returned to her lips.

Jamie didn't like the blatant passion and the harsh hunger in his kisses, but she couldn't forget that this was Ren. And when she at last slid her arms around his neck and pulled his face against hers, his lips softened and tenderly touched hers again.

But before emotion and the sweetness of that kiss could take over, he pushed back, breathing heavily, and looked away from her out the other window. After a long minute's awkward silence, Jamie ventured, "Well—good night." Then she felt like a fool. After their heavy, unsatisfactory exchange, "good night" was so tame as to be ridiculous. She opened the truck door, and he said one word.

"Jamie."

She froze. His voice was as scary as his fierce kisses, and he didn't look at her, not even when he spoke.

"My mother died when I was ten, but she'd been dyin' for years. She had a problem with her heart that they couldn't make right. Everybody thought she should never have kids, but she did anyway. She risked everythin' for me. I used to think that her kind of love was what love really was."

He looked down at his hands blindly. "Then there was my father's kind. He knew she was dyin', and couldn't give her up. In the end he died the very night she did, except it took his body six years to admit it. That kind of love is no good, because it ruins a man. It won't let him face what's real or admit even that a woman's out of his reach."

Ren looked at Jamie at last. "I've thought a lot about Daddy's kind of love lately. Ever since I came to Logan Farms. I won't be another John Garrett. Not for anybody."

Jamie didn't understand why he was telling her this now, or what it meant. She didn't know what to say to ease the pain on his face and in her own heart, so she spoke what she wanted to, whether it made sense or not. Her voice was too emotional, but it was gentle.

"I really did lose that bet after all, Ren. Because there's nothing ordinary about you."

Something else hovered on her tongue wanting to be spoken, but she couldn't get it out, so she stepped away from the truck and into the house. From there she watched him pull out of the circle drive. She had a sick feeling inside her. The man she'd been with tonight did not seem like Ren.

Saturday morning started glumly. It was drizzling rain, and Jamie got up with the same depressed headache she'd gone to bed with. Eli and Eve were both at the breakfast table when she got downstairs. Jamie sat down and picked at her food listlessly.

Eve spoke in a rush. "I'd like to know what you meant with that appalling lack of good manners last night. I have known the Sheffields all my life and Harry since he was a baby. You behaved scandalously. His mother was extremely upset when I met her at the festival. She would barely speak to me. From what I can worm out of your father, you deserve everything she managed to say about you, young lady."

Startled by the attack, Jamie glanced uneasily at Eli, who was eating eggs as if his life depended on it.

"I'm sorry, Mama," she said contritely. "Harry does have a right to be angry. I did stand him up."

"Then you can just get on that telephone and apologize. Or better yet, we'll ask him and his mother to dinner tonight and you can give your apologies in person," Eve snapped.

Jamie said meekly, "I don't think that's such a good idea. And I don't think Harry would come."

"Of course he would. Why in the world wouldn't he?"

"He doesn't like two-by-fours?" Jamie offered.

Eli choked on his eggs as a spasm of laughter crossed his face. He wiped the expression off with a napkin and said to Eve blandly, "Sorry, honey."

Eve stared angrily from one of them to the other. "There's obviously some kind of inside joke here that I don't understand, and both of you are plainly not going to enlighten me. But I've got something to say to you, Jamie. When Eli hired this Ren person, I thought it was a bad, bad idea. I was right. He's using you."

"Mama, you don't know the—"

"Let me finish without interruption, please. Your manners really are atrocious these days. This boy is plainly using you as a substitute for the girl you look like, that Jennie person. There's nothing healthy in that. As if that were not enough, he's nothing like the young men you're used to."

"Thank God for that!" muttered Eli to himself, and his wife glared at him.

"I suppose you think she'd have a happy marriage with this man if—God forbid—things went that far. Even if she didn't remind him of another girl, Jamie with her money and background wouldn't be happy with a—a farmer!"

Eli looked at her steadily, "You have been, haven't you?"

Eve looked down at her hands, and a reluctant smile spread over her lips, "Yes, I have," she admitted, then protested, "but you're a good, loving man, a hard worker, a fine husband and father."

Eli pushed his plate away. "So is Ren Garrett. Or he will be, for some girl. I know. I've been around him for weeks now. I know about his background, about him."

Jamie's heart warmed as her father spoke of Ren. Eli looked at her sharply. "I'm not real surprised that Ren's comin' around the house lately. It's always been plain as day to me that his feelings run deep where you're concerned, in spite of everything. But you, Jamie, you're walkin' a mighty tight line. This time you better play straight. It's not about love anymore, not for him. Now it's about trust. He's not like Harry or Todd, or any of these artificial, shallow social climbers you're used to. He means business. So the question is, what do you mean?"

That was easy. "If he'll ever forgive me for all I did, I mean to marry him. I love him," she said steadily.

Eli's face broke into a slow smile, and Eve said in frustration, "What is going on? And what did you do that he has to forgive you for?"

Jamie glanced at her father and took a deep breath. What a way to start a Saturday. "You're not going to like what I'm about to tell you, Mama...."

She made up her mind to tell Ren the next time he came to see her. She'd just say it. "I love you, Wrendon Garrett. Please, will you marry me?" But she didn't get the opportunity, because Ren stayed determinedly away.

That strained feeling, the dread that something was wrong, kept her from seeking him out, even when he was on the farm, which was not often the next few days.

Her mother's words returned to haunt her, especially when she remembered the way he had behaved at the festival. Maybe Ren really was using her. Maybe he didn't love her anymore at all. What an ugly, dirty feeling. Was this how he'd felt? Was this revenge? Maybe he'd just wanted to see how far she would go, and then he'd laugh. He might be turning the tables, planning on taking all he could get and then walking out and letting her bleed to death. Maybe he'd been warning her with that story about his mother.

No, her rational self said firmly. One thing about him, he was not devious or mean. But as Saturday faded into Sunday and Sunday into Monday and he neither came nor called, Jamie's emotional side shouted that something was very wrong. On Monday night after work, Jamie drove past the farm office and saw his truck there. In fact, he was leaning against the hood of it, laughing at something Beau, across from him, was saying.

Jamie hit her gas pedal in a furious expression of hurt and temper and shot past them home. They must have recognized the sporty little blue convertible, but she didn't care. She *hated* him.

Nevertheless, she waited for hours for him to come up to the house, and when he never did, she slammed angrily up to bed and lay staring at the moon through the oak tree outside her window. Part of her wanted to slap him, part wanted to yank his shirt off and wipe that laughter off his face with her hands and her kisses.

Eli knew something was wrong the next morning. He looked keenly at her tired face and suggested she stay home from work.

"No," Jamie said quickly. "I need to work."

"But you look—"

"Don't worry, Daddy. The biggest thing I'm going to do today is drive to Tyler to check on the new office building and pick up the construction invoices. I'll be fine."

She pulled her hair back in a delicate snood to keep it from blowing too much. She didn't want to be businesslike and put the top up. She wanted to be rebellious. She didn't even glance over when she flew past the place where Ren always parked, too afraid she might stop and yield to temptation. She hadn't seen him in three days. A man could do a lot in that length of time, maybe even with somebody else.

She fumed to herself all through town, nearly missing the red light in front of Cody Nichols's office. Then she slowed down. After all, the last thing she needed today was to get a speeding ticket and one of Cody's it-hurts-me-to-have-to-give-this lectures.

There wasn't much traffic in town; there never was unless it was Saturday. She pulled past the town limits, and the road began to curve around the Kentucky hills. It was nearly sixty miles to Tyler, the larger town in yet another neighboring county out of which Eli and his brothers ran their construction business. Maybe the drive would calm her.

The morning was crisp and a tiny bit cooler. The fresh scent of new-cut hay struck her nose and she breathed it in. The cool wind blowing in her face and the hot sun beating down on her hair made a contrast of sensations that was pleasant. The sun glittered off the green fields, and as she turned a sharp curve and the road straightened out for a short distance to accommodate an old, narrow, steel-beamed bridge, its rays struck the deep water of Danton River so brilliantly it nearly blinded her.

The river ran like an icy, twisting snake through the edge of the county. It was deep and greenish-blue and treacherous, yet it had a wild beauty that Jamie had to appreciate even when she felt as awful as she did this morning. Usually a heavy fog hung over it and the trees that leaned over its banks. But today was hot and clear, and Jamie could look down over the side of the car on the tops of the trees far below and see every branch, every ripple of water. Again the sun sparkled and promised, and she reached for the sunglasses that lay on the seat beside her. She glanced down and with one hand she started to shake them out.

That was the reason she never caught more than a fleeting look at the speeding red sports car and the scared face of the driver who smashed into her like a sledgehammer halfway across the high bridge spanning the Danton.

She thought she cried out, but it felt like a horrible, long, soundless scream that bounced off the skull bones inside her head. Everything was slow motion, yet it was so fast she could do nothing, and in the deadly cushion of silence inside her terrified mind, her thoughts were slow and loud and crystalline in their clarity.

I'm going to die.

Hold on to the wheel. Don't hit the brakes. Straighten the car.

Ren. Daddy. Oh, Tory, is this what death is like? So fast that you don't even have time for it?

The cars tore apart with a wrenching and grinding, and her convertible spun like a slow top released into motion by a string, spinning slowly toward the gray beams of the bridge behind the red flash of the other vehicle that was spinning, too—two metal dancers in a deadly ballet. Jamie saw the sky, the trees and, in the dreamy distance, the tower of the courthouse back in the little town she'd left behind. Far beyond that were long rows of cornfields.

She saw it all in clear, slow, distinct frames. Then the silence and the slowness ended. Her car struck the bridge with a terrible violence and the noise exploded around her. She could hear herself screaming and the metal cracking. The bridge was bending, the car was going over, her arms were being pulled out of their sockets. She was torn from her grip on the wheel—no seat belt—oh, God—and she was thrown by force against the passenger door. The car was sideways, she was sliding, slipping—slipping—falling out. The world spun crazily, the sky was above her and the water below. She could see it down there. She and the car were plunging toward it. A hard blow struck her on the top of her skull. Pain, throbbing and pounding, nearly took her head off her shoulders.

Oh, Daddy, Mama, how will you survive this grief?

I love you, Ren. How can I die without telling you?

Then a gray and red and black haze washed across her, and a sick buzzing went off in her ears. She thought she was awake, but she must be dead. It was only her soul that hung there between the shuddering car and the twisted bridge, caught between the water and the air.

Then there was silence. No, birds were singing. Somewhere. About a million miles away.

Chapter Fourteen

It was funny how she kept waking up from the same dream. It kept coming back to her. She dreamed she was half lying on a hot concrete highway, looking up at the blazing ball of the sun, and half hanging off a high, suspended bent bridge. For a while her head would rest on the steel beam somewhere behind her; then it would roll sideways to dangle in the air like her arm and shoulder, and she was looking far, far down into water. She wished the dream would go away. She wanted to play dolls with Sharon, and the dream hurt.

She wanted the doll with the lacy dress, the one Sharon had been playing with all morning.

"No, it's mine," cried Sharon, clutching it to her.

But Jamie knew exactly what to do. "Tory," she shouted. "Tory, make Sharon give me this doll. It's *mine*."

"Tattletale!" Sharon flung back. "You always run to Tory."

Not anymore. Tory's dead, and now I know the secret of that trick.

Tory came, frowning, a tall pretty girl of fifteen to Jamie's skinny seven. "Sharon, here. Why don't you play with this doll? See, it's got little pink shoes to match its pink dress. It even has a little hat."

"I don't want it," cried Sharon. "I want this one."

"But that one is Jamie's favorite. Let her have it. You can have any of these others." Tory reached out for the doll Sharon held, and Sharon threw it at her and ran crying into the grape arbor on the other side of the house.

Oh, Tory, how can you and I love so much and do so much damage? The sun is hot, and I'm too sick to move out of it.

Jamie stood alone in the backyard. She could hear Sharon crying. Tory said impatiently, "Here, angel. Take it. But you have to let Sharon have whichever of the others she wants. Now, stop fighting with each other."

Tory went back inside. Jamie watched her go. Then she looked down at her favorite doll. It really wasn't very pretty, not as pretty as Sharon's face when she smiled. Jamie felt mean inside; something was wrong with what she and Tory had done.

I didn't even want Todd, Tory. I never even loved him. God, tell Tory that I'm happy with Ren. A fly buzzed across Jamie's face.

"Here, Sharon," she said to the thin little back of the sobbing child, who'd thrown herself facedown in the heavy shade of an oak tree. "Don't cry. You can have this doll. I don't really want it."

I don't. You, Sharon, you're important. Not the doll. There's a blackness between me and the sun now, did you know? And I want a drink of water.

Somewhere there were sounds. Car tires. A woman's scream. I didn't scream. It wasn't me. Then there were voices. And after another blackness, more voices and an arc of light that kept circling and circling. Now there were snatches of conversation, voices she thought she might know if she could just concentrate on them.

"Did you get Eli?"

"...and they got the message to him and out to the house. I can't believe she's alive. Are you sure? Look at that car!"

"...the other driver...cut him out with a torch...car smells like a brewery...dead, probably killed instantly..."

"...a special rescue unit out of Tyler. They think they can save her...."

"Damn, how much longer do we have to wait? For all we know, she's dying."

It was a long way down there to that shining water. It was peaceful, tranquil. Maybe she could just slide into sleep for a while.

A fight was going on when she awoke again. There was a lot of yelling and scuffling. She could hear moving feet and panting. And Ren's voice, like a light in darkness.

"She's slippin' a little more every minute! Turn loose of me! Eli, for God's sake, let me try now before it's too late. The rescue unit won't make it in time."

Cody's voice. "You might do more harm than good. Push her over the edge for sure. Leave her be."

Ren's voice was pleading and tortured. "Eli if you're my friend, make them turn loose of me. I can't watch her die. Let me go to her."

Somebody spoke, then Ren cried in a voice so anguished, it cut through all the mists in Jamie's mind, "I love her! *Please—*"

She smiled to herself and contentment welled up in her. I love you, too, Ren. I wondered if you'd ever say that to me again. She tried to turn, to find his face, and screams went up from somewhere out of her line of vision. She winced away from the sound. Now her hip was over the water and her leg wanted to slide with it off the bent beam it rested on. She frowned. Maybe she should be still. She wasn't sure what to do.

But Ren came through. His voice, that slow, gentle, steady, rich voice, was beside her head now, soothing and cajoling. It was a little too husky and broken, but she knew it and clung to it.

"Don't move anymore, Jamie. Please, baby, be still. No, don't look for me! I'm comin'—I'll be there. I'm here. Here. I love you. I love you, Jamie. I can't let you go like this."

His murmuring voice was coming a little closer and a little closer, then the voice changed, and he was telling her something. It was important. His voice was too insistent on her ear. She tried to concentrate.

"Don't move, don't turn a hair. I'll reach for you. I've got a rope. Let me . . . slide it . . . I'm goin' to slide it on this wrist. No—no! Be still! I'll reach for your hand."

His hard panting breath was right over her, and she felt the terrible heat of his body. Ren was really here. His scared, intent face was above hers now. He must have been lying nearly flat because he strained across her shoulder to reach toward her wrist. Sweat from his cheek dropped onto her face. She felt the brush of his shirt on her hair, then something rough and abrasive under her fingers and up. The rope. He pulled it taut. Then he let go of his breath in heavy expulsions and relaxed back, the side of his head touching the top of hers.

"Jamie," he gasped. "Listen to me. We're both hangin' out over the water on the beams the car bent. You're slidin' a little farther all the time. All that's holdin' you is one foot and leg still on the road and your skirt. It's—it's caught under part of the car door."

He stopped to breathe. She could feel the trembling in him. He made an effort to speak again.

"I don't know how hurt you are—even whether you understand me. The rope on your wrist will stop you from falling if... but it could break your arm, or add to whatever hurt you've already got. But I'm—I've got to take the chance. I'm gonna try to pull the skirt out from the edge of the car. If I can't, I'll cut it. Then—then I'll slide backward with you, off the beams. Please, be still. Trust me. Let me do it all."

Jamie wanted to speak, but her mouth was too tired. She wanted to tell him she'd trust him with her whole life, if she had one left. Then he was stretching, straining again, his face beside hers, his cheeks taut, the cords in his neck pronounced with stress. His hand was at her side, barely touching her. He seemed to fumble there forever, and she closed her eyes. The sun was too bright.

She registered the same relaxation of bone and muscle and breath as before in him after a minute or so. Then he was sliding sideways, away from her.

Panicked, she tried to clutch at him, and he shouted hoarsely, "No!" Cloth tore, then she was falling, screaming; and his arm swept out to grasp her roughly around her chest. His arm was too tight, his fingers pinching her skin through her clothes. Her head snapped with the impact against his ribs. She knew he had her in one arm, in a brutal clutch, her feet dangling over the water way, way down there. He was straining to hold on to the beam beside them. The muscles stood out in his arms wet with sweat, and the blood vessels in his temple throbbed against her face in his agonized, straining posture.

There were shouts and noise behind them, and Jamie, sick with her pounding head and churning stomach, saw the blackness around her again and then she knew nothing.

They roused her in the speeding ambulance, and she was dazed and inarticulate. She saw Eli's tormented face above her, and said "Daddy?" in a croak. A smile so bright it hurt her to see it broke across his face.

"Jamie. Oh, baby, you're goin' to be fine. Do you hear? You're not seriously hurt at all. It's a miracle. God is good."

Her mother's weeping face was beside his, and she was clutching her daughter's hand wordlessly again and again.

"Love you...both," Jamie tried to whisper. Out there on that bridge it had become important that they know that. She twisted to look for someone else, but it hurt her torn, bruised muscles too much, and a stab shot through her head.

"Be still, honey," said her daddy, anxiously reaching for her.

Where was Ren? Was he—he hadn't fallen reaching for her? He wasn't *dead*.

"Ren?" she gasped frantically.

"He saved your life," Eli said. There were tears on his cheeks.

She looked around again and this time Eve understood. "He pulled some muscles. The paramedics wanted to look him over. He wouldn't let them put him in the hospital. He's coming to see you, though."

They examined her and poked her and x-rayed her. Afterward an amazed doctor told her that besides a blow to her head that had left her face sore and bruised on one side, a slight case of shock and numerous scrapes and bruises, she was fine. They would let her go home after a twenty-four-hour observation period.

Then she had to talk to Cody and tell him what little she could remember. She shuddered at the only truly clear memory she had—the red car's driver and his terrified face, the face of a man about to die.

Cody put his notebook away. "He'd been drinking from the looks of it. Empty bottles everywhere. The autopsy will show how much. And you, Jamie, you're mighty lucky. You got pitched out'an open car. That kills most people, that and not wearing a seat belt. But it saved you. If you'd 'a been in that car when it turned over and slammed into those steel beams, you wouldn't be here now."

"Maybe I needed...another chance," she tried to say, but her throat muscles hurt.

She tried to stay awake because Eli told her Ren would come that afternoon, but her eyes kept shutting. When she awoke, it was late, nearly midnight. She called the nurse.

"Yes, honey, your young man was here. We were all dying to see him after all we've heard. He sat right there in that chair for nearly three hours, but he wouldn't let us wake you up. Don't worry; he'll be back. And you're going home tomorrow."

But Jamie wanted to cry, "Ren, why aren't you here? I waited with you. You said you loved me!"

The doctor released her at noon the next day. By that time her room looked like a bower of flowers, and when Eve helped her to her room at home, there were more of them everywhere. And there were guests: Sharon and Beau, her aunts and uncles, Claire and other friends. Even Harry, and for protection, his mother; both of them were still stiff with resentment but determined to do the proper thing.

Sharon was the last to leave. "Sharon," Jamie called after her. "I want to tell you that I love you."

Sharon's face worked and she began to cry.

"I lay there on the bridge and I remembered you when you were little, the way we fought and the way I've always had my own stubborn way and you let me."

"No, Jamie, don't—"

"I want to say this, Sharon. For once in my life."

Sharon smiled through the tears. "Don't, because I'll get soppy, too, and tell you how alive and sweet and—and human you are."

"Sure," said Jamie dryly. "You're getting tactful in your old age. You mean I was—I *am* a brat."

Sharon laughed. "Well, so am I. And you'd better hang around for the rest of my life so I'll have somebody to be rotten with me."

Eli came in after supper. Jamie was pacing in front of the windows.

"How's the face?" he asked tenderly, putting his hand to the dark circle on her cheek and up into her hair.

"It's there," she said, trying to laugh. "Daddy, where's Ren? What's wrong? He told me out there over the water he loved me. So why hasn't he come?"

Eli turned away. "Something's botherin' him. I don't know what. But he's worked all day, and this afternoon when he asked to see you, Harry and his mother were here. Ren wouldn't come in. I knew you were waitin', so I sent him home early to take care of his stock. He'll come back when he's through, and he can spend the night here, at the house. You can talk to him in private, and tomorrow morning you can surprise me by tellin' me I'm goin' to have a son-in-law." He grinned at her, and she blushed in flustered happiness.

Then Eli fell silent and serious.

"I couldn't have lived if I'd lost both my girls. Tory's goin' nearly killed me; yours would have finished me off. Life's too breakable. All I want is for you to be happy. Out there yesterday, watchin' that boy—no, that *man*—reachin' out with his own life to pull you back, I thought my heart would crack. I knew then that I could trust him with you even when I'm dead and gone. He held you there till they pulled him back in. I could tell—they could tell—he'd fall, too, before he'd ever let you go." Eli cleared his throat and his voice lightened. "So I'll trust you alone with him tonight, I guess."

She smiled at him tremulously. "I don't think he's the one you have to worry about."

He shook his head, his cheeks a little flushed at his daughter's bluntness, and said dubiously, "I'm beginnin' to think you're right."

She saw the lights of Ren's truck when he pulled in the drive, and her heart started pounding. Roberta had stayed late tonight because of all the excitement, and Jamie had enlisted her help before she left. She knew exactly what room Roberta would show him to. It was the one all by itself on the first floor. She wanted to be with Ren tonight. Just them.

Within minutes she had slipped down the hall and the stairs. Roberta, smiling at her as she got ready to leave, said in a loud whisper, "He just went in. He was asking about you."

Jamie's heart was beating like a winded racer's, her face flushed and shy. She reached for his doorknob—hesitated, scared to death—grasped it and slid inside the room. He saw her instantly from where he stood by the bed. A dim lamp behind him was the only light, and she couldn't see his face clearly.

Had he always been so tall? She took a step forward, then another, and suddenly she saw the leaping flame in his eyes and the still, heavy longing on his face. She went blindly into his arms, seeking his lips passionately. When his met hers, it was as if an explosion went off somewhere inside her heart. She could barely stand, and he wrapped his arms around her so tightly she couldn't draw breath. His sweet,

sweet mouth opened on hers and she responded instantly, trying to draw him closer to her.

When the kiss ended at last, he kissed her unbruised cheek, her throat. Then she felt his tongue against her ear, and it was not enough. She reached for the buttons on his shirt, finally tearing it in her haste. He was breathing heavily as she spread kisses across his chest, and he closed his eyes when she kissed his throat and the line of his jaw.

She fumbled for his belt and at last his hands came down to help her. When she had finished, she pushed his hand away, kissed it and tugged at his jeans.

"Oh, God," he whispered hoarsely. "Jamie—please."

She leaned against him heavily, intimately, her face drowsy with love and passion. He fell backward off balance against the bed behind him, and she followed him down.

"I want to please you, Ren," she whispered back.

"No, Jamie. You don't have to. Your parents—"

"My parents know that I love you. The rest is... is between you and me. You're the only one, ever. In my whole life, just you. Ren, please, I *want* to."

He looked at her flushed, pleading face, reached out and touched her cheek tenderly and said in a voice so low she hardly heard him, "You're so beautiful. So beautiful, baby."

"So are you," she half laughed, half sobbed. He started to say something, but she smothered the words on his mouth.

And then there was no more talk. There was only his capitulation, his hands under her gown, easing it off, his lips gentle and healing on her bruises, his legs tangling with hers. But this time Jamie meant to satisfy all the yearnings she'd suffered through lately. She was no passive virgin tonight. She twisted and writhed in his hands, ran her fingers feverishly through his hair and over his smooth, broad chest until at last, gasping, he caught them and stopped her torture.

That night seemed to go on forever, but when he at last gave her what she'd never experienced before, when he'd left both of them satisfied and satiated, she felt so excited and alive, she wanted to run.

Instead, she cried. Not a little, like the other time, out of regret. But great heaving sobs against his warm throat, tears that she laughed through. He was completely bewildered, trying to see into her face, at last just holding her against him and stroking her shining hair.

She fell asleep in his arms finally, but just before she did, she said drowsily, smiling up at him, "Thank you."

She awoke at dawn, and Ren and the night before were in her mind the instant she opened her eyes. She could have been dead. Instead, she'd gotten to celebrate life with him. She felt good, and she smiled, remembering her father's words: "Surprise me by tellin' me I'm goin' to have a son-in-law."

She turned to find Ren and he was not there. Startled, she sat up, and then relaxed. He was standing before the window, his back to her, looking out at the rising sun. He was already dressed, but she admired his build anyway. Clothes could be disposed of easily; she'd learned that last night. Among other things. Her cheeks burned with a heady embarrassment.

"Hello," she said, after three tries. He turned to look at her. It was then that the dread of the past week came to life again inside her. Something was terribly wrong. His face was as grim and set as death. He looked older and tireder than his twenty-five years.

"What's wrong?" she gasped.

He spoke abruptly. "I'm leavin', Jamie. Today. I meant to tell you last night, but you—I—I didn't have the guts, or the desire, or the something, to say so after you..."

Jamie could think of nothing to say. It felt as if she hadn't really heard his words, like when they'd first told her Tory was dead. She felt stupid, slow, stunned.

"You don't love me. You never have. You feel guilty about me. And after yesterday it's worse. You want to thank me." He rubbed a weary hand across his face. "Well, I took last night when I never should have. So I've been thanked."

"Ren, you don't know what you're talking about," she cried. "I do love you. Can't you understand English? I want to be your wife."

He made a gesture of despair and negation. "Stop it. You're killin' me. You don't want *me*. And I don't belong here. Yesterday all these fancy people and photographers were everywhere. Even the governor called to talk to Eli while you were in the hospital. Me, I didn't even know where to get you flowers. And I couldn't have afforded one bunch like some of those. It just hit me how damned rich you Logans are. I've got nothing."

"You've got everything I need."

"You don't belong with me, Jamie."

"So who do I belong with, then?" she said fiercely, choking back tears. "Harry?"

He winced but he said stubbornly, "He's got the same money, the same kind'a family."

She flew out of the bed, clutching the sheets to her. "Harry Sheffield's got no money. His daddy lost it all playing the market years ago. Why d'you think Harry's such a good stockbroker? He knows who's a loser, that's what. All the whole family has is a name. Oh, and a house and a mortgage up to their teeth. They're a bunch of snobs who try to make up for their losses by reminding me that Daddy was a sharecropper's son. There's no blue blood in me, Ren."

She moved closer to him, pleading with him to reach for her again. "I want *you*."

He drew away, then said with a terrible finality and dignity, "I saw you on those beams and I hurt like I've never hurt before. I knew then how much I cared and I knew that you couldn't ever care that much. That's all there is to it. I told God if he'd just let me get to you, I'd walk out of this county for the rest of my life. I remembered how I'd wanted to hurt you, use you like you did me. If I stay, we'll turn into mean, disappointed people like Sidney. Or my father. I told you, I saw what tryin' to hang on to a woman did to him."

"How can I make you believe me?" Jamie asked in quiet despair.

"You can't. I'm facin' truth and turnin' loose. I never had you, anyway. I still love you. I reckon I will when I'm an old, old man. But I won't let it break me." He reached to touch her hair gently and there was a great sadness on his face. "I just want to forget the hurts and remember the love." His hand lingered near her cheek, then dropped away. "I want to go home . . . Jennie."

She watched out the window, watched him go into the early morning sun, the dew sparkling on the green grass all around him. Hot, salty tears burned up in her nose and throat, and her face twisted as they ran down her feverish cheeks. She hurt all over.

When he got to his truck, he paused with the door open, looking up at her one last time. She'd remember him that way forever. He'd never looked more handsome than the morning he said goodbye.

Chapter Fifteen

She cried all day, sick and aching. She had lost him. He would spend the rest of his life within a heart's beat of her. The two of them would live and grow old and die under the same Kentucky sun, and he would always be just out of her reach, just beyond her fingertips.

She had wealth and a loving family and a gracious home. She had beauty and the promise of years before her.

But she did not have Ren. And she wanted him. If he would open the door of that little farmhouse and let her come in, she'd walk into his arms and stay forever. She'd love his children, brown-eyed, shy little children, and she would love him. But he had locked her out, so she had nothing.

Her heart was not easy; it was as true as his. She couldn't forget Ren with another man or ever be casual about him. If she'd only known what she had back in Roswell, if she'd only known when she'd opened that old high school annual six months ago that the face she'd looked at would become everything to her.

She couldn't even fight. He didn't believe in her love, so there was no great truth to tell him. He'd proved to be beyond jealousy, so that was no weapon. She'd played every card she had, and she'd lost it all.

Jamie Logan didn't know how, but she lived through that day, then the rest of the week. She lived to see Eli's white, shocked face and her mother's worried one. Her father wanted to go after Ren, to drag him back. But Jamie told him she would leave home for good if he did, and he read the seriousness in her tone and reluctantly gave up the idea.

She spent whole days listless and lethargic. She couldn't sleep, she didn't eat. But she tried harder after they called in a specialist to check her.

She thought of going away. She'd run to Nashville, get a job, live on busy streets. She'd shake this little town and this grief.

But she knew all the time she wouldn't. There was no happiness that way. The new Jamie would live a real life, without the artificial drama of wild bets and impulsive, futile escapes. She wouldn't forget the lesson of the bridge. There were her parents and her family to think of, so she'd fight out her problems here. No more running.

Someday she'd be in her car on the highway and Ren would pass in his truck. She would survive it; it would be all right.

When Jamie reached that point in her thinking, she returned to work, trying to ignore the anxious faces of the people around her. Their kindness hurt her almost as much as her own heart did.

It was impossible not to think about Ren. She looked forward to the nights because, alone in her bed, she could remember him in peace. Jamie wondered if he had gone back to his old job, to his old life completely. Then finally, she got angry. She hoped he was as miserable and as heartsick as she was.

Six weeks of hell later, Sharon got mad, too. "You make me sick, Jamie Lynn Logan. Moping around here like a dying cow. What's the matter with you? The man said he loved you. You've always been able to handle him like a charm before, haven't you?"

"He never did anything I wanted him to!" Jamie practically shouted at her cousin.

"Really? He fell for you hook, line and sinker; he came after the job you wanted him to take; he took you to the festival when you asked him to; he nearly died for you on the bridge. Good Lord, what more do you want him to do? Save the planet? You march yourself right over to Roswell and tell him you love him, too, that you're dying without him. And killing the rest of us in the process."

"I already told him. He didn't believe me."

"Oh." Sharon was thrown a minute, then she said flippantly, "Well, so what? You also told him once you were Jennie Lynn. Why should he believe you now?"

"I did more than just say it," Jamie muttered and looked down at her twisting hands. "I tried to—to show him."

Sharon stopped short, diverted. "And it didn't work?"

"It made no difference to him at all."

"I'm not really surprised," she said with wry humor. "If I remember right, you 'did more' as Jennie, too."

"So there's nothing left," Jamie said dully.

Sharon thought a minute, then spoke slowly, seriously, "I know you love him. And he loves you. I could feel it every time I was around."

"He told me all about how he loved me just before he walked out," her cousin answered bitterly. "But I have too much money and I don't love him enough and there's too much between us—oh, the list goes on and on." She stood up quickly. "Let's forget this. Do you—"

But Sharon, frowning, motioned Jamie into silence. "I'm trying to figure this out, to put it into words. I don't think this—this situation is about love, Jamie."

Where had she heard those words before? Something Eli had said. "It's about trust," she said slowly.

Sharon's face lightened. "That's the word. And pride and self-respect, and all those other words in the Constitution." Sharon grimaced. "I keep remembering the day Ren crawled out on the bridge after you. I was there with Aunt Eve. He was dying inside, and I heard part of what he said to you. It was as still as death out there—most of us heard him. Sure, he came out of that little episode looking heroic and brave. But there was something else. There was this—this shock that he would do that for you. Nobody expected it. If only others had known you cared about him, if Ren had been your boyfriend or your husband, it would have been all right. But you never treated him like that so others could see how it was."

"I don't understand you, Sharon," Jamie said, but she could almost sense what was behind her cousin's stumbling words.

"I mean that he probably came out of this situation feeling the same way he did after everybody found out about Jennie in Roswell. See, he ran because he felt that he'd made a fool of himself over you again, and you'd never really given him any assurances that you were willing to do the same for him. There wasn't any trust." Sharon paused, looking pleased with herself. "Yeah, that's it. That's what I'm trying to say."

"So that's the big revelation that's supposed to get me through the rest of my life?" Jamie said shortly. "Well, thanks anyway."

She started toward the door, but Sharon, who stood still in thought, stopped her just as she got across the room. "Hey, made any good bets lately?"

"What?" Jamie asked, laughing in bewilderment.

"I'm willing to make one with you. I say that if you corner Ren Garrett in front of a bunch of those people who think you made a fool of him before, and do something drastic—get down on your knees and beg, or throw yourself all over him—if you'll go that far for him, he'll pick you up, or catch you, or whatever. And he'll hold on. I'll bet he will."

Jamie stared at Sharon in surprise, then horrified comprehension dawned. "You mean you want me to set him up again?"

"Is it a bet or not? What's the matter, Jamie? Chicken or something?"

"But . . . but I can't," she protested. "I can't go after him, not another time."

"Why not? He's used to it by now. And this time will definitely be different."

"He might say no. Or laugh."

"Will it hurt any worse than you do this minute?"

Jamie glanced at Sharon. "No," she whispered.

"Good. Then it's all agreed," Sharon said briskly. "Here are the terms: If Ren says yes and grabs you up, I win. That means I get to be head bridesmaid. And I want your first child, too."

Jamie just laughed, still bewildered. But a hope and an anticipation that she'd not felt in ages were stirring inside her.

Sharon was frowning. "No, forget the child. He might turn out like Beau."

"And...if you lose?" Jamie asked far more soberly.

"I won't. But to satisfy you, pessimist, I'll agree to sing at your wedding whenever, wherever and whoever you do eventually marry."

Jamie's mouth dropped open. "Sing at my wedding! You? The one they threw out of junior choir back in Sunday school?"

Sharon raised her eyebrows at her. "Exactly. So you'd better get Ren Garrett to marry you, hadn't you?"

It was such a temptation to think that there might be something she could really do, something besides suffering, that might bring him back to her. But Jamie knew better.

"No. It won't work, Sharon, and I'm not willing to start this hurt all over again when it fails. Even if I agree to all you've suggested, I still have too much money, and my family still has some sort of position. And it won't change how we met."

Sharon said angrily, "What's wrong with how you met? If you hadn't made that deal with Beth, you'd never have known Ren. You'd be married to Todd now. How'd you like that?"

"I'd hate it. Ugh." She shivered.

"Since you got involved with Ren, your stupid social position hasn't changed—you haven't stopped enjoying life—or stopped having friends. You've got one fantastic one standing right here, and I'm trying my best to help you. Listen to me. Something in you wants him, and you're not the type to turn away from that, money or position or not."

"I'm not the one worried about it. But he said—"

"Ren will work out any problem of his. He always does, if it's worth it to him. So it all comes down to this, Jamie: Do you want to live the rest of your life prim and proper and rich without him, or can you stand to add a little red blood to all the good things you've already got and have a life with him? Well?"

Jamie stood in the dark back bedroom upstairs in Sidney's house. She was nervous and afraid. She wanted the night to hurry up and be over; she wanted time to stand still so that, if she was going to be hurt tonight, it would never happen; she didn't know what she wanted.

Sidney had finally agreed to give this dinner for her, but only after persuasion and pleading. Over the phone she had adamantly refused.

"He's in a worse state every time he comes back from you," she'd snapped. "I'll not be a party to anythin' concernin' you anymore."

But when Jamie had shown up on her doorstep, Sidney had looked her over keenly and questioned her at length. At last she said, "I'll say this: I believe you look more miserable than he does."

Then, out of the blue, Sidney called two days later to tell her of a pre-Thanksgiving supper she was having the next Friday night. Ren's friends would be there. So would Ren. Sidney added, "I won't say no to your comin'. Just don't start thinkin' I'm feelin' sorry for you, because I'm not. And if he shows you the door, you'll have to go out it. I won't help you."

So here she was. Sharon had picked out her clothes for her, and Jamie had been too wound up to care what they were.

Now she gazed at herself in the mirror. "This looks sort of like a—a wedding dress," she said accusingly to her cousin.

"Well, I thought we'd give him an idea of what you want, and what he's missing," Sharon chuckled gleefully, motioning to the low V neck. The dress was a creamy antique-white with long tight sleeves. It fit snugly from bodice to hips, five layers of delicate material wrapping around her flatteringly. Below her hips, the layers became soft, sheer skirts that twirled and swayed around her knees with every move.

They pulled her hair back in a dramatic sweep, and lessened the bridal look with big earrings, drops of emeralds and diamonds.

"I guess you look like a bride," Sharon said mischievously. She eyed the low neckline and the tight fit. "If your groom likes a—a naughty one. Parts of this dress definitely appeal to the sinner in men, not the saint."

"Maybe I'd better not wear it," Jamie suggested nervously. "Ren might not like all this."

"You certainly will wear it," Sharon said firmly. "You haven't got the farmer yet, remember. And there's no man in good health who wouldn't like this dress."

So now Ren was downstairs. Jamie didn't know for sure, but she thought Dan and Sylvia, Enoch Johnson, Ben Dalton and Cheever were, too. She didn't know who else Sidney had invited, and she was too sick with nerves to care.

Just before the supper started, Sharon went to the kitchen and returned, helping Sidney laboriously up the stairs so she could give Jamie one last piece of advice.

"Ren's too quiet, girl. He'll be gone as soon as he thinks he can get out without hurtin' my feelings. You'd better make your move soon." Then she looked the white dress over, and said dryly, "Let him eat first. I don't reckon his mind's goin' to be on food after he sees this." She poked the filmy skirts with her cane and, motioning Sharon away, left by herself.

Sharon stared after her in shock. "That old lady is a terror. I wonder if that's me in fifty years?"

Jamie clutched at her cousin with clammy hands. "Did you see him? How does he look?"

"I just got a glimpse through the door. He looks wonderful, just like Ren. You're going to be all right, Jamie. I promise you."

The hour slipped by, and she could stall no longer. On the dark stairs she stood trembling, her stomach sick and her legs about to give away. It didn't matter what happened if he only believed. God, let him believe.

"Go on," Sharon whispered down the steps to her, and Jamie shakily slid down them to the door of the living room. She took several pulls of air into her starving lungs, opened the door and walked in. Sidney had been watching for her, and she signaled her where Ren was with a glance.

Among the talking, laughing groups of twos and threes, he stood alone, leaning on the wall looking out the window at the night. He was wearing a sort of brown plaid shirt, and one hand was shoved down in his jeans pocket. He had a glass in the other. So big and broad and tall. Jamie ached to brush his hair back and touch the wide, strong hand that she remembered so well against her. Looking at Ren was pure pleasure. It made her feel as if she'd gotten everything in the world she'd ever wanted.

Then Dan noticed her. Like a dark cloud he rose to touch Ren's arm, and when Ren looked at him, Dan motioned toward her.

When Ren saw her, he sucked in his breath sharply and dropped the glass. It shattered at his feet and he never noticed. He stared at Jamie as if he'd seen a ghost. For an instant, there was a pull so strong between them he actually started toward her. Then he remembered and halted.

"Jamie," he said steadily. The others gradually fell silent in surprise. "What are you—" he began, then anger flashed over him. "You," he said accusingly to Sidney. "This is the second time. You promised me. I'll never trust you again."

"Yes, you will. Listen to her," Sidney said calmly.

He looked back at Jamie, and this time he swept her in one look from head to foot. There was a flicker of longing and hopelessness in his voice when he said, "You look beautiful. Like always. So get it over with. What do you want?"

She swallowed. She had to tell him now. "Ren." Saying his name made her somehow stronger. "I love you. *I love you.* There. Did you hear me? I'll say it again if you didn't. I can't help having money and I can't change my family, but I can't stop loving you, either."

"My God!" he gasped, his face flushing red.

She could not even really distinguish the surprised, avid faces around them. They were a blurred sea surrounding her and Ren and her desperate, earnest voice.

"You said I made a fool of you. How? How can my loving you enough to chase you across two counties all summer make you feel like a fool? Is it because, like Sharon says, I never told anybody else how I felt about you? Because if it is, I'm telling the world, beginning right here. Ren Garrett, I'm dying for love of you. I'm the one like your father. I can't let *you* go."

Dazedly, wildly, Ren spoke to Sidney, "Who is she? This can't be Jamie Logan."

But the girl in front of him answered. "Jamie, or Jennie, or whatever. Do you want proof?" she said, trying to tease. There was a light on his face that made her heart jerk in hope. She put one hand just under her breast on her side. The other started toward the zipper at the back of her dress.

He choked out, "Don't you dare!" Then in two long strides he was in front of her, his hands catching hers, pulling her to the door after him. Her skirts tangled and wrapped lovingly around his blue-jeaned legs when he stopped to yank the door open and jerk her with him out across the darkened hall and into some sort of parlor.

In the silence there, still held by his side, she could hear his thrumming heart as well as she could her own. Breathing harshly, he struggled for several minutes. At last he looked at her, surveying her from head to toe. "I never thought I'd ever see you again." His voice was vibrant and rich. "Why did you do that out there?"

"I'm sorry...if you didn't like it," she faltered. Had Sharon been wrong?

"It sort'a took me off guard. But I'm not complainin'. I just need to know why. Why, Jamie?"

"Be—because I didn't know what else to do," she stammered. She pulled her hands free and dropped her head into them. "If there are two sides to me, Ren, a Jamie and a Jennie both, like you say, then they both love you. You're what makes me complete. Oh, Ren, I've missed you."

His hands pulled hers from her face then. Looking down into her green eyes, he said hoarsely, "I don't know what to do with you. Or what you want out of me."

Well, she knew. "Marry me. I want a husband. And maybe four or five kids. Yours, Ren."

Still he stood there, watching her face in shock. Why didn't he move? What else could she offer him? Tears made her eyesight blur, and she tried to speak. Her words came out in a half whisper.

"I'll give away all of Daddy's money. I'll be happy to stay in your little house forever. Your terms. Please, Ren. Just don't send me back to live with all the misery I've been living with since you walked out." Her voice cracked and shivered into nothing.

"Jamie," he breathed, and his eyes were tender. He cupped her face in his hands, and she reached up to hold his brown wrists. "I love you, Jamie. I always will. Yes. Yes. I want to marry you."

"Do you believe that I love you?" she said tremulously.

"I'm startin' to," he whispered in the old gentle, half-laughing way, and then his warm mouth settled on hers. Her arms slid desperately, eagerly, around his neck, and his own bound her tightly to him.

After the most satisfying kiss she'd ever known, he pulled away from her lips to kiss her cheeks and her throat, still holding her in the prison of his arms.

"I know—" and his lips touched her bare shoulder "—about misery." He bent and kissed between her breasts, on the edge of the deep neckline, and she shivered a little. "An' about dyin' a little ever' night." Back to her mouth. "An' about wantin' you," he breathed just before their lips met and clung. Suddenly, sharply, Sidney's voice from the door made them break apart.

"Well, I reckon he didn't throw her out, after all," she said gruffly.

Ren was as flushed as Jamie when they turned to face the old woman and Sharon, who was hovering anxiously behind Sidney. Nevertheless, he kept a firm hold on Jamie's arm and, grinning at the two in the door, he said, "Throw her out, nothin'. I'm takin' her home with me."

Sidney snorted in disgust. "If I'd known it was goin' to end up in all this mush, I'd never have started this. But you, miss," she said, pointing the cane at Sharon, "you just won a bet."

A moment's scared silence ticked by. Then Ren stiffened and pulled sharply away, but Jamie grabbed at him. Not again, not ever, ever again.

"It's not what you think," she said quickly.

Sharon rushed in. "I did it, Ren. We wanted you to come back. Beau's been driving us crazy. So has Jamie. Nothing but moping and crying for six weeks now. She said she couldn't make you see the truth—that she loved you. I bet her that she could. That's all. Except I think I won. So guess who's going to be a bridesmaid at your wedding, Ren?"

"I'm glad she won." Jamie laughed up at him, a little nervously. "She threatened horrible things if she was wrong and you didn't come back to me." Her face suddenly passionate, she looked up into the eyes of the man who stood close beside her. "It's the best bet of my life. It got me to you again."

He relaxed slowly as he looked at the woman clinging tightly to his arm. Then at last he smiled. "As long as it's your last one," he said teasingly, but with a hint of warning. "Please. No more bets. This is about to kill me."

"I don't need to make any more. I've got everything I want. You, Wrendon Garrett. For the rest of my life." She reached up a hand to caress his face.

"Mush," said Sidney.

* * * * *

INDULGE A LITTLE SWEEPSTAKES

OFFICIAL RULES

SWEEPSTAKES RULES AND REGULATIONS. NO PURCHASE NECESSARY.

1. NO PURCHASE NECESSARY. To enter complete the official entry form and return with the invoice in the envelope provided. Or you may enter by printing your name, complete address and your daytime phone number on a 3 x 5 piece of paper. Include with your entry the hand printed words "Indulge A Little Sweepstakes." Mail your entry to: Indulge A Little Sweepstakes, P.O. Box 1397, Buffalo, NY 14269-1397. No mechanically reproduced entries accepted. Not responsible for late, lost, misdirected mail, or printing errors.

2. Three winners, one per month (Sept. 30, 1989, October 31, 1989 and November 30, 1989), will be selected in random drawings. All entries received prior to the drawing date will be eligible for that month's prize. This sweepstakes is under the supervision of MARDEN-KANE, INC. an independent judging organization whose decisions are final and binding. Winners will be notified by telephone and may be required to execute an affidavit of eligibility and release which must be returned within 14 days, or an alternate winner will be selected.

3. Prizes: 1st Grand Prize (1) a trip for two to Disneyworld in Orlando, Florida. Trip includes round trip air transportation, hotel accommodations for seven days and six nights, plus up to $700 expense money (ARV $3,500). 2nd Grand Prize (1) a seven-night Chandris Caribbean Cruise for two includes transportation from nearest major airport, accommodations, meals plus up to $1,000 in expense money (ARV $4,300). 3rd Grand Prize (1) a ten day Hawaiian holiday for two includes round trip air transportation for two, hotel accommodations, sightseeing, plus up to $1,200 in spending money (ARV $7,700). All trips subject to availability and must be taken as outlined on the entry form.

4. Sweepstakes open to residents of the U.S. and Canada 18 years or older except employees and the families of Torstar Corp., its affiliates, subsidiaries and Marden-Kane, Inc. and all other agencies and persons connected with conducting this sweepstakes. All Federal, State and local laws and regulations apply. Void wherever prohibited or restricted by law. Taxes, if any are the sole responsibility of the prize winners. Canadian winners will be required to answer a skill testing question. Winners consent to the use of their name, photograph and/or likeness for publicity purposes without additional compensation.

5. For a list of prize winners, send a stamped, self-addressed envelope to Indulge A Little Sweepstakes Winners, P.O. Box 701, Sayreville, NJ 08871.

 DL-SWPS

INDULGE A LITTLE SWEEPSTAKES

OFFICIAL RULES

SWEEPSTAKES RULES AND REGULATIONS. NO PURCHASE NECESSARY.

1. NO PURCHASE NECESSARY. To enter complete the official entry form and return with the invoice in the envelope provided. Or you may enter by printing your name, complete address and your daytime phone number on a 3 x 5 piece of paper. Include with your entry the hand printed words "Indulge A Little Sweepstakes." Mail your entry to: Indulge A Little Sweepstakes, P.O. Box 1397, Buffalo, NY 14269-1397. No mechanically reproduced entries accepted. Not responsible for late, lost, misdirected mail, or printing errors.

2. Three winners, one per month (Sept. 30, 1989, October 31, 1989 and November 30, 1989), will be selected in random drawings. All entries received prior to the drawing date will be eligible for that month's prize. This sweepstakes is under the supervision of MARDEN-KANE, INC. an independent judging organization whose decisions are final and binding. Winners will be notified by telephone and may be required to execute an affidavit of eligibility and release which must be returned within 14 days, or an alternate winner will be selected.

3. Prizes: 1st Grand Prize (1) a trip for two to Disneyworld in Orlando, Florida. Trip includes round trip air transportation, hotel accommodations for seven days and six nights, plus up to $700 expense money (ARV $3,500). 2nd Grand Prize (1) a seven-night Chandris Caribbean Cruise for two includes transportation from nearest major airport, accommodations, meals plus up to $1,000 in expense money (ARV $4,300). 3rd Grand Prize (1) a ten-day Hawaiian holiday for two includes round trip air transportation for two, hotel accommodations, sightseeing, plus up to $1,200 in spending money (ARV $7,700). All trips subject to availability and must be taken as outlined on the entry form.

4. Sweepstakes open to residents of the U.S. and Canada 18 years or older except employees and the families of Torstar Corp., its affiliates, subsidiaries and Marden-Kane, Inc. and all other agencies and persons connected with conducting this sweepstakes. All Federal, State and local laws and regulations apply. Void wherever prohibited or restricted by law. Taxes, if any are the sole responsibility of the prize winners. Canadian winners will be required to answer a skill testing question. Winners consent to the use of their name, photograph and/or likeness for publicity purposes without additional compensation.

5. For a list of prize winners, send a stamped, self-addressed envelope to Indulge A Little Sweepstakes Winners, P.O. Box 701, Sayreville, NJ 08871.

© 1989 HARLEQUIN ENTERPRISES LTD. DL-SWPS

INDULGE A LITTLE—WIN A LOT!

Summer of '89 Subscribers-Only Sweepstakes

OFFICIAL ENTRY FORM

This entry must be received by: October 31, 1989
This month's winner will be notified by: Nov. 7, 1989
Trip must be taken between: Dec. 7, 1989–April 7, 1990
(depending on sailing schedule)

YES, I want to win the Caribbean cruise vacation for two! I understand the prize includes round-trip airfare, a one-week cruise including private cabin and all meals, and a daily allowance as revealed on the "Wallet" scratch-off card.

Name______________________________

Address____________________________

City__________ State/Prov.______ Zip/Postal Code______

Daytime phone number____________________
Area code

Return entries with invoice in envelope provided. Each book in this shipment has two entry coupons—and the more coupons you enter, the better your chances of winning!

DINDL-2

INDULGE A LITTLE—WIN A LOT!

Summer of '89 Subscribers-Only Sweepstakes

OFFICIAL ENTRY FORM

This entry must be received by: October 31, 1989
This month's winner will be notified by: Nov. 7, 1989
Trip must be taken between: Dec. 7, 1989–April 7, 1990
(depending on sailing schedule)

YES, I want to win the Caribbean cruise vacation for two! I understand the prize includes round-trip airfare, a one-week cruise including private cabin and all meals, and a daily allowance as revealed on the "Wallet" scratch-off card.

Name______________________________

Address____________________________

City__________ State/Prov.______ Zip/Postal Code______

Daytime phone number____________________
Area code

Return entries with invoice in envelope provided. Each book in this shipment has two entry coupons—and the more coupons you enter, the better your chances of winning!

© 1989 HARLEQUIN ENTERPRISES LTD.

DINDL-2